OTHER BOOKS BY JOSEPH BATHANTI

Communion Partners (poems)
Anson County (poems)
The Feast of all Saints (poems)
This Metal (poems)
East Liberty (novel)
They Changed the State: The Legacy of NorthCarolina's
  Visiting Artists, 1971-1995 (nonfiction)
The High Heart (short stories)
Land of Amnesia (poems)
Restoring Sacred Art (poems)
Sonnets of the Cross (poems)˙
Concertina (poems)
Half of What I Say Is Meaningless (creative nonfiction)
The Life of the World To Come (novel)
A Conversation with Ronald H. Bayes in 1988 (nonfiction)
Twelve Poems (poems)
The 13th Sunday After Pentecost (poems)

COVENTRY

JOSEPH BATHANTI

LIVINGSTON PRESS

THE UNIVERSITY OF WEST ALABAMA

Typesetting and page layout: Sarah Coffey
Proofreading: Nick Noland, Joe Taylor
Cover layout: Nick Noland
Cover photo: Joseph Bathanti,
with gratitude to Jimmy Davidson, Vivian Davidson, and
Amy Galloway

This book won the Novello Prize in 2006.
The author has made slight revisions from that edition.

COVENTRY

JOSEPH BATHANTI

For Joan always

In memoriam: Fielding Dawson: 1930-2012

FOREWORD

After my first ever meeting with Joseph Bathanti at his favourite restaurant in Winston Salem on a sweltering North Carolina summer's day, I came away thinking to myself, "he's inexplicable in remarkable ways". Joseph's exuberance for life, interest in people – alongside his intelligence and compassion – is difficult to elucidate unless you have met the man. His 2014 collection of autobiographical essays, *Half of What I Say is Meaningless*, begins to illuminate something of his persona – when reading it recently I laughed out loud to the amusement of my fellow passengers on a long train ride to London, while also welling up, nodding vigorously and then finishing the book with an affirmative grunt. (Someone next to me asked what I was reading, but I don't think I did a good job of selling it and don't think she jumped on her smart phone to buy it, apologies JB.) *Half of What* won the Will D. Campbell Award for Creative Nonfiction, given to "the best manuscript that speaks to the human condition in a Southern context". In interview, Bathanti has confirmed he identifies as a regional poet having spent more than two thirds of his life in North Carolina.[1] He has established himself as a seminal author/observer of America's prison culture, particularly that of the South.

Bathanti's preoccupation both with the South and with humanity similarly permeates his 2013 collection *Concertina*. These poems detail his experiences as a young Italian-American leaving Pittsburgh in 1976 to become a VISTA volunteer with the North Carolina Department of Correction. The arresting image of the Concertina wire – "a colossal Slinky / ribboned with scalpels" – metaphorically and literally encloses a world "so utterly strange". Bathanti writes of bounty hunters and bloodhounds, the prisoners who

1   Marina Morbiducci, "An Interview with Joseph Bathanti", *RSA Journal (Rivista di STdui Americani),* issue 28 (2017): 215-227, http://www.aisna.net/sites/default/files/rsa/rsa28/28_Morbiducci_ Bathanti.pdf [accessed 10 December 2018].

I

look "like schoolboys" exposed to rape and overdoses. If prison is strange, it is also often tragic: Bathanti speaks from experience about accompanying children – including some "so young, they can't help wetting" – to see their mothers in prison. These may be the only visitors to ever "smile at the twirling jagged grandeur". There is the boy at prison camp who "stuffed pillows under his prison greens" and "then crabbed / up the fence like a movie creature". Once caught in the wire the boy hung all night "undetected" until he was shot in the morning by a tower guard. But *Concertina* is also about the South – its religion, the spittoon, the cowboy hat, the African American cook who averts his eyes from the prison Captain.

The year before *Concertina* was released Bathanti was appointed Poet Laureate of North Carolina by the state governor, reflecting his commitment to the region. Bathanti's 2006 novel *Coventry* is set in a rural work camp where the protagonist Calvin Gaddy is – like his father before him, MacGregor Gaddy – head guard. The novel won the Novello Literary Award, an annual prize for a North Carolina writer. The popular English idiom, *to send someone to Coventry*, entails ignoring a person and acting as if they are invisible or non-existent. Ironically Bathanti brings all those involved in the prison – inmates as well as guards, "brothers after all" – into clear visibility in this wonderfully written and poignant novel. All the while, the concertina quietly encapsulates everyone and everything, whether Mac's hair ("spiked along his neck like concertina"), the innocence of the newborn baby who has no need for language ("Words were like stones, sentences like concertina that pent people up in prison"), and the building of Mac's residential wall ("what [it] lacked was concertina, that final inevitable punctuation").

In his memoirs of life in Angola, former inmate Wilbert Rideau explains the prison lifestyle in thought-provoking ways: "I was surprised to learn that it was a world unto itself, with its own peculiar culture, belief system, lifestyle, power structure, economy, and currency. It has its own heroes..."[2] In Bathanti's *Coventry*, time is another aspect prison life makes strange – it is "spatial, not chronological". I teach a university module entitled "American Prison Culture of the 20th & 21st Centuries" in which we explore Hollywood movies varying from *I Am a Fugitive from a Chain Gang* to *Dead Man Walking* alongside poetry from Guantanamo Bay, memoirs by Sanyika Shakur, novels by Chester Himes, and short stories edited by Wally Lamb. We use these texts as a springboard into discussions of US history, society and politics more widely, and we talk at length about what we *should* do, what we *can* do, as scholars with these "peculiar" pieces of culture. How do we articulate a viable view of prison, without making it *too* literary or *too* artistic? Should it be educational as well as entertaining? What do we do with representations of something which is so authentically engrained in real-life American society? Discussing such prose, poetry and films, we are forced by default to situate text alongside context.

Indeed, as I write new study notes nearly half of all American adults (113 million) have had an immediate family member incarcerated at some point in their lives.[3] At the time of the research 6.5 million had an immediate family member currently in prison; and, African Americans were 50% more likely than white Americans to have had a family member incarcerated. (North Carolina today has a relatively low incarceration rate with "only" approximately 132,000 people in prison or on probation and parole.[4]) What is perhaps most shocking is that these statistics no longer shock many of us. By the end of 2006 – the year

2   Wilbert Rideau, *In the Place of Justice: a Story of Punishment and Redemption* (New York: Alfred A Knopf, 2010):
3   "Study: Half of US adults have had close family member jailed", *BBC Online*, 6 December 2018, https://www.bbc.co.uk/news/world-us-canada-46471444 [accessed 10 December 2018].
4   "Department of Public Safety Statistics", *North Carolina Department of Public Safety*, https://www.ncdps.gov/about-dps/department-public-safety-statistics [accessed 10 December 2018].

when *Coventry* was first published – Federal and State correctional authorities had jurisdiction over 1,570,861 prisoners, an increase of 2.8% since 2005 and the number of women in prison increased by 4.5%, reaching 112,498 prisoners.[5] In 2006, the 'Dirty South' rapper Ludacris released a memorable song about prison, advising "Do your time, don't let your time do you" in order to survive horrific conditions in a system that is "so close to being slavery".[6]

Burgeoning statistics and concerns over conditions are certainly valid reasons why we should take prison cultural texts seriously. My students are often at their most passionate when debating representational politics: do we all have the *right* to represent incarceration when it affects so many of us? Or who has the *right* to represent prisoners, especially when they are of different classes and races to the director / poet / novelist? In particular, can a prison novel *only* be classified as such when it is written by a prisoner? The wider ramifications of these questions echo well beyond the confining walls of a prison. While *Concertina* has been explicitly inspired by his VISTA experiences, Bathanti claims in *Half of What I Say*, that "fiction maintains a looser gait, yet a panoramic canvas. You can get away with more." One reviewer on the back cover of the original edition of *Coventry* flags that Bathanti writes "with a power rooted in his own first-hand experience" while another deemed it a "terribly beautiful piece of truth-telling". Bathanti is not naïve; he knows his middle-class status as a university professor or VISTA volunteer enables him to return home at the end of the day (since his VISTA days he has been regularly involved with creative writing projects in prisons across North Carolina in some capacity). Nor is his writing as immediately politicized in the same ways that some other prison texts seek to raise awareness of the prison industrial complex. His ingrained activist outlook is evident throughout *Half* and *Concertina*,

5   Bureau of Justice Statistics, "Prisoners in 2006", https://www.bjs.gov/index.cfm?ty=pbdetail&iid=908 [accessed 30 December 2018].
6   Ludacris, "Do Your Time", *Release Therapy* (Disturbing Tha Peace & Def Jam South, 2006).

but really *Coventry* is first and foremost about humanity, about the capacity of humankind to survive in the face of adversity. From this viewpoint, the setting of prison is not incidental, but essential.

Coventry carries naturalist elements, much like Chester Himes's equally affecting novel, *Yesterday Will Make You Cry*. First published as *Cast the First Stone* in 1953, Himes's narrative was callously edited by publishers, "forcing him to delete his more literary touches" and "forcing him to dumb-down his masterpiece before agreeing to publish it".[7] The editors refused to believe that an African American man could go "beyond ghetto experience" and write a literary masterpiece, instead insisting he turn it into a hard-boiled prison novel, particularly given Himes's first-hand experience of prison.[8] It was not until 1998 that *Yesterday* in its original form was "rescued from oblivion".[9] Though Himes's publishing experience and context are far removed from Bathanti's, their novels draw logical points of comparison, not least because of their naturalist tendencies. A literary movement at the turn of the century, Naturalism engaged with realism to suggest that social conditions and environments <u>have</u> inexorable influence in shaping human character and consciousness. Despite the oppressive conditions in Coventry– where Cal is comforted by a dormitory stabbing because "it's predictable. The way things were supposed to be" – it is a place where the protagonist "couldn't help" caring about convicts. It comes as no surprise that in establishing Foucauldian machines of total control over mind and body, prison not only houses but encourages animalistic and monstrous behavior among guards as well as inmates (there are numerous instances of this in both *Yesterday* and *Coventry*). Yet Himes and Bathanti remind us <u>that the human</u> experience is not so limiting; rather extreme

7   "Introduction" by Melvin Van Peebles, in Chester Himes, *Yesterday Will Make You Cry* (London: W.W.Norton, 1998): 19.
8   "Editors' Note" by Marc Gerald & Samuel Blumenfeld, in Himes, *Yesterday*: 8.
9   Ibid: 9.

V

circumstances can paradoxically prompt humane responses. Both novels suggest the incarcerated – and incarceration staff – always have the potential to rise above their associations with prison.

A key event in both Himes' *Yesterday* and Bathanti's *Coventry* is a horrific prison fire that results in multiple deaths (in the former, this was based on Himes's real-life experiences of the 1930 inferno at Ohio State Penitentiary which killed 320 of his fellow inmates). An authorial spokesperson in *Coventry* declares that "There is not a damn thing you can do about fire and convicts. It's the nature of the beast". Cal's father similarly notes "Fire is natural to convicts", reflecting widespread public beliefs that the (fiery) devil is alive inside criminals even before they reach the prison entrance. The fire in both novels serves as a reminder that death affects us all the same, whether criminal or lawful, convict or guard, black or white, male or female. And in the immediate aftermath of both fires, we witness emotions coming forth in even the most hardened of convicts. During the actual blazes, we are privy to a reaffirmation of humanity within confinement, a "typical" characteristic of much prison literature. Himes's protagonist, Jimmy, is astonished by the convicts "working overtime at being heroes" to save their peers, despite any pre-prison involvement with mutilating people.[10] The night after the fire and envisaging death, Jimmy realizes that "no matter what you had been, or ever hoped to be, a foot of greenish vomit hanging from your teeth would make you much the same as any other bastard".[11] Along similar lines, in *Coventry* the Frankenstein-inmate, the conflicted guard and his ailing pregnant wife, the delusionary grandfather haunted by chain gang devils; are all one and the same.

Bathanti is one of those rare individuals you cannot stop thinking about in inspired ways, long after you leave the room; his writings perform the same feat long after you get

---

10   Himes, *Yesterday*: 99.
11   Ibid: 153.

off the train. He is an extraordinarily *humane* human being and such humanity pervades his essays, his poems, but above all this novel. Like many university lecturers before me, I have thought long and hard about my role in the classroom, and like many others I regularly return to a quotation from Martin Luther King Jr.: "the function of education is to teach one to think intensively and to think critically. Intelligent character – that is the goal of true education". When you finish reading *Coventry* I defy you to deny that Bathanti has guided you to do your own intensive, critical thinking and that you do feel more intelligent (and ever more humane). Such feelings speak to the sheer literary power of this (prison) novel, the relevance of its content, and its impact echoing far beyond the final page.

Josephine Metcalf
December 2018, UK

"They humbled his feet in fetters: the iron pierced his soul,
until his word came."
— PSALM 104:18.

"There'll be smoke and confusion everywhere when God
sends his dark messenger to roll over the rooftops and loose
the prisoner from his sleep."
—*Salvation on Sand Mountain*, Dennis Covington.

CHAPTER 1

The night Zedda Pate was electrocuted in Central Prison, Calvin Gaddy surrendered his virginity to a blushing, matronly whore in The Heart of Dark Motel. All he remembered of it was the woman, in her black under-things, lowering herself onto him, whispering, "You remind me of my son." He never even had the chance see her without clothes, which was all he'd really bargained for.

He'd been a first semester engineering student at the state university in Raleigh and had gotten feverishly drunk at a frat house kegger celebrating the execution. It was Thursday, November 1, The Feast of All Saints, which honors the holy souls who during life loved Jesus Christ and strove to imitate Him and practice His virtues. Black and orange crepe, skulls and tissue specters still hung from the Halloween party the night before.

The fraternity brothers had fashioned togas of bed sheets dyed red, cinctured with wash-twine, and toasted Zedda Pate with plastic cups of beer all night until 2:15 a.m., the precise moment the black-hooded executioner threw the first switch in the killing cycle – the morning of November 2, All Souls Day, the feast commemorating the faithfully departed souls in Purgatory, the first time in twenty-two years that America had marched a woman into one of its death houses.

To get to The Heart of Dark, Calvin and his friends had had to drive by the governor's mansion. People stood there at vigil, crowded against the black iron gate. Two factions. One cheering and carrying signs that said, *Kill Zedda, An Eye for an Eye, I believe in Affirmative Action*. A few hundred of them. Of the abolitionists, but a single circled enclave. Like statues holding candles, several weeping. Calvin, who had never had so much to drink before that night, propped himself up in the backseat to stare at them as the car rolled slowly by. An old white-bearded man, looking through his blazing candle, seemed to recognize Calvin, because he smiled, even though he wept. The newspapers had reported for the last many weeks leading up to the execution that Zedda Pate had come to Jesus. But Calvin knew that was bullshit.

Some years later, at his job on the prison yard at Coventry, Calvin occasionally found himself telling the story of that night, how he had given in to the whore and what she had said to him. Each time he told it, the men around him laughed because somehow the story pained them, though they never could have said how or why. The more he related it, however, the more harrowing it became. Eventually, even the inmates turned away. Calvin realized that what had happened was his alone, taboo, to be kept secret. Thus, the little hours of All Souls, 1984, had reconciled themselves in Cal's mind in the images, like a double exposure, of that aging whore invoking her son as she winched down on him and the guttering candle of that clairvoyant old man outside the governor's front door.

Eleven days after the Pate execution, Calvin's mother, Elizabeth Gaddy, unexpectedly died. He quit school on the spot and traveled home to live with his father. He figured he would go back to his studies, but he never did. College was a dream his mother had had for him. As long as she was alive, he entertained that dream, took solace in it when the side of him that was indisputably his father bubbled up: harrow blade, the lash, unlabeled mash in a Dixie cup by firelight.

His mother: string of pearls and set of teeth to match, the Holy Bible and biscuit flour, the condensation on her tea glass, lipstick on the straw. Sunday was her claim: church, cake and chicken, *Sweet Jesus* till everyone around her was fit to tear Him off the tree. But no one crossed her. She had about her something spooky that comes from living in the mystery of the body and blood. She really believed, and a mallet to her cheek or the sky teeming buckshot would not change her.

Calvin's father was set opposite. He would not pray with her, not MacGregor Gaddy. Cal prayed with her, though, even after his belief fell off. He loved his mother; he couldn't break her heart. That was his father's province. She adored

Calvin, wrote it in letters and poems, saved everything he had ever drawn or written. She insisted he would build bridges and dams, missions and cathedrals like the ones he scratched out on paper as a child, those last two slashes on the steeple tip that looked less a cross than an X.

His father said Cal would end up at the prison camp. It had been good enough for him. Hadn't he spent thirty some dad-blasted years schooling convicts - more Christian work than most? And hadn't every red cent of salt and meal and thread come from it? On and on like the avalanche of empty bottles hidden in the beadboard the night of Cal's conception, the night the gale took Saint Joan's County. But the house didn't fall. Not Calvin's father's house, his mother crying, her muslin dress blowing about her on the piano bench as she played *Vesti La Giubba*.

"Breakheart," she would say breathlessly. "Breakheart." Crying, throwing her arms around her husband when finally he returned from tracking an escaped convict. Nearly dead himself and filthy in her white arms and dress, near-smiling over her shoulder at his little son gazing up at him. This was his woman. MacGregor Gaddy had no doubt. Nor did she. Even the worst blow to light in a hundred years could not shake his house down. Calvin's father had been right. His son ended up at the camp.

CHAPTER 2

From half a mile off, Cal made out the concertina idling cursively along Coventry Prison Camp's perimeter, the sun imbedded in a wall of blue. Above it, though not another cloud to be seen, stretched a long black brow. It was in the glint of the wire in the sun that everything about who he was came back to him, anchoring him in a consciousness that was both wistful and unreal.

He passed a pasture of black and white belted Herefords and turned right at Prison Camp Road, then swung into the camp lot, parked next to Sergeant Thrake's perfectly manicured two-toned '57 Chevy, and headed for the office to check in.

Count had just cleared. The shift was changing from first to second. Inmates slipped slowly out of the dormitory. Except for the cooks, who dressed in white, they all wore brown clothes to mark them as felons, though at a distance the bled-out fabric looked grey.

In the parking lot, just beyond the main gate, stood a big young guard named Friend who held a mammoth shotgun, the guard and shotgun each exaggerations of the other. Coventry was a gun camp, its two towers manned with armed guards twenty-four hours. At shift change, they counted. Three times daily. It was protocol to have at these times an extra gun – in this case, Friend – facing the front gate.

He turned to Calvin. "Gaddy."

"Afternoon, Friend."

"I'm fixing to clock out directly."

"Okay," said Cal. "Let me check in and I'll be right out to relieve you."

Coventry's captain slumped behind an immaculate desk in his office. He was either asleep or in a stupefied, capitulant reverie, as if the effort at remembrance had made him terribly sad. In his tie and coat, bent back and poor shave, he looked completely blameless. He had that drugged, though expectant, mug of a felon waiting for promotion to honor grade. Above his nodding head pined a picture of the governor; and, just to the left of it, the mounted head of a jackrabbit to which the taxidermist had somehow attached the small rack of a new buck.

In one corner, the United States flag fell from its pole, in the opposite corner the state flag. The only other piece of furniture in the tiny office was a three-tiered glass case filled with contraband. Mostly homemade: shivs, zip-guns, pieces of the everyday – toothbrushes, combs, spoons, shoelaces – fashioned to lay a man open. Among them was a spiked leather collar, with an attached leash.

Calvin stared at the leash for a moment as he waited for the captain to come around. When he didn't, he walked across the hall and into the secretary's office. He grabbed his card and hit the clock, then dropped it back in its slot. The secretary, Blish, wore a yellow patch over one eye, which made more provocative her black-headed, red-lipsticked good looks. A different colored patch every day to match her outfits. She was the captain's girl, though each was married.

She talked on the telephone, reading off a notepad: "Yes. Concertina wire for the perimeter. With the new long barbs. SS 1289. Excalibur."

She looked up at Cal and waved. "Uh-huh. The organic finish, chromate coated and galvanized, cold-formed, high tensile yield. Uh-huh. That'll be fine. Thanks. Bye now."

"Hey, Cal," she said.

"Hey, Blish."

"How's that wife of yours getting along?"

"Just fine. Rounder and rounder."

"That goes with the territory."

"I reckon."

"Is the captain still asleep?" she asked.

"Yeah."

"Bless his heart."

"I better get. Friend's waiting for me to relieve him."

5

"Take this damn thing," said Friend, handing Cal the shotgun. "I think you'll find everything in order. Happy trails."

"Later."

"Keep an eye out for Thrake. He's on the warpath."

Cal immediately broke the shotgun, took both shells out, pocketed them and replaced them with two others. The fence line filled with apparitions of men who stared at Cal, men filled with words, but without language, dozens of stories sealed off by chain-link and razor wire. The sun had been eclipsed by the brow above it. The sky turned the color of felon clothes.

Thrake lumbered across the yard, his mouth going up and down like a pump. The men at the fence shouted. Cal looked up at the tower where Ernestine, Coventry's first and only woman guard, threw up her hands like *I don't know*.

Thrake marched right up behind the men at the fence and yelled, "Get the hell away from that fence." Then he yelled at the tower, "Goddam move them off that fence." Then at Cal: "What the hell do you think is in your hand, Gaddy? Your dick?"

It was posted on the fence that inmates should at all times keep five feet between themselves and the fence – a rule to which no one, especially Cal, ever paid much attention. He walked toward the fence, the shotgun held casually up toward the sky.

"Move back from there, fellas."

Backing off, they laughed at what Thrake had barked at Cal, but not at Thrake. He was the shift sergeant, one of the old-liners and there wasn't anything about anything he cherished save his reputation on the yard and his automobile. He walked right through the throng, opened the first gate with his key, then the tower buzzed him through the second one.

"Got one gone," he said to Cal. "You're coming with me."

"Who's gone?"

"That goddam witch doctor or whatever the hell he is."

6

"But count just cleared."

"Well, it ain't cleared."

Cal glanced up at the tower again. Ernestine was on the phone. Guards fanned into the yard from the sergeant's office. Cal wondered where the captain was, but the front office door never opened.

"Lock'em down," Thrake yelled over his shoulder. "C'mon, Gaddy."

Cal followed Thrake into the parking lot, climbed into the passenger seat of one of the vans and racked his gun. It started to rain the second Thrake turned the engine over, and in five minutes Cal was asleep.

CHAPTER 3

When he was just a little boy, Cal had gone on escapes with his father. Two days of water and kill everything else they needed to live: possum, squirrel, geese, quail, deer. His father had once killed a cow and carved steaks out of it. They camped and tracked, barely speaking. A canteen with Mac's whiskey. Take the pickup, the bloodhounds, and a dog-boy named Frankenstein, an old convict who smelled out inmates, half-dog himself, still doing time at the camp, long past the point of ever going home, of even remembering a home.

Frank had been on the state since he was twelve. Convicted of raping a white girl down east in pickle country, they had castrated him, then put him away for life. It had all been legal; it was on the books. They made Frank a eunuch and then sent him off at twelve to live with men in the penitentiary. He never had grown a beard or sprouted hair except on his head. Stayed smooth and pretty. So did his voice. In the joint, they just ate the boy alive, tore him to pieces, went at him like cotton candy – cloy and venom.

Over time, Frankenstein found himself in a jackpot between a convict and guard, both of whom, as Frank told it, were punking him. Who Frank belonged to became a battle between them. The convict believed Frank was just another thing the man wanted to take away. He and Frank were, after all, of the same pedigree, though the convict white and Frank black. The guard had to show he had control – complete, unquestionable. Custody has to do with entering someone, and the only way the guard could enter the convict was through Frank. A game the convict knew he could not win.

One night Frank dreamt about that imperceptible tear that had all along been there in the tether that held his life on course. Before the chain gang: a road with orange flowers, a kid on his first bicycle, a spotted dog. The instant before his real life had torn like threadbare into a strip of hell.

As Frank dreamt, the cuckolded convict smeared Frank's face with airplane glue and torched it with a Zippo. The glue annealed fire to the boy's countenance. Even as he screamed and pin-balled about the cellblock – beating his face against the concrete, the bars, beating himself with his fists – his opened mouth transformed into a tiny hole just inside of which his teeth melted. No one made to help him. Finally, the very guard who had chatteled Frank, that night's duty man, opened the block, and blackjacked and jackbooted out his flaming face the way he might a brush fire.

Eventually, Frank recovered, his face torn apart: cut, crushed and incinerated, then all hinged back together again in a crazy graft that gave it the consistency of paraffin and the profile of Idaho's eastern border. No one ever bothered him again – he was too hideous, hence the name, Frankenstein – but they made a place for him, prison a place where horror lacks a threshold. Frank swore he never raped that girl.

Cal's mother never wanted him to go on escapes with his father and Frank.

"Leave the boy, MacGregor," she would say. But by then his father already had on his boots and gun belt. Frank sat in the truck bed with the dogs, munching a pimento cheese sandwich Cal's mama had carried to him. She would not have him in the house, though never would say such.

"Leave the boy, MacGregor." But with no heart in it because she believed in her husband, and allowed he knew best what made a man. Knew what made a man run too.

"Elizabeth," Mac said, kissed her, then they walked out to the truck and she prayed. They all had to join hands, even Frank. His father gave in to this praying and hand-joining, hating it, wanting to get on with it, crushing Cal's hand in his whenever they found themselves linked in that prayer circle, the mother crying softly, then taking Cal in her arms: "Oh, if only you knew, my sweet boy."

As a child, Cal had been mesmerized by Frank. Could not look away, yet looking robbed his breath. His mother admonished him not to stare, that Frank was bearing in his face the aberration of others. This is the way of the Creator, she

9

told him. Mystery. Signs. Parables. Love that face or do not look at all; but Cal saw the times she gasped when suddenly she ran up on Frank, her eyes darting about their sockets. His father never seemed to notice Frank's frightfulness and felt any talk to try to accept it or explain it away dignified the lowdown way of things. Frank was a convict. This was the beginning and end of it.

Though gentled and quite old, Frank was a monster, literally. He looked nothing, however, like Shelley's monster. That would have been a relief to Cal. Sitting out in the woods around the fire with his father and Frank. The way the monster caught the light, like looming nightmare, mumbling something occasionally while Mac just stared at the fire and sipped; and somewhere, maybe watching them, the convict they sought.

"Little Cal," Frank would say, his voice like air escaping a balloon. "Listen. We got a Mr. Fox or a Mr. Rabbit." Then Frank smiled, a smear in soft yellow wax, and from his lotus position put his nose on the earth and sniffed.

"Mr. Fox," he'd call out into the woods where the running boy hid. "You a Mr. Fox? Mr. Rabbit?"

On their spits, skinned squirrels cracked. Before MacGregor passed the bottle to Frank, he tethered him to a tree by a thirty foot chain and let him talk all night about his old days as a dogboy with Ruther, the bounty hunter:

"Be all night at the catching. Color boy. White. I blood Ruther's hounds and save me a whipping. That simple. State pay him twenty dollars on the head. He bring them in, he get paid. Otherwise, no. Ruther a bad son farmer who do on the side what the man can't do for hisself. Out here in the dark, it don't pay to make a step unless you a dog or Ruther. I yip so real a rabbit convict think I'm a bloodhound and go to confound me through a creek, circle back, leave cowlick in the pine pitch and little sprinkles of his mess just like a fox do. And there be Ruther with his sawed-off in one hand and logging chain in other. And that Mr. Fox, he kneel down right there in the creek bed and pray him not shoot while I creep up behind and press the steel like the shivering word of

10

Moses on him. Then Ruther have me strike up a fire and shin down a possum and we eat the glassy meat in front of Fox, his eyes big-like. All them stories that Ruther's roundup be a convict boneyard, that the quarry behind Coventry yard seasoned with his bounties. We feed the camp dogs the tails and ears. Bones. We eat off fire-sticks."

When the squirrels were done, the eyes fell out. Then Frank handed Mac and Cal a stick and kept one for himself. Out in the woods came whimpering. Could have been anything. Mac never looked at his son, as if to do so was to admit something. Frank swigged off the bottle whenever he felt so moved.

"Will we get him tomorrow?" Cal asked.

"This one, he smart. This fox-rabbit." Frank let out a keen that shook the boy. He wanted to go to his father. Mac spit in the fire. Frank keened again.

"I yipping, though what voice I got when I ain't yipping is screech or what you might call hawk whisper. Come from them making me eunichoid in '15. Judge told the doctor put me to sleep and when I wake that that. And never had nary the first woman."

"Shut up, Frank," said Mac. The dogs ripped at the bones.

They always collared the fugitive. He'd simply wear out. Find him slumped against a tree or crouched in a corncrib, all the fight and swagger gone, the dogs swarming him. Cal's father would lay back and send Frank on. Frank had a way of approaching the convict, his arms out like the Good Shepherd. Cal had seen more than one throw himself into Frank's arms and weep, then allow himself to be led back to the truck. Mac never touched a fugitive, never said so much as a word, and the convict knew to hush. After Frank had buckled him to the bed, and jumped in too with the dogs, Mac slide behind the wheel and they started back to Coventry.

Once they found an escape dead in a cottonwood, wedged way up at the top as if he had lighted there from the sky rather than climbed. Dogs sometimes pushed a running man to impossible feats. Doctor said he had died part of fright, part melancholy. There had not been any other way to land

11

him back to earth, but shoot him down.

Found a man once sitting in a field of orange poppies, eating the heads off the flowers. They watched him for a long time, Cal's father's eyes, just behind the impervious irises, registering with absolute fidelity the entire scene. They came up on men in every conceivable manner, brought them back to camp and threw them in the Boot.

But if a man bucked, Mac would do whatever. His temper was ingenious, exquisite. Were he holding a gun, he'd shoot, spraying pheasant-shot with both barrels. The convict jumped, legs bicycling midair, then crashed in the weeds, shanks and loins punctured with growing red periods.

MacGregor Gaddy threw rocks. He hit a convict with a dog once, beat another with a live black snake. He'd run him down with the truck, throw himself on him from the speeding vehicle. Pound him with his fists, with a coffee pot, never saying a word. Few of them tested him, but came on out, solemn as church, and surrendered at the sight of him.

When they arrived back at the Gaddy house after a manhunt, Mrs. Gaddy sent Cal up to shower, then led her husband into the downstairs bathroom, locked the door and bathed him.

Cal was not the same sort as his father. He did not really believe in prison, nor own the proper temperament. He knew how to do his job at the camp and that was the end of it.

CHAPTER 4

Thrake turned onto a dirt road running between two sets of power lines under which Angus cattle grazed. A man and a boy fished at a little pond. Thrake stopped the van.

"You seen a man come by here? Black man in white clothes and hair all up in knots?"

"No," said the man. The boy stared at Thrake.

"You have not?"

"No," repeated the man.

"Son of a bitch," oathed Thrake, driving off.

He turned up a rutted clay drive. On both sides of it fell fallow cornfields out of which gray chopped stalks stubbed. Foraging crows went up as the van passed. A trio of deer regarded them for a moment, zigzagged toward the trees and stopped. When they drove up on an abandoned homestead, Thrake stopped the car again.

"You go on in there and scout for him. I'll ride further down the road."

Cal turned and looked at Thrake. "Alright," he answered and stepped out of the vehicle.

Thrake handed him the shotgun. "Check them outbuildings too."

Cal stood in front of the house in the misting drizzle. He looked out where the deer, now a long way off, still stood. They had their heads down. Wisps of fog rolled out of the woods. The crows settled back to the ground. Cal wanted to shoot the gun off – to see the deer run. He yelled at them, but they didn't budge. He heard the prison van, though it was out of sight.

The front door of the house hung open. He walked quickly through the four downstairs rooms leading off a shotgun hall. Nothing. Spider webs, dauber nests, dust and the acrid smell of abandonment. On one wall was red-crayoned: *Jesus Saves*. There was nowhere to hide. Not even a closet.

The stairs were solid, not a creak to them, packed with

dust. At the top lay an ossified crow. Cal kicked it out of the way and stood on the landing. There were only two rooms. Nothing at all in the first, but an open flue hole. Through it whispered the darkening day tunneling toward him, then the clipped flutter of bird wings. The door to the other room was tightly closed.

Cal knew pretty well the man they were looking for. His name was Tarl Benefit. He cooked first shift in the kitchen. The other men called him Pitch, sometimes Conjure Man. He was the camp mystic and also one of its racket kingpins. He had started out reading palms and predicting outcomes of football and basketball games by consulting his augur, an ancient-looking rust-stained mason jar in which, floating in a yellow brackish liquid, were three turkey wishbones, an eyeball, and locks of wiry hair shorn, Pitch swore, from the heads of his ancestors. According to Pitch, the augur was three centuries old and had been passed along in his family to the chosen one of each generation. The Coventry inmates testified that Pitch could come and go, astrally project himself from his body, that at night when the rest of the population was locked down, he consorted with the night.

His biggest game was reefer and Thrake was hell-bent on busting it. Cal was not sure how politic this was. A stoned population was a docile population. Everyone knew that reefer kept the lid on the camp. There was a certain amount of give and take that had to go on among the convicts and the guards. The guards let the inmates go so far, and the inmates knew how far to go. An unspoken code. And Thrake had decided to violate it. Once he had a hard-on for something. Not that he was idealistic. He was simply a jack-raising son of a bitch.

Having been on the state nearly twelve years, Cal knew a few things. Not to mention he had been raised in it. For some time, he had been mulling over sitting for the Sergeant's Exam. Rachel, his wife, had encouraged him to take a crack at it – if he was going to make a life of prison – and there was the baby coming.

He cocked the shotgun, and spoke to the door. "Pitch,

14

if you are in there, I'll give you ten seconds to come out and then I'm coming in. This is Gaddy and I will brook no nonsense."

The doorknob stared at Cal. He put his hand on it and turned. Locked. He stepped back a pace, lowered the gun and kicked. The molding splintered. When he kicked again, the door shot open. The room was empty. Not a stick, just the two words, *Jesus Saves*, again on one of the walls. Cal released the hammers and set the shotgun in a corner. Walked to the window. Through the antique glass, the landscape undulated. He lifted the window, but it would not stay. He propped it with the shotgun, dug from his pocket one of the shotgun shells Friend had given him, and with a pocket knife slit the casing.

Inside were five joints. He lit one and stared out the window. Beneath him sprawled a dead pasture trussed in rusty barbed wire. In it were a big barn, a corn crib and a wooden silo that looked like a minaret. He could see for a long way. Tobacco grew in the surrounding fields. For a moment, a swath of sun cut out of the mist and darted across the tobacco, the plants the size of a small boy, leaves splaying out from their stalks and eerily glowing in patches where the light hit. Far beyond the fields, Cal made out a single-steepled whitewashed church sitting in a band of light on the horizon. Then the sun disappeared and it began to rain a little harder.

Cal burned half the joint, stubbed it out on the sill and returned it to the cartridge. He retrieved the gun, walked out of the house and stood in the rain. It felt good standing there, stoned, washed in the downpour. He heard the van again and soon Thrake came into sight. He was by himself.

"Well," he said.

"He's not here," said Cal.

"You check the barn and outbuildings?"

"Every inch."

"Son of a bitch." Thrake banged on the steering wheel. "You think there's anything to this black magic of his?"

"I don't know, Sarge."

"Shit."

Pitch had hold of Thrake. Cal could tell, and he relished it. The hell with Thrake. He wanted to play John Wayne. Let him go on. For true, he could break most men. He was that hard. But Pitch had gotten next to him, had planted in his skull a hexing. Pitch had Thrake believing he could witch him.

CHAPTER 5

When Thrake and Cal got back to the camp, they found that Pitch had not escaped at all. He had been in the cookshack all along. Someone had botched the count. Thrake marched into the office. Cal followed, checked his gun, and stood for a while outside the captain's closed door. Thrake was in there. Blish, typing in the office right across, had her back to him. She turned and looked at him, and he walked out to the parking lot. It was still raining.

A dump truck, loaded with the tar squad, pulled up. The prisoners wore leg-irons and orange highway vests emblazoned with black letters, *Inmate*, their boots caked with asphalt and gravel. Two guards climbed out of the cab, pulled out shotguns and walked to the back of the truck. Each man slid off the tailgate and lined up at the fence to be patted down. The stench of burning road rose off them.

Cal looked at these men through the gauze of marijuana. A scene he had witnessed all his life. He didn't know what it meant, but it had a familiarity which was both comforting and disorienting, and for a few seconds he lost himself among them. He shivered. He had not eaten for a very long time.

"Ernestine," he yelled up to the tower, and Ernestine buzzed him in the first gate. He let himself in the second. Two guys played catch with a baseball and fielders' gloves in front of the canteen. He nodded at them and walked to the chowhall. The hoops were deserted. Pinging from the horseshoe pit as the iron shoes hit the stakes. There was a tiny garden next to the canteen: tomatoes, carrots, squash, okra, green beans. Just one man in the stocks, a booster queen, still decked in his make-up, eye-witnessed at prostitution. Mascara had run down his cheeks which, along with the smeared rouge and lipstick, gave him the sad look of a clown. A crow sat on the collar-board through which the booster's head peeked. His hands dangled from the lock-holes like limp white gloves.

Close to chow, the cook crew, dressed in white, hustled about the kitchen. Giant stainless steel pots and pans. Smoke rising from the steam tables. The deep fry boiled with blonde grease, the ladle going up and down, fetching out dripping fried catfish and potatoes. Cal liked the kitchen. It was big and white and clean, airy, well-lit and reminded him of the camp parties he had come to with his father and mother at Christmas, and on the Fourth of July. It was the only place at Coventry where he could lower his guard. He poured himself a cup of coffee.

Brotherton, the chow-boss, bulled out of the walk-in with a fifty pound sack of potatoes, and nodded at Cal.

"Cut up these spuds," he bellowed at one of the cooks. "And bring Mr. Gaddy here a plate."

"You have a pleasant wild goose chase?" Brotherton asked Cal. He wore a long white coat over his uniform, sleeves rolled off massive hairy forearms.

"Pretty fair," said Cal. "As these things go."

They both laughed.

"I never thought Thrake had room in his head for more than one thought at a time. But, you know, I believe he's got him an imagination. Hoodoo and whatnot. He's shitting green apples over that witch doctor."

"Yeah," said Cal. "He's got himself worked up pretty good."

"He has done made a proper ass of hisself this time. I hear Pitch was in his bunk the whole time. He's sitting in the cook-shack now."

"Yep."

"There'll be hell to pay," predicted Brotherton, walking off. "Step it up, boys. Fifteen minutes."

A gangly, jet-black cook laid a plate of fish, potatoes, slaw and hush puppies in front of Cal.

"Thanks, Snoo," he said to the cook.

Cal had eaten his share of chaingang food. Since he was old enough to remember. Right there in the Coventry kitchen, almost every day at the shift change when his father sat after clocking out and drank a glass of buttermilk and Cal was given something sweet from one of the bakers. Cornbread in milk and sorghum, pie or cake. They'd give him anything his father would allow. MacGregor sitting there with the Stetson off his sunbaked face, a rosette of blue and red tiny veins coiled on each cheekbone, the eyes like no eyes because they were colorless and without pupil or all pupil; and Cal, though he wanted to be near his father, had no specific recollection of his ever smiling.

Back then, the guards had not worn uniforms. They favored the dress of field men and mechanics: khakis, denims, wide brims and work boots. No one mistook his father for anything but what he was: the first shift ramrod whose yes was yes and no was no. He had been purely afraid of nothing, including God. Not a bit of play about him, although the old captain his father had sergeanted for had been an equal son of a bitch.

It was Frank who always sidled over, wary, obsequious, with that tall glass of buttermilk. They kept the glass special for Mac in the kitchen. The inmates were permitted only plastic and tin. Mac had to have it in a glass and ice cold. He wrapped around the glass his big fleshy fingers, lift it and look at it. White and impenetrable, clots of clabber bobbing just at its surface, the glass sweating. In one swallow he took it down, his throat a stump his head fell back from, cording. Then the glass came down on the table and Mac wiped his lips with the back of his hand.

The glass, like an oracle, mapped with greasy threads of butter, horrified Cal. Got to where he couldn't look at it without growing queasy. How was this glass his father? He knew that it was, but he could not connect the two. Every day that glass at that table at that same time when count had cleared and the yard men shouted the number to one another and on up to the towers, the gravel in the parking lot crunching as the second shift wheeled in.

Years later, after Cal had taken a job at Coventry and his father retired, Frank had been the one to tell him about that daily pint of buttermilk, that every day before Frank so meekly set it down in front of Sergeant Gaddy, each man

19

working the kitchen took the glass and dipped his business in it. Then, with veiled eyes, never so much as smirking, they watched the sergeant drain it, just as his only child had watched. Cal had to laugh and nearly cry every time he took a bite in the chow hall. There was always that glass in front of him, the vision of those men passing it on, unzipping and zipping back their white state britches, and then Frank, almost curtsying, delivering it.

In an easy chair tkept for him in one corner of the big room, next to the piano where Snoo played a slow, slow *Chinatown*, Frank nodded. Maybe to the tune or because he was drifting off. He was up past ninety now, and blind, stick thin so that his ugliness was caving in on him, scars on scars of ashy pellucid, like wax rolling down a taper.

The food was good. Cal figured if it had been subjected to some obscenity for his benefit, then he probably had it coming. Hell, they all had it coming.

He went over to Frank and put his hand on his shoulder.

"Little Cal," squeaked the old monster. "My ace poon coon."

Cal laughed. "You're a sight, Frank."

"Life to die, Little Cal. Just making my time."

Cal patted him. "You take care, Frank."

"Care take me. Lights getting low."

CHAPTER 6

In the yard, the men massed for chow, catching last drags on their cigarettes before throwing them down and going in to eat. Snoo held a plate for the guy in the stocks who had his head in the food like a scarfing dog. The weather felt like it was changing a little. Cool. Cal was still wet.

The cookshack was a little concrete, barred building that stood alone from the others. Always overheated in a carnal, enveloping way. Fans whirling and the thermostat jacked up. And always, winter and summer, year in and year out, there were flies; and a stink Cal could not make out, something cooking – and the ubiquitous stench of custody at close quarters.

Most of the bunks, three-tiered, narrow, steel, gray tick and bedclothes, were filled with lounging and sleeping men who had risen at four in the morning to work breakfast and lunch. The others sat around, smoking, watching TV or plugged in with earphones to radios, milling in and out of the tiny latrine, two piss stalls and a shit jacket, to void and shower. No one paid Cal much mind. Those who noticed him come in nodded as to a fellow convict. He was accorded a kind of acceptance among them, thin, but not without substance. They had heard of his father and this tithed him to an earth still wet and burning with their blood.

On television played a soap opera, the scene a stark jail cell with two men in it. One, a young, handsome, perfectly-coiffed, falsely-accused rich guy taking the fall for his beloved girlfriend. The other was a big, drooling seasoned con out to have his way with him. The camera cut to the face of the jaded guard who obviously knew what was going on, but refused to step in. The young man pleaded for mercy. There was the close-up of his contorted face, then the big con's leer. Pan to two sets of feet on the floor, one behind the other, planted in the same direction. The guard's face in his hands. The young man's pleas of *No, no*. Violin and bass

21

piano. The cooks watching burst into laughter. Others, trying to sleep, sat up in bed, bleary-eyed, cussing.

In the middle of the concrete floor sat Pitch, sweat standing out on his upper lip and forehead as he sat over his book and hotplate.

"Heard you escaped today," said Cal. "In fact, I just got back from trying to find you."

Pitch glanced up from the pot he was stirring and smiled. "Did you find me?"

Cal thought he smelled buck on Pitch's sweet breath, but it was hard to tell for the aroma wafting out of the muddy stew.

"No. But I didn't look very hard."

They both laughed. Next to Pitch, on the floor, was his augur; and next to it a shoebox. In it were labeled jars: *cat and snail fat, oil of rain worms, spiders, pigeon talons, chicken gizzards, sheep manure.*

"What are you doing, Pitch?"

"Incanting."

"Run that by me again."

"Preparing a spell for the man."

"Thrake?"

"The same."

"Well, it's your constitutional right to practice freedom of religion; and this great state supports you in that exercise. So you go on and incant away. Just so you stay this side of contraband."

"Of course."

"Why didn't you turn up at count today? Where were you?"

"I was asleep in my bunk. Any of these men can verify it. Your colleague, Icemorelee, made the count. I was here all along. He sometimes falters in his numbers. I've noticed it before."

"Well, I reckon you were. I've yet to see a man escape and then beat it back here in time for evening chow."

"All things are possible."

"I will not discount that fact."

"This morning in the kitchen I dropped a ten pound sack of salt."

"So?"

"A sign. Signs have been thickening for weeks."

Pitch's eyes were glazed and bulging. Cal figured him for drunk or stoned, one. Maybe both. Cal knew he had a little buck operation going on on top of the reefer. It was nothing for him and the other cooks to smuggle out of the kitchen enough potatoes and fruit, anything, really, to brew it. A little sugar, yeast. A bucket. This did not bother Cal too much. But he was at a loss about the reefer. How it was coming in? How big was it? He wanted to get to the bottom of it before Thrake, but it would mean serious busts, an all-out shakedown.

"What would you have done, Mr. Gaddy, if you had found me out there today on escape?"

Cal saw himself in front of the closed door on the second storey of that abandoned farm house, the shotgun in his hand coming up belly high, the hammers' inflection, the smashed door veering in on the void.

"I would have saved your ass from Sergeant Thrake."

On television the ruined man lay whimpering face down on his mattress. In the bunk above him, his cellmate smoked a cigarette and read a magazine. The guard passed along the block and paused at the cell. The young man hushed.

"Everything all right in there?" the guard asked.

"Aces and eights," said the man in the top bunk.

The scene faded with a shot of the lower bunk, the sodomized man curled up, a corner of his blanket stuffed in his mouth. A commercial for perfume: a long-haired woman in a flowing white gown galloping in slow motion through a field of larkspur.

"Good God Almighty," one of the Coventry cooks whispered prayerfully.

Cal went into the latrine. He stood at the trough and urinated. Next to him, on the lone seatless sit-down toilet, was a man with his pants around his ankles, arms crossed on his knees, head on his arms. He seemed asleep. In one of his hands was a roll of gray toilet paper and in his other a Bible. A waist-high wall stood behind the trough and toilet. On the other side of it was the shower, a length of pipe descending from the flaking ceiling with a spigot on either side of it. A man, lit by the light from the high, barred naked window, stood in a trance under its labored stream. The walls blued with mildew.

CHAPTER 7

Talfont hurried into the cook shack, slamming the door behind him. Giant flies rose up from the doorjamb, buzzing noisily, before settling back down. Again, the sleeping cooks murmured obscenities. Talfont was one of Pitch's boys. He had long black hair sheathed in a bandana and a black goatee cut to a point. His favorite quip was that he was doing life on the installment plan.

"Thrake just busted the coffee," he announced. "And he's on his way up here."

The coffee game was another of Pitch's enterprises. He simply stole instant coffee, sugar, whitener and Styrofoam cups from the kitchen, then turned it all over to Talfont who ran the racket from the dorm. Coffee was served only at breakfast. After the canteen closed at five, the only place to buy it was Talfont's bunk. Hot water from the latrine tap was used to mix it.

Pitch's eyebrows shot up and he nodded toward the latrine just as Cal walked out of it.

"I'm not interrupting anything, I hope," said Cal.

"My ass is cooked," said Talfont.

Thrake stormed into the room, picked up over his head the little black and white TV and slammed it to the floor. The machine sputtered, skittered along the floor for a few seconds, then sent out a white arrow of light and exploded.

One of the sleeping men screamed. Then they were all awake, cussing and yelling until they saw Thrake standing there, panting and sweating, moving his eyes from face to face around the room, holding for a little longer, Cal felt, on him. Icemorelee, a guard who had come to back Thrake, was trying not to look at anyone. He stood in the doorway, batting flies from his face.

"Out of the bunks, girls," Thrake shouted, undoing a riot baton from his belt. "And stand-to like count."

The men climbed out and lined up. Pitch kept his seat.

Thrake turned to Talfont: "You like a good cup of coffee, boy?"

"I don't drink coffee."

"Don't drink coffee? You sure got a sight of it under your bunk for one who don't drink it."

"There ain't nothing under my bunk but fucking cockroaches."

"Under the bunk. In the bunk. That whole dorm's full of cockroaches," said Thrake. "Put the jewelry on Maxwell House here, Icemorelee, and Boot his sorry ass up."

Icemorelee stepped up and handcuffed Talfont.

"You like coffee so good, I'm going to see that you get all you want," vowed Thrake.

"I said I don't drink coffee."

"Yeah, I heard that. Now you run along. Good to the last drop."

Icemorelee grabbed one of Talfont's arms and led him out.

Thrake wheeled on Pitch. "I know you're at the bottom of this. At the bottom of every shady lick on this camp."

Pitch stared at Thrake as if memorizing him.

"You're just as smooth as a baby's ass. Ain't you?" said Thrake. "Stand up."

Cal looked around the room and counted. Ten plus Pitch and the two in the latrine. He stayed stock-still, not wanting to upset the precarious balance, moving only his eyes to look at the shocked faces of the cooks. The room tightened, got smaller. A fly landed on his cheek. Thrake kicked over the hotplate along with the steaming pot that held Pitch's potion.

The little building tilted slightly. Everyone jumped, though Cal could swear that no one had moved. Men held on to their bunks. The shower trickled. Pitch stood, his whites brown-splotched like the coat of a snow leopard, his face dripping. The room reeked with the overturned liquid.

"We better get you out of them wet clothes. We don't want you catching cold," sneered Thrake, running his shirt sleeves across his splashed face.

Pitch smiled. His teeth were perfect, white as arrowroot.

He studied Thrake. "I don't catch colds, Sergeant Thrake."

"Strip, Houdini."

Pitch did not move. Thrake shouted, "Strip, you piece of shit," and banged a metal locker with his stick. The room again seemed to list.

Cal wondered where the hell the captain was. Hadn't Icemorelee reported this? Pitch took off his T-shirt, then his pants, shoes and socks. In just a pair of white boxer's shorts, he had the fanatic body of a light heavyweight ready to rush across the canvas and destroy his enemy. The white-ridged crescent beneath his bulging right pectoral where he had been shot. Another scar checked across his upper lip. Cal felt like he was being stripped. He wanted out of the building. What the devil was Thrake trying to prove?

"Everything," Thrake ordered.

Pitch raked the shorts down and stepped out of them. One man let go of his bunk and slid as though on ice a few feet forward. Thrake raised the riot baton over him and held it there.

"No one move," he said. "No one. I cannot be scared. I cannot be hurt. You don't know what all I have in me to do to you with no conscience at all. I can have you dead and it will be like you never were."

The man fainted and lay in the stinking spell-broth. The other men gasped as if they had just witnessed a miracle. The heat of the building smelted them. Cal could barely breathe. He felt faint himself. The man with the Bible walked in from the latrine. Thrake whacked him in the head. He went over like a dead sapling, his book landing open at Pitch's wet feet.

"Now you turn around and relax," said Thrake. "We are going to conduct a little skin search."

Pitch glanced at Cal, then turned.

"Step over here with me, Gaddy," said Thrake. "Your superior understanding of convicts might come in handy."

Cal left the doorway and stood behind Thrake.

"Assume the position, Houdini."

Pitch spread his legs, then leaned at forty-five degrees into the wall, his arms extended ahead of him. Standing behind Pitch, Thrake took his stick and ran it along his arms, then into the armpits, then up and down his legs.

"Where were you today?" Thrake asked Pitch.

"In my bunk. I have witnesses."

"Witnesses. You were out there somewhere. Weren't you?"

Pitch was the color of whitened coffee. His head fell forward as he pushed into the wall. His scrotum hung like a peach, visible from behind through his opened legs. Thrake stuck the stick in between his legs and banged it around. Pitch did not move; the electricity coursing through his body sent out sparks.

"Now spread them."

Pitch reached back and with his hands spread his buttocks. Thrake prodded him with the stick.

"Bet you like that," Thrake cracked.

Pitch's face was a mask.

"Alright. Get dressed," said Thrake, walking to the door. "Take him to the office for a piss test, Gaddy."

CHAPTER 8

Cal drove slowly through Coventry, a town dug into the slag-lands of Saint Joan's County and quit by everything but the church, post office, mortuary, and general store, each holding down a quadrant of the town square. A cadre of old mill houses, uniform in their anonymity and once-whiteness, staggered along the road where neurasthenic Guernseys mile-posted the way out of town.

He took the long way home, through the deep country. It was cold. Snowflakes feathered down among the drizzle.

"Jesus," he said and turned on the heat, pushed in the lighter and lit the last half of the joint he had started earlier. He was worried about Thrake and Pitch. Bound to be serious fallout. Exactly how it would play out was another question, but he wanted to stay as far away from it all as possible. The hell with it. Let Thrake stew; let him go crazy.

The road banks rose up in pines and beyond that stretched endless land no one had ever owned. A man could park, stand all night on the double yellow running down the middle of the road and see nothing but wild turkey, deer and bobcat. Cal braked when he came to Michelle Baptist Church, its congregation a constant throng of deer. From its lone steeple, a neon cross blazed in perpetuity. Deer, phantom-eyed and burning in his headlights, spread all over its grave-heads. They moved against the black wood-line like picture negatives, appearing and disappearing as Cal swung his truck around to better see them.

It was there one night in front of Michelle that Cal, on his way home, had looked up into the sky and seen a chaplet of rotating red and blue lights fuming as they skittered the sky and finally gyred into the black night curtain. Whatever could it have been that night, along with the deer beneath the gas cross, the moon levitating as it was now over the trees above the marsh, its broken face catching in a thousand pieces along the sluggish water? Way up where nothing could have been, nothing man-made. Angels? Flying saucers? These things he kept to himself. Rachel: he could her tell anything. But no one else. More often than not, these eleven miles of road home were all he had. The prison things, however, he refused tell his wife.

He drove on past the four dead cottonwoods called *The Four Sisters*, their thick arms gesticulating like hired mourners, startled bodies hairless and mottled. He swerved to miss a dead possum and saw at the last instant the motherless young nursing from the carcass. He thought of his baby in Rachel's womb. A spectacular brown-maned daughter who would never have to enter the doomsday universe of custody.

They had kicked names around. Elizabeth for his mother. Erica. Patricia. Never a boy's name. But he knew it was a boy. Despite the ultrasounds which revealed undoubtedly its girlness. He and Rachel kept magneted to the refrigerator a triptych of ultrasound photos: the little unmistakable head mounted on a shifting zodiac. How could a machine see into a someone and see another someone living there? Cal saw in that shadowy film pictures of a soul.

"Life to die," Frank liked to say. All those lives on the yard that had been given utterance through the sheer ignorance of instinct. Men and women cleaving together in the dark like animals making young that would someday do the same. Convicts: babies once, conceived in their deathbeds.

Cal feared fathering a boy, a boy like him who would be state-raised; and as a man do hard felon time, be electrocuted in the state's death house. The specificity of this vision terrified Cal, so much so that in his stoned trance he saw in his mind's eye the lavender eye shadow of the he-she giving head behind the cookshack, heard the click of buck glasses in the unpoliced dorm, smelled the invisible scurf that choked the air whenever guard and convict came in contact.

Suddenly he envisioned himself in felon browns, sitting on visiting day with his feet beneath a picnic table, hands folded in grace atop it, head bowed. Fresh from Sunday worship, in crinoline and white gloves, his mother sat across from him, praying. For him. Between them on the table were

30

her Bible and his daddy's pistol. Calvin saw who he was like words on a page.

In his daze, he ran off the road into a flat patch of scrub and briar. The swamp had been timbered out years ago. Among gleaming stumps, deer chattered. Cal rolled down the truck window. It was snowing.

CHAPTER 9

Calvin and Rachel lived in a trailer set in a tiny meadow on Gaddy land. Around it were ancient hardwoods and a rocky stream. From their front door, the land rose abruptly half a mile to the house where Calvin had grown up, a white two storey farmhouse in a dying pecan grove. Across from it were a barn and a cow pasture, and all around green corn, and wheat not far from harvest. There was one parcel of land, however, about thirty acres, that for the first time in memory had not been planted because it had been sold off by its owner for auction. Little plastic, pink flags waved among the broom sage and volunteer stalks of wheat. A few houses had already been framed. Backhoes and tractors leered out of the site.

Cal turned into the long, unpaved drive that wound past his parents' house and down the slope to his trailer. His father, up on the rise behind the house, watered his garden. The entire back of the house was trained in spotlights so that MacGregor Gaddy appeared in relief against the gray bank of clouds swelling up around him. The silver water shimmering out of the can looked like it spouted from the old man. Silver too was his hair, which of late he had neglected to have cut; it spiked along his neck like concertina. Next to him sat May, an old, once blonde, now rusty, shepherd-collie mix with a black tail. Cal shook his head and drove on, the image of his father watering in the rain and snow arranging itself in his head alongside the misty photos of his unborn child.

All the lights in the trailer were on. Rachel, eyes closed, lay on their bed, her nightgown hiked up over her naked stomach. One hand rested on it and in the other she held a wristwatch. Cal froze in the bedroom doorway and stared at his wife's white belly rising in a parabola above the bed. Six months into the pregnancy, he was still surprised by its beauty, its unlikelihood. Whatever high he had, coming into the house and seeing her like this turned him shaky. She was having contractions. It was not even fear that halted him anymore, but the dull fatigue of powerlessness.

"Hello, sweetheart," she said without opening her eyes.

"What's going on?"

"Not even a greeting, a dry peck for your wifus extremis?"

She opened her eyes. Blue. No color blue. Blondish brown hair. Freckles. She smiled. So tired. Cal went to her and kissed her lightly on the mouth, then kissed her stomach.

"What's up?" he asked.

"Oh, just a few contractions."

"How far apart?"

"Irregular."

"Have you ... ?"

"Yes, Daddy. I called the doctor."

"What did he say?"

"Come in if they get down to five minutes."

"God."

They had had this conversation so many times over the past weeks it was like a rehearsed script. Rachel had had trouble from the outset: spotting and gestational hypertension, swelling, terrible nausea which had never abated. She threw up every day. Preterm contractions at eighteen weeks.

Cal looked at her – worn out, lovely, smiling. *God, God*, he prayed, sat down on the bed and brushed the hair from her forehead.

"It's snowing," he said.

She started to cry.

"Everything will be alright," he whispered.

"I know."

"Does it hurt much?"

"I think they've stopped."

"Really?"

"Yes. They've stopped."

Rachel pulled down her gown, put the watch on the nightstand and shifted to her left side, a position that kept down her blood pressure.

"Everything will be fine." His refrain which he only half-believed. What he had come to trust in was doom. He wanted shed of doom.

"What are you thinking?" Rachel asked.

"Nothing really."

"Don't be worried, Calvin."

"I'm not." He brought her hand up to his mouth and kissed it.

"How was work?" she asked.

"You know. Alright. Nuts."

"What? Tell me."

"Just the system, honey. Bunch of crazy men running one another around."

"You don't tell me anything. Can't you see I'm starved for news of the outside world?"

Cal laughed. "That's not the outside world. Was my father down here today?"

"Uh huh. Twice. Once to cook me grits and once just to see how I was getting along. He's pretty distraught about those houses going up."

"Did he upset you?"

"No. He was fine. Just preoccupied in that silent rumbling way of his. Why don't you go up and look in on him?"

"Not tonight."

"For me?"

"Why?"

"I don't think he's eating."

"He's eating."

"Baby food, Calvin."

"Rachel. Listen. He's watering the damn garden in the rain and snow. Never mind. I'll go up there." He bent and kissed her. "You look tired."

"I am."

"Go to sleep. I won't be long."

"Calvin, I love you."

"I love you too." He kissed her again.

"You've been smoking pot."

He smiled. "I'm allowed. I'm not pregnant."

CHAPTER 10

Calvin walked slowly up the meadow hill to his father's house. Snow came steady at a slant. The wind picked up. It hit him in the face. He opened his mouth. Snow had begun to catch in the trees. As he walked, he felt smaller and smaller, so that when he came upon the house, its looming stature struck him as it always had when he was a boy. Off to the side of it was a massive satellite dish, its stamen pointed toward the moon.

His father, who had always had a garden, was on his hands and knees, his face hanging inches from the brown furrow, the lights making day around him, the snow like bone chips flecking their beams. It had stopped raining entirely.

Cal came quietly. The old man had a pistol on his hip. May let out a little grunt and sidled over to Cal, dragging one of her rear legs. He squatted down to pet her.

"Hey, girl. There. Yes, now. Good girl."

Her face was sad and grizzled, eyes filled with regret and recognition. MacGregor Gaddy lifted his head and looked at his son. The hair of his head fell to his face, raveled in a stringy silver beard. He wore overalls over a brown state convict shirt, and his prison jackboots. He looked astonished, as if he gazing into a looking glass, trying to deny himself. Everything about him said, *No.*

Cal remained fascinated by his father. For a long time, when he was little, he had thought his father more than just a man. There were times when he thought MacGregor might turn into something else – a bear or a wolf. That he might be about to come out of his skin or turn himself inside out. Rachel had said it perfectly. There was about him a rumbling. As if he were contemplating his own detonation.

"Papa," Cal called.

His father again regarded the soil. Then with his hands he dug at it for a moment. "I am seeing faces in my dirt," he said.

"Let's go in the house," said Cal.

Mac stood up, half a head taller than his son. His patch of corn flapped behind him. "Convict faces," he muttered.

Cal figured his father had always been crazy. A crazy that hadn't clashed much with the world Mac had lived in. He had toiled with men, fellow guards and convicts alike, who took his manner as his will and word for them. They tried to copy him like they would a preacher. How could he not be crazy? Now without the prison to grind his teeth down every day, without Cal's mother's Bible and doilies, her row of dresses in the bedroom closet, every inch of her livery that kept MacGregor sane and panting, he was just a man. A man without limits. Now he was seeing faces – the curse – what they called *devils* on the yard.

Cal did not want to call it *devils*. Did not even want to say the word in his head, but it said itself and blinked on like a hazard inside his eye. Devils were what too much prison work could do to you. Take a man like his father who would run an escaped convict three days on foot and lower himself into a bear tunnel just to make sure his man was not in it. A man who would have fought a bear for his prisoner, who Cal had seen once walk away from a bear, simply turn his back and walk as the bear lowered to all fours and stared. "Don't ask a bear a single question," his father had said. "He won't tolerate foolishness."

Mac Gaddy had once driven a truck through a barn because there was a man hiding in it, put out Cal and Frank and the dogs, then floored it. A ready-to-die man who could not be killed. Not a bounty hunter. Like Ruther. Not even a duty man. Though he was honor-sworn to whatever, right or wrong, he attached himself. And now he had devils. Convicts in his dreams, in his plowsoles and sunsets. He was being haunted.

Cal knew a little about it. His father had told him, but he had never seen it. Cal thought of it as *karma*,. Though that word had a cause-effect to it. Devils were arbitrary. There had been – were – worse state men, harder men, than his father. Maybe. But no one had stared so long and so deeply into what it took to separate a man's heart from his soul, then take each, nail it to a tree and let the dogs fight over it. He had made the shackle sacramental and now he was being visited. Cal would not say it. Say it and then it's out. Then his father would go to war against it. But his father knew, was already fighting it.

It grieved Cal to approach the house, which had always been a testament to order. It had fallen apart since his mother. In small accruals: flaking paint, listing gutters, trim wanting battening, Virginia Creeper twining the balusters, porch furniture rusty, spider webs in window cornices, the score of birdhouses empty.

But Elizabeth's lavish flower beds had gone on wildly without her. Cosmos, black-eyed Susans, moon flowers, zinnias, canna lilies, chrysanthemums rioted among the weeds. Every year they died unpicked in their beds. The snapdragon were tall as swords and bearded, bloody, nothing like flowers. Roses sprayed off their trellises and climbed the old-fashioned accordion window screens.

Cal's mother had spent every spare minute with her flowers, singing to herself the same hymns she played in the *Baptist Hymnal* that still sat on the forgotten piano: *It May Be At Morn, O Happy Day That Fixed My Choice, I Surrender All*. Cal had been able at one time to name each flower. She had had him repeat their names as he stood looking over her shoulder as she pressed them with her bare hands into the earth that had looked to Cal like chocolate. Now he could not remember the names of the flowers, but words to hymns came unsummoned: *All to thee, my blessed savior, I surrender all.*

Cal's mother had died before he had time to verify her existence. Her life, like gossamer, had appeared and then vanished. Yet he kept expecting her to turn up – there in her garden where she would walk of a night in white linen bed gowns, and traipse out in storms and dare the lightning, counting the strikes about her. It was only when Cal would cry out of fear for her that his father would leave the house and bring her back in.

"Fifty-six bolts," she might say. Or: "Two hundred and one. I am not afraid of my Savior."

His father, who didn't like lightning, looked at his wife and said: "I am not afraid of your Savior either, Elizabeth. But if that lightning hits you, you'll be dead."

It got so his father locked her in a room during a lightning storm, while Cal crawled under his bed and waited for the world to stop exploding – on his back, gripping the bed slats, his mouth against the grainy mattress batting, listening to her a floor below at the window, watching, singing: *All to thee, my blessed Saviour, I surrender all.*

All Cal had was his father's account of her death. MacGregor had been watching television, having had installed against the house-side the electronic saucer that looked like a giant black sundial. What had alerted him to the storm was a crash and then instant darkness, the TV fizzing from the jolt. He grabbed a flashlight and walked to the door. Elizabeth stood in the jamb, the drenched gown coating her; and her hair, though soaked, shooting from her head like the spikes of a globe thistle. She walked straight at her husband, and past him. He followed her with the beam down the hall where she stopped at the piano, sat and played *Vesti La Guiba.* Then she stood, sang *The Doxology,* and fell over.

Mac swore his wife was dead the second she took the charge. Had seen it in her eyes. Dead standing there at the door. Dead walking down the hall. A dead woman playing the piano. On the floor where her bare feet had rested remained two black prints, and a black smudge on the piano bench. Smoky shadows swirled across the white keys she had fingered.

She was dead a day before Cal's father called him at the university. When he arrived home, he found draped across his bedstead a new blue suit, a shirt and tie. After dressing in them, he had gone down to the living room where his father, in his only suit, had waited, smoking for the first time within the walls of his home his tailor-made Piedmont cigarettes. Mac had taken him by the hand, as Cal had no recollection of his doing when he was a child, and led him down the hall to his parents' bedroom.

It was a tomblike room, immaculate, still and polished and perfect. Not a fold in the white chintz spread making the monstrous chestnut bed, not a speck of lint on the blue carpet. Each piece of furniture stood at attention, a doily beneath the bare necessaries: Cal's baby picture, the bronzed shoes worked into the frame; the formal wedding portrait of MacGregor and Elizabeth Gaddy; the profiled picture of androgynous Jesus. Motes of dust flicked in through the translucent shears as though on a film beam. A room in which one held his breath.

MacGregor sat his son at his wife's vanity and brushed his hair with her silver monogrammed hair brush. Eleven, twelve strokes before Mac stopped and said, "That'll do." But in that interim, as Cal sat on the backless bench and watched through the mirror his father brush his hair – again with no memory of it ever having happened before – he recognized on his father his own face. He looked at himself, dropped his eyes, and forgot what kind of man he was.

The funeral was discreet and tidy. Cal and his father stood to the side as Elizabeth's sister, Ruby, her only living relative, saw to it "the way Elizabeth would have wished." MacGregor said he had no druthers, just wanted her decently in the churchyard. Cal stood by. He too had no druthers. That whore's breath and body still clawed at him, the dissenter's candle of conscience threatening to set him afire. He had the blood of dead women on him.

Mac set to the short wake, funeral and interment like he might a shakedown: dogged and with a ragged fury kept in check by the fact that he could make it through without crying, or the benefit of comfort or giving comfort.

She was a good woman. She was a good wife. She was a good mother. I will dearly miss her; we all will. MacGregor Gaddy could say these things. He could take a man and hogtie him, throw him in the Boot with a dead skunk for company, drink his buttermilk, clock out and go home and have supper. The next morning that man in the Boot worshiped Mac like

Jesus Christ.

Cal did not cry for his mother until she was left sunk in the churchyard, and then not in front of his father. Rather he waited until he was alone. Then he squeezed beneath his old, boy's bed where he used to wait out lightning, banged his head on the slats, and let loose in weeping howls the long-stored query of *Why*. Cal had known at that moment that he would never return to the university, that he had no future. He screamed and bashed his head again and again as if against bars.

CHAPTER 11

After his mother died, Cal moved back home. Stoned and drinking beer, he simply drifted: in his mind, behind the wheel of his truck, along the back roads of Saint Joan's County – electric guitar music like a chainsaw splitting the dashboard. He threw the empties out on the road for the paupers from Shantytown who hiked ten miles out in the country just to load a trash bag with bent beer cans and drink the spit left in them.

He let his hair grow long. Wore baggy jeans and T-shirts. He liked living in bags: of fast food and beer on the road, of reefer, and then finally tiny bags of cocaine. Out there strung out and wasted on the blacktop, with only wild creatures and impervious swamp-scrub and timber to intrude on his buzz, he was able to imagine his life.

Mac Gaddy did not seem to notice what was going on with his son. He had replaced the blasted satellite dish and spent his evenings in the dark, watching and listening to the TV as if it were an internal monologue. When he slept, he slept on the couch. At dawn he left for Coventry.

Cal steered clear of his father. They lived like two strangers in the house which, without Elizabeth, had lost its center; yet she haunted it with the life she had left behind. Something which now they could only remember, yet refused to talk about. They smelled her fragrance, heard her piano music. Every time one of them touched a thing of hers, it flew from his hands: silverware, glasses and plates, needle and thread. The tablecloth split. The houseplants shriveled: fichus, begonias, jade, Wandering Jew. Just above her trousseau the roof began leaking. Her clothes dry-rotted. Finally, Mac summoned Ruby and had her spirit out of the house all of Elizabeth's things. He closed the door on the bedroom he had for years and years shared with her, hasp-locked it from the inside, climbed out a window and nailed it shut. Her flower gardens went wild, strangling the house, commingling, mutating.

The piano, with its brimstone angel-prints, stayed. And a photograph, that had hung in the living room for as long as Cal could remember: MacGregor and Elizabeth's wedding day. One of those dated, earnest, iconographic black and white tableaux that grace homes, attempting to describe a secret past that had never existed, and with every passing day fades further into dream.

Cal had always noticed it merely the way one notices a lamp or a sofa. The principles of the photograph, four of them, had obviously been posed by its phantom photographer. Cal's mother wearing not a wedding gown, but a white dress printed in what looked like dahlias, white gloves and white hat over a wreath of black shoulder length hair, white open-toed shoes.

The picture made the point of Elizabeth's youth explicitly, as if perhaps the photographer had been in love with her. Her face was open and unhurt, shy and smiling. Unadorned save for the candor of her loveliness, even beauty, her eyes obedient to the photographer, yet looking through him, through the pane of glass that confined the photograph, as if through a window at an onlooker. At Cal. At me, Cal had always imagined. His secret mother.

Cal's father, a foot taller than his new wife, and then some, even slumped as he was, stood on her left. A brand new state man, still green, guarding chained-up convicts on the road. In a dark suit. The brown one it would have been. His hair dark and tufted at the widow's peak. He too unhurt, hopeful, bemused; yet preoccupied, as if he were meeting the eyes of someone else across the room, not pictured or in any way specified. The obvious contentment on his face centered on this doppelganger and not on anything temporal at that moment when the shutter convulsed.

On Mac's left was Cal's grandfather. The man who had built the house. The only image of him extant, and even there he did not show up. He, another hand taller than his son, but only the dome of his black head visible, and the necktie sliding up the middle of his white shirt. His entire

42

face obscured by the brim of his wife's hat – MacGregor's mother's hat – fanning across it from forehead to chin. The grandfather could not be identified. Never. As much as Cal wanted to peel back that imperious hat brim and see him. But, never. He remained hidden.

His wife, however, Mac's mother, of whom Cal had no recollection of his father ever speaking, was exaggerated. A great corsaged, floral matriarch with matching white everything, literally twice the size of her new daughter-in-law, perhaps an optical illusion in the forced perspective of the camera angle she occupied. But bigger by far than anyone in the frame. Her implacable smile clearly for posterity, her arm extended to the far cropped border to receive her tithe of white cake from an invisible hand. Her long alabaster arm – it had been a summer wedding – cutting everyone in half, the hat obscuring the faces of her husband and son. No one having any say-so, but her. Cal's mother, however, nonetheless, determined in her pretty tininess, the beauty of her derivative dress, the arm of her mother-in-law sliced across its bosom.

Elizabeth's own parents were in the photograph too, but only in the shrunken periphery. Kindly and sheepish. Fortitudinous. Excluded. They died young. All of them. Mac's parents too. Cal knew nothing of his genealogy, but this framed artifact. The only one able to divulge anything was his father, a man who refused to believe in the past.

Occasionally, after Elizabeth's death, Cal's father would ask him if he needed anything. The boy always said, "No," and they left it at that. In the morning, Cal found money tacked to his door.

CHAPTER 12

Cal bumped down a two-track for a mile, then over a dead field through woods to the mouth of Merton Creek where deer came to drink. He sat on top of the truck cab with the spot off and waited, cupping the joint flame and drinking Red, White and Blue beer. He liked to hear the deer gather, the tentative pawing at the water as they drank, the sound of their hooves sluicing in and out of the mud around the pool, their voices, half fay, half funereal, telling secrets. When he knew he had a herd in the dark in front of him, he turned on the big flashlight and there they'd be. More like ghosts of deer than deer themselves, marble in the light.

Cal held them in the beam, then moved them around with it like a film director. As if they had come to expect him, their maker, every night there on Merton Creek where he clicked on the light and, like magic, they appeared, their eyes burning green holes in their skulls. Ultimately, he screamed or reached in the cab and sounded the horn, and they knifed off, white-tailing in slow motion, the bucks nickering, the does pushing ahead of them their painted fawns. "Amen," invoked Cal, and drove back across the black-scape home.

One night, while Cal studied the deer, frozen in the traction of his big Eveready, lights appeared behind him. Wasted, he was unable to fix their origin, but they seemed gliding down from the sky. Fascinated and paralyzed in the strobes rolling out of the pitch at him, he hoped for something unbelievable. Abduction into a realm of vapor. Other planets. He had read of it. People disappearing. Crop circles. He was the perfect candidate, Saint Joan's County the perfect locus.

Looking into the lights, Cal felt at that moment as if his life had all the clarity of film. Something he, like the deer, could stand away from and see with complete objectivity. He had that perfect white, white-powder edge that made him the fiction. And behind him were the deer in his movie, now doubly tranced by the oncoming second set of lights. He stood on the truck cab and waved his arms and legs like a gandy dancer.

"Take me," he yelled.

The deer bolted. The approaching lights had under them an engine, behind them a captain, who looked like a space man as he came out of the craft, holding a cylinder of light which blinded Cal. There was the sound of bone grinding bone which Cal realized, as the figure came closer, was his own teeth.

It was the game warden, with a flashlight in one hand and a .44 Magnum in the other. Saint Joan's County police were scarce and placid, but the game rangers were hell for punishing and double hell on spotting deer. One of them might be in a tree or sitting a stump in the middle of black swamp at midnight. They came out of nowhere. Without a word, the warden spread-eagled Cal against the cab and rifled through the truck. He wasn't much bothered by the beer; and there were no guns, so he knew Cal hadn't been poaching. But when he went over Cal he found a good sized roach and a pinch or two of coke left. He shot out the four of Cal's tires and threw him cuffed into the county jeep.

"I know your daddy," the only words he uttered.

Cal knew better than to plead.

Cal sat behind the wire that fenced off the jeep's back seat from the front and watched the two uniformed, stone-faced men in the vague glimmer of the Gaddys' porch light. It was late. The game warden's fist against the front door had roused Cal's father from the couch. The living room window flickered from the TV's limelight. The dish sat on the horizon, contorting robotically at the whim of some distant signal.

The men kept their hands in their pockets. Probably talking by then of the weather, or a load of pea gravel. They might have just been tasting each other's air. All they really wanted was to get on down the road. Finally they came over to the jeep. The game warden opened the rear door, guided Cal out by his elbow and removed the handcuffs.

"Take off your glasses," Cal's father commanded his son. Cal gazed at his father through the circular lenses of his wire glasses. When Cal, after removing his glasses, glanced at him again, his father had softened. He seemed to be smiling, his closed right hand moving slowly out of his pocket as if it contained something he had all along been saving for his son.

The blow broke Cal's jaw and knocked him to the ground. His father looked down at him. His hand was back in his pocket. The game warden looked down too, then got in his jeep and drove away. May sauntered down from the porch and licked Cal's face. Still holding his glasses, he noticed the ghost of his mother on her knees, picking weeds in the flower garden. It was so dark, he could barely see her. He put on his glasses, his father's boots next to his face. He placed his hands on one of the boots and got to his knees. His face was numb; the inside of his mouth felt packed with batting.

Mac, his face fixed almost in tenderness, helped Cal get to his feet. But the boy did not recognize his father, only the scales of justice superimposed over the state seal which formed the Department of Correction insignia on his breast pocket. Cal peered into the garden at the last of the cosmos lashing itself to a dying Pecan tree, and wept. With his eyes only because his mouth did not work. Not even to say the word which made him faint from pain when he tried it: *Mama*. His father caught him and carried him into the house.

Nine weeks later, after his jaw was unwired and he was able to eat with a knife and fork instead of a straw, Cal emerged from the house. His hair was an inch long and he was clean-shaven. Contact lenses instead of glasses. He wore grey trousers with a deep blue stripe running down the outseam of each leg, a short-sleeved sky-blue shirt and a blue baseball cap. On the cap's crest and on one breast pocket of the shirt were identical patches: the scales of justice on a bed of fire, a saber crossed over a pine bough with a cardinal perched on it. On his belt hung handcuffs, a blackjack, and a can of mace. He climbed into the passenger's side of his father's truck. Mac forced it into gear and they lurched off together toward Coventry Prison Camp.

Going to Coventry every day did not seem unusual to Cal. He had spent so much time there as a boy that its rhythms seemed natural, almost soothing. There was a sameness about it in which he took refuge. But as time went on, the place began to change as he accepted state wages every month in exchange for keeping men penned. He wore the uniform, and in a few weeks it wore him. Dangling from his waist were keys which locked men for the night in dark rooms with one another. He, Calvin Gaddy, had entered prison. His new mother with whom he bartered his soul for what he thought might be his own freedom. Yet he had within him an unresolved gnawing and the two halves of his face no longer fit. He was nineteen years old.

Not long after Cal started at Coventry, Mac and Frank went out in the middle of the night on escape. Not Cal. Once he signed on with the state, Mac would not have a thing to do with him on the yard. It was a young fellow they were chasing, a first offender in for drug-taking and stupidity mainly. Frank told it that the boy was so scared that he and Mac could smell him from the gate; they didn't even take the dogs.

The boy holed up in an old privy standing next to a fallen-over house. Mac and Frank built a fire and sat around it drinking buck Mac had taken from a convict. They knew the boy was in the outhouse. The whole field smelled of his scariness. They drank a while and then Mac went to the truck, got a drum of gasoline and set that privy afire. The boy rocketed out of there with his browns flaming, and Mac would have let him cook had it not been for Frank who threw himself on the boy and quenched the flames. Frank claimed that since having been set afire himself he was fireproof. And truly every stitch of clothing was burned off Frank, but he was not even singed. The boy was hurt badly. Had to be helicoptered to the burn hospital at the state university. Mac was lucky the boy didn't die. Even so, they made him retire.

CHAPTER 13

From his parents' porch, Cal watched the newly framed houses coming like ships up out of the field. His father noticed him looking. He raised his hand and leveled it against the houses as if to chop them away.

"I won't have it," he declared.

"There's nothing you can do about it, Papa."

"The hell."

"You have to accept it. Look. Those are houses going up over there. Not too long there's going to be families living in them."

"I will not abide any godforsaken families. I want the world to end as it is right here."

Inside, the television prattled on. A news show about a boy who had been molested by his parish priest. On the coffee table were the remote control and empty jars of baby food, each with a spoon sticking out of it. The couch was sunken with Mac's indentation.

"What have you eaten today, Papa?"

Mac looked at the little jars and read the labels. "Had some peaches and carrots and beef."

"Pa, you're eating baby food. Why the hell are you eating baby food?"

"It's all I can tolerate."

"You can't survive on baby food."

"Can't I?"

"Let me take you to a doctor. I'll make an appointment for you. Maybe something's wrong with your stomach."

"It's not my stomach. Maybe something's wrong with *your* stomach."

The priest was explaining that he didn't know why he had done the things he had done, but he still loved God and he believed God still loved him.

"Why are you watching this junk, Pa?"

"It's the truth. Turn away if you choose."

Mac pointed at the priest, a bewildered, kind-looking old man with spectacles. "They should do him the same way they did Frank," he said.

The priest began to cry. The cameras left him that way, his face in his hands and the sound of his sobs as the credits rolled over his black suit.

The lead story on the news was the upcoming execution of Lindrey Vance who had murdered two young women. He was scheduled to die in three days, and there was little chance for a stay. There were a few words from one of the girls' mothers who said she would be glad when it was all over. A picture of Vance flashed on the screen. A very young, sweet-looking white man with long brown hair. A shy smile on his face. Around his neck hung a cross. Just a boy, really. He looked harmless. It could not have been a very recent photograph. Mac reached for the remote and clicked off the television.

He threw a couple of logs on the already roaring fire, took from the mantle an unlabeled bottle of clear liquid and sat down in one of the chairs by the fireplace. With the spots turned off, it was black outside and not one light on in the house. Cal sat in a chair next to his father and they drank.

"I'm going to sit for the sergeant's exam," Cal said.

"Well," said his father.

"I don't see another way, and with the baby coming there's no turning back."

"I should have discouraged you from it."

"It's not your fault."

"I don't believe in fault. My daddy beat me with his fists and I appreciate him for it. Every man makes his own choice. Good or bad. You are either guard or convict. The line between is not so wide as this" – he held apart his thumb and forefinger – "and it doesn't take but one moment of inattention to find yourself crossed over."

"I don't know," said Cal.

"Hell, boy. You know. You been doing it long enough to know you are not cut out for another thing."

Cal took a long swallow of the liquor, then another before

passing the bottle to his father who stared into the fire. The old man took a drink, then spit it into the fire. The flames bubbled up.

"There, you son-of-a-bitch," snarled Mac to the flames, and then he drank.

He stared into the fire and Cal stared too. Mac was looking at something Cal could not reckon. Mac's eyes, glassy, glittering, were on the ledges of their sockets. Cal saw in them the fire, then glimpsed in the reflected flames the faces in the fire his father stared at.

"I won't speak to them, Calvin. I can't help but look at them. They have gotten behind my eyes. But I will not converse with them because the words will look different out in the air than they do in my head. Every man I ever put steel to is come back to visit, to rebuke me, telling me to hang myself, shoot myself, cut on myself. I won't have chat with them. On this I will not be buckled."

Mac stood, drained the bottle and smashed it in the fire. The fire spit the glass back and started out at them. Mac pulled his pistol and fired twice into the flames. Something sounding like a sprung guitar string ricocheted off the firebrick and hit the piano. The first few strains of a song played. There came the scent of Elizabeth Gaddy's perfume, then smoke. The keys tinkled, then froze – a bullet hole in the piano cabinet.

"I better go home," sighed Cal.

"Go," said his father.

CHAPTER 14

Two inches of snow on the ground and still it snowed, only now in sparse pricks of ice. The ground was slick and twice Cal fell. The second time, he lay there a long time in the snow. A crow circled him and called three times. The moon lit the snow and the trees, and the crow came back again and called several more times. Cal lay face down in the snow and ate a little of it. Then he got up, retraced his steps back toward his father's house and looked in the window. Mac was asleep on the couch, May at his feet, asleep too. Cal walked into the house.

The TV had been turned back on: Hyenas chased a wildebeest calf while the adult wildebeests tried with their horns to ward them off. The butted hyenas skidded and rolled, but remained undaunted. There were too many of them and finally they cut off the calf, pounced on it and dragged it off. The wildebeest herd scattered. The cameras closed in on the hyenas eating the calf, a jagged red cavity in its side, their muzzles smeared with blood and gristle.

Cal turned off the TV and looked down on his father. He wanted him to wake up and see him standing there. He went to the fire, picked up the heavy poker and pushed the fallen logs off the hearth back into the fireplace. A few coals burned red on the carpet. Cal picked them up with his hands, threw them into the fire and stamped out the circles where the carpet smoked. Then he pissed on the fire. It hissed and smoked, but did not go out entirely. Neither dog nor the old man stirred. Cal paced back over to his father, threw an afghan his mother had crocheted over top of him and left the house.

It had stopped snowing and was bright enough from the moon that he saw his footprints outlined perfectly in the snow. He was about to lie down in it and rest, but was suddenly so exhausted, he knew if he did, he would never make it home.

There was a light on in the kitchen. Rachel was asleep, on her left side as usual. Cal undressed and got into bed and curved up on his side against her for warmth.

He had first met her in autumn on the yard at Coventry not long after he had gone to work for the State. A social worker, she had been sitting at one of the picnic tables, under a sycamore tree, with a converted Muslim inmate named Mutasid who carried a pouch filled with dirt and sticks and stones, from which he occasionally took something and nibbled. Rachel was trying to help the kid establish a home and work plan, so he could get paroled. Rachel had worn a brown hat with a wide brim, pushed off her face. The sun shone on her hands, folded on the table.

She had sat at that table with inmates for months, years, through all kinds of weather. Women were not allowed in the cellblock and she refused to use the sergeant's office to interview the men she called her clients. She arrived dressed for winter and, in damp weather, hold an umbrella over herself and her clients: Mutasid, the queens and boosters, hard-hearts and jukers, he-shes and scalpers, old and young, black and white, red and brown. She visited their homes in Blackbottom, Monktown, Cashion, Sugartown, wherever she had to go in her blue county car, talking to the mothers and grandmothers of those gone men. Where they would sleep, how they would get to work, bank accounts, bus routes. Did they have alarm clocks? Some of them she got back home. And if there was no one else, she was there in the blue car to drive them, and the pittance they had first stumbled into Coventry with, to the shelters the day they were turned out.

Mutasid finally got written up for eating dirt, so he tried to escape. They gave him more time and he ran again. Stayed gone six months and when he walked back on the yard, trailing a couple dimes for armed robbery and possession, he had back his Christian name – Horace Truesdale – and a Crack jones. He didn't want any more truck with the Help-lady, what the inmates called Rachel.

Cal curled tighter against her, ran a hand over her stomach and held it there until he felt a thump and then another. *Be a girl*, he hoped. Rachel sighed. He kissed her shoulder.

After they had married, Rachel worked with pregnant girls. Kids sometimes as young as twelve. The whole gamut of prenatal care, adoption, counseling. Abortion. She had to mention it. She was legally bound. She had to counsel them about their babies, one way or the other. Death before or after. They were cursed, those little ones, wending their ways through the world until they came to the jailhouse gate or maybe even the death house – like Lindrey Vance. An aborted baby cannot be executed. Right-to-Lifers. The only lifers Cal knew were pounding the Coventry yard. *Life to die.*

Had Vance been aborted, had all the Vances been aborted, there would not be anyone living in the zoo up on death row. No Vances to kill. No killers like Vance. For a moment, with a hand on his quickening baby, Cal was Vance's diary and upon him Vance's inscripted memory, as if it had happened to Cal: two suicide attempts, amnesia, siphoning gas out of cars and stealing drink bottles off back porches, being convict-raped, shunned as an ex-con, kinless, B & E, stuck in the hole for protection, nose broken by a guard, shanking a guard, showering in restraints for a year, punked and repunked, double murder, lawyers, fourteen years on death row.

Cal drew his hand back from Rachel's belly, sick at himself for maybe having cursed his child. He went into the bathroom, ran his head under the tap, then staggered back into bed. Rachel had not moved. Cal thought he heard banging off in the night – and a dog barking. He felt for Rachel, took into his hand a fold of her gown and held it in his fist, listening to her breathe as if eavesdropping on someone's confession.

CHAPTER 15

Pitch had a child who had died. A little boy named Journey. The boy lived with his mother, but Pitch had made sure to spend time with him. Took him to the park and for drives, bought him presents when he had extra money. Rolled a ball back and forth over the floor. Pitch had shown Cal the picture he carried: Pitch holding Journey holding a red ball. The baby looked like a little black savior Jesus Christ fondling the planet in his tiny hands. Beautiful boy who got dead one day because his father got wasted, forgot about him, and the little boy pulled an iron by its cord down off the ironing board onto his head.

That was the story Cal had from Pitch; and, even though they were on the prison yard when Pitch told it, he had no reason to think it untrue. Pitch claimed the blood of his son on his hands made him a devil man. He no longer had a soul.

Cal told Pitch this was not true. About his soul. Burned into Cal's brain as if from that deadly iron was the image of Journey tugging the world down on top of himself. Pitch had cracked under it all, sold his soul for a pistol and a package. Armed robbery, Smack possession, Strong-arm, Larceny. Two concurrent prison jolts of twenty-five years.

"I didn't care," Pitch had confessed to Cal. His eyes were like sour milk and blood. They filled with tears. "I want to be punished."

Cal put his hand on Pitch's shoulder. The conjure man just hung his head.

The next Sunday, Cal sponsored Pitch out of Coventry, got him a pair of jeans and a gaucho left behind in the camp clothes-house and came from home to pick him up in the truck. Rachel had agreed to it, had more than agreed when she heard about Journey. She was pregnant and it was nothing for her to cry, overcome in turns by beauty and sorrow, taking them into her womb with every breath.

Cal and Pitch sat in front of a football game on TV while

Rachel finished preparing the meal. She fixed a special dinner, things she knew Pitch never got at the camp, a meal that would welcome him into a new world. Cal served him a glass of beer, and when he finished, he asked for another. Cal was reluctant to say no, even though he knew it was a bad idea. Pitch stretched out on the couch and watched football.

Rachel came in and sat with them for a minute. She drank her own glass of beer, something she should not have done because of the baby. Cal looked at her as if to say this. But she just smiled at him. She looked very beautiful. Pitch smiled too. He said, "Thank you for this day, for bringing me into your home." Tears stood out in his eyes. In Rachel's too. She walked over to Pitch and kissed his cheek, then walked back into the kitchen.

There was wine at dinner. Rachel insisted. Cal looked at her, but she would not meet his eyes. The meal was something they had never eaten before, yet Pitch and Rachel talked about it with great familiarity. An African stew with chicken and okra and chick peas, cinnamon, cayenne, saffron and hard-boiled eggs. It was to be eaten with the hands from a communal bowl by dipping into it a spongy, wet bread.

The dish was far too spicy for Cal and he could not manage the bread without getting his fingers into the bowl. His hands streamed with the crimson sauce, his throat and stomach on fire. All he could do was drink wine. Rachel and Pitch ate heartily, handling the bread and stew masterfully, never dripping any of it onto their fingers or the table. They talked and talked, occasionally glancing at Cal with what seemed to him a growing concern, but he could not make out what they were saying. They had drunk much, the pregnant woman and the prisoner; and then they were clinking their glasses together, then leaning across the table to kiss, then walking together out of the room, Pitch's hand on Rachel's belly.

This is all Cal remembered until the three of them were in the truck, delivering Pitch back to Coventry. Pitch drove. Rachel sat next to him. When they pulled into the Coventry lot, Pitch got out of the truck, came around to Cal, helped him out and walked him to the double gate.

Thrake was waiting. "Welcome back," he said, grabbing Cal by the arm and leading him through the first gate. Cal pulled back and Thrake snatched a handful of his hair, bowed him back and forced his face against the second gate.

"He's been drinking, Sarge," said Pitch.

"Is that right?" answered Thrake.

Cal tried to speak, but words would not issue forth, just the garbled syntax of a drunken convict. He heard Pitch clip back to the truck, open the door and turn the engine over. He heard Rachel laughing, the baby inside her swooning. Then the truck drove off.

"You been drinking, boy?" Thrake needled him. "You been drinking?"

Then the second gate opened and Cal found himself on the yard, handed over by Thrake to Friend and Icemorelee.

"Get him back in brown," said Thrake. "After a little skin search. Then throw him in the Boot."

Cal woke before Rachel. It took him a few seconds to pull himself out of the dream, and then out of the dream of the dream, so that when his consciousness finally checked in he was merely sick with his father's white liquor. He got up and looked outside. Barely a trace of the snow. The sun bore down. Rachel opened her eyes.

"Calvin, what time is it?"

"About ten."

"You'll be so late."

He sat on the bed next to her. "It's okay. I'm pulling second shift."

"Oh, yes. That's right."

She slid her face from the pillow to his thigh.

"How do you feel?" he asked, running his hand through her hair.

"Hungry."

"I'll make some breakfast," Cal offered.

"Wait. Stay here for a little while."

They remained like that a moment: Rachel with her head on Cal and a hand on the arm he leaned on. Cal, his hand in her hair. Both staring in different directions, neither of them able at that moment to think past the other and the baby, already hatching its clairvoyant narrative, curled in Rachel's womb. Cal could not think of the things he had to do. Only of going back to the prison, of the terrifying dream he had just come out of. He could not remember what month it was.

"You stayed at your father's so long last night. Did you talk?" Rachel asked.

"Some."

"About what?"

"He's all to hell over these houses going up."

"I know."

"He's headed for something black, Rachel."

"What do you mean?"

"He's got devils."

"What are you talking about, Calvin?"

"He's seeing faces. In the dirt. In the fire. Everywhere."

"What kind of faces?"

"Convicts. It's an old chain-gang superstition. If you're the kind of son-of-a-bitch hard man Papa was on the yard, then you get paid with devils. You see the faces of the men you chored to death."

"Do you believe that?"

Cal laughed. He felt sick, like he was going to vomit. He laughed some more and put his hand on her stomach. Her look softened.

"What exactly is he doing, Calvin?"

"Shooting into the fireplace and breaking bottles and sitting in front of that TV. He sits in front of it like it's an altar. All he eats is baby food."

"He's lonely."

"He's crazy. He's always been crazy. He's paying hell now."

"Don't talk like that. He needs to see a doctor."

"That's what I told him."

"What did he say? She took his hand from her stomach and, as she pressed it against her face, noticed his burnt fingers – red with a brown crust at the tips. "What have you done to your hands?"

"I don't remember."

"Can I tell you something and you promise you won't get mad?"

"I don't get mad."

"You're mad now."

"No, I'm not, Rachel."

Rachel's face became a mask of implacability. She looked past Cal out the window. A hummingbird dipped its stiletto beak into an orange feeder. The bird hovered, its wings vibrating. Cal recognized in Rachel's face that something had just broken. He didn't know what he had done, but he knew he had done it. Not her. And he simply could not stop himself or make it better.

"What do you want to tell me?" he asked.

"Nothing."

"Don't do this, Rachel."

"I'm not doing anything. It's alright. I'm fine."

"Then tell me what it is."

"It's really nothing."

Rachel got up, went into the bathroom and locked the door. She flushed, then water ran from the sink. Then she was sick – over and over. Through the door, Cal felt her shuddering. He got up and put his head against it.

"Rachel."

"I'm alright," she called tiredly.

"Can I come in?"

"I'm alright. I'll be out in a minute."

Water splashed again in the sink.

"Rachel," he said to himself and rapped his head lightly against the jamb.

The door opened. Rachel stood in it, her stomach huge and round, low on her torso. Her hands rested on it. She smiled like someone with no reason to smile: like a child, her eyes big, whitish blue, the hair around her face wet from the water she had rinsed with. She leaned in the doorway. Cal put his arms around her.

"I love you," he said.

"I love you too. I'm going to lie down." She walked through his arms and got back into bed.

"I'm sorry," he said, pulling the blankets up around her.

"You didn't do anything."

"I upset you."

"No." She closed her eyes.

"You just need to eat. I'll fix some breakfast."

"I'm going to close my eyes for a little bit."

"Shouldn't you eat?"

"I really can't right now." Her eyes still closed.

"Rachel." He put his hand in her hair. "I'm sorry."

"It's alright." Her voice, barely.

He kissed her forehead. "I love you."

Her lips moved toward the words, but she was asleep.

Cal walked outside and sat on the terra cotta chimney flues that served as steps into the trailer. A beautiful day, the sky turquoise with high, dense milky clouds floating across it. He lit one of the joints from Friend and stared at the line of hardwoods spread in front of him.

No wind, yet at their tops the trees tossed madly. The trees his mother had always told were reminders of God's invisible mercies: the way they held themselves up to Heaven while sucking at the grave, embodying the mystery of His love. The trees around his parents' home had been filled with birdhouses. When Elizabeth died, MacGregor had fed the last of the birdfeed to May, and the houses rotted. To a tree Jesus was slapped. Nothing fancy.

CHAPTER 16

Lindrey Vance, pondering his last meal, lay on deathwatch now. Zedda Pate's last meal had been chicken and dumplings. The journals she had kept while on the Row had been published along with her letters. By all accounts, she had been innocent, a martyr, a hero come to Christ. She had died in the odor of sanctity. No state had dared kill a woman in its death-house since. Cal had been ridden by a whore at the exact instant Zedda Pate joined the communion of convict saints. He could not remember what he had been thinking then. Not of Zedda Pate.

He had been in the State death-house once. Back when he was twelve years old on a school trip. Coming in sight of the century-old penitentiary, the entire yellow school bus had hushed. Fifty schoolchildren faced with the nightmare fairy tale, the haunted castle incarnate. Grey stone after grey stone, coiling and mounting in glassed guard towers and Thomson machine guns, an electrified fence topped with concertina.

Inside was dirty. Stinking. Not in the way of mere filth and vermin, which were in plain sight and abundance. But in the way of fear. The same way one felt the sacred loom upon entering an old church. The maximum joint, however, was a cathedral of anguish, the thrum of two thousand men beating their ways among tunnels tiered one atop another, metal on flesh, the stench of custody and surveillance eternal.

The children had walked single file, winding lower and lower, through the catacombs, the sound of invisible armies shuffling about them. Damp. Cool. The walls sweated. Rats and occasional lizards. They came to a wall pocked with ellipses, a sentence left hanging.

"Machine gun holes," their guide, Mr. Strang, explained, smiling. His tie-tack was a silver set of miniature handcuffs, his white hair fluffed over his ears.

They travelled along a catwalk beneath which were

Blocks I and J, the criminally insane, padding about with balls and shuttlecocks in their specially wired court. T-shirts and green pants, dilapidated tennis shoes. Staring at the children passing above them.

Then on to Death Row where the children were too afraid to look at the condemned. One to a cell, they were dressed as bakers. All white, like the truce flag at Resurrection. A revolving camera in a ceiling corner, sink, toilet, bunk. Their hands through the bars and folded outside of the cells, free, bird-like. They smiled, but the children would not look at them.

They crossed through a little yard and walked up a few short steps to what looked like a chapel. A giant key opened the steel door. The sound of the tumblers revolving as the lock undid. Mr. Strang pulled on the door and it yawed open. Daylight crept in, and a shape in the middle of the chamber within etched itself. Then a door of bars, another key and they were in.

Strang switched on a light. In the center of the room, glassed off in a booth with a light bulb lynched from a still black cord, rested the electric chair. Modest. Unremarkable. Convict-made. Slabs of oak on slabs of oak. Like a deacon's chair. At intervals across it – to buckle down the chest, lap, biceps, wrists and ankles – were leather restraints. Another at the neck. Then, depended over the top of the chair, a silver helmet with a chin strap. In the wooden floor were electrical outlets and a grey panel that looked like a fuse box.

Outside the booth, directly in front of the chair, were two dozen witness seats bolted to the floor. Behind them, a black curtain behind which the hidden executioner actually began the killing cycle. Strang invited them to inspect the chair closely.

"Sit in it," he said. "Sometimes when I want to be to myself, when I can't take the noise on the range a minute more, I come down and sit right there and take my lunch. It's the quietest place in the house."

The children sidled up around the chair, touching it, running their hands along the wood and belts.

"Three hundred and two convicts have died in that chair," Strang told them.

A few of the boys sat in the chair, Cal among them. Strang lowered the helmet to his head.

Finally they were escorted to a room and given gingerbread and lemonade the inmates in the kitchen had made for them. The warden came in and asked if they had any questions. He wore a uniform like a fire captain's. A little girl asked if any of the prisoners ever killed themselves. Mr. Strang and the warden looked at each other.

The warden smiled at the children. "I don't believe so," he answered.

CHAPTER 17

The trailer door opened behind Cal. There was Rachel, smiling.

"I made breakfast," she announced.

"Why? You shouldn't have. I would have done it. I should have done it earlier."

"Calvin. It's alright. I felt okay, so I cooked a little meal. I didn't dig a ditch. What have you been doing?"

"Just sitting."

He mounted the flues and kissed her. He knew she smelled the reefer, but she said nothing. On the kitchen table were omelets, grits, biscuits, tomatoes, glasses of orange juice.

"This looks great, Rachel. I'm starved."

"I made coffee."

"I'll get it."

"No. Sit. I'll get it."

Sun flooded the room as they ate.

"Can you believe there was snow on the ground yesterday?" said Rachel.

"It was a spell."

"A spell?"

"That's what some of the guys on the yard said. Said Pitch – he's a witch doctor – said he made it snow."

"The one who's your friend?"

"He's not my friend."

"He sounds very talented."

"He's got his ways. That's for sure. There's something brewing between him and Thrake."

"What?"

"Not sure."

"Is he violent?"

"Which one?"

"You know, Calvin, I have to interview you every time I want to hear something about your life outside of this aluminum shoebox."

"I know you don't like living in this aluminum shoebox."

She smiled. "Actually I love this aluminum shoebox as long as you're in it with me."

"I'm going to sit for the sergeant's exam."

"If that's what you want, then I'm happy. But I don't want you doing it for my sake. We were doing fine before I had to quit working. I can go back after the baby's born."

"But you don't want to go back. If we're ever going to break ground on our own house, I need to make a move."

"Is that the move you want to make?"

"What other move can I make?"

"You could try something else. You could go back to school."

"I'm thirty years old, Rachel. With my first child on the way. I'm too old to go back to school. Besides, when we do move, we can't move far. I don't feel like I can leave my father."

"There are other things – if you want them, Calvin. I just want what you want." She reached across the table for his hand, but Cal pretended he didn't notice.

"Realistically, Rachel, what else can I do? I'm vested in this system."

Rachel retracted her hand. "You talk about it like it's a blood-born pathogen."

"It is."

"So will this be our child's birthright?"

"No. No, it won't. I'm not going to haul him around the job the way my father did me. I thought you wanted me to take the goddam test."

"I said that if you were going to stay in the system, then you owe it to yourself to move up in it. And you agreed. I just want you to do what will make you happy." She stood and carried dishes to the sink.

It would have been easy for Cal at that second to throw it all up, tear it apart, raise hell with Rachel and leave the house angry. He stood, stacked a few dishes and carried them to the sink where Rachel scrubbed plates. He put his arms around her and rested his hands on her stomach. He kissed her hair where it hung over the back of her neck.

"We're not far from breaking ground, Rachel. We'll be in our own house by the baby's first birthday."

They both knew this was not so, but it was something to say. Rachel didn't turn, but placed her hands on Cal's.

"It'll be fine. I pass the sergeant's exam, I'll be bringing home a lot more money. This pregnancy has you dragging. We're just in a spot now. We'll be alright."

She turned and put her arms around him. "I know we'll be alright; but there's something I have to say to you, Calvin. Even if you get mad, I have to say it. I'm really worried about it."

Cal looked into her eyes, her familiar, frail and lovely face. He believed in Rachel.

"What is it?" he asked.

"I'm worried about how much you smoke pot."

"How much do I smoke pot?"

"A lot. Constantly. And I think you drink too much."

"Drink too much? I hardly ever drink."

"Calvin, what if they give you a drug test at the unit?"

"They're not going to test me."

"How do you know? Maybe as part of the sergeant's exam."

"They are not going to test me?"

They had edged away from each other. Rachel turned back to the sink. The water ran. Cal heard it as if it were running within him, as if part of him were filling. He had the sensation of tilting. Silently he left the room, left the house, tiptoed across the yard to the truck, got in as quietly as he could and turned the key. Then, because whatever inside him was washing away his kilter, he bashed the truck into gear, floored it and slid screeching and snaking through fifty yards of gravel until the tires caught and he was barreling along the pasture two-track toward the state road.

A wall of grit hung in his wake. Behind it, he imagined Rachel weeping and tearing at her hair, convulsing over the toilet, cursing him. Everything ruined, bad, all to hell.

He pounded the dashboard with his fist, then pounded his thigh until he raised knots on it. But it was his own raucous weeping he heard splashing the cab, threatening to drown him as he passed his parents' house. His bedraggled father, beyond whom the newly framed tract homes looked broken, stood in his garden. At the approach of Cal's truck, he raised a plaintive hand. Hunkered behind the wheel, crying, Cal floored it again, fishtailing onto the blacktop.

CHAPTER 18

Coventry gleamed in the mad sunlight: the fence with its two mile icing of concertina, the shotguns in the towers, escutcheon and insignia. All gleaming. Glad. Another day of brown clothes. Cal pulled into a space next to Thrake's Chevy. Every window in it was gone. Smashed. Pieces of glass strewn inside glittered in the sunlight.

The yard was abandoned, the men put up for count. The captain's office was empty. Blish's door was closed. Beyond it, Cal heard her and the captain. Like they were rearranging furniture. He knocked. Then noises like mice in the joists. Coughs. Rustling. Drawers going in and out. The door opened. The captain walked by Cal, crossed the hall to his own office and turned.

"That looks fine, Blish," he said. "Make sure it's posted in the sergeant's office and that each of the custody people gets a copy." He looked at Cal for the first time. "Good afternoon, Mr. Gaddy."

"Good afternoon, Captain."

The captain was nervous, in a hurry. The collar of his sports jacket was turned up on one side and his matching necktie hung up inside his jacket sleeve.

"Blish and I just finished drafting a memorandum on key control," explained the captain. "You'll soon be getting a copy. We have to know at all times where the keys are around here." The captain looked from Blish to Cal. Blish was nodding her head.

"Yes, sir," said Cal.

The captain mumbled something to himself, walked into his office and closed the door.

"He works too much," Blish said. "He really cares about these convicts."

Cal said nothing. He followed Blish into her office. "I want the application for the sergeant's exam," he said.

"Well, that's wonderful, Calvin. You're a regular chip off

the old block."

"Just looking to make a few dollars, Blish."

"Being a daddy's going to make an honest man out of you."

"I reckon."

Cal was hung-over; he didn't want to talk to Blish. Nor to anyone. He had no idea what he was doing with the sergeant's exam. *The devil with this place*, he thought. Blish took a form out of a file drawer and handed it to him.

"There you are."

"Thanks, Blish.

Blish called him back as he was leaving. "Cal, Frank died."

Cal figured this was as good a time as any to walk out of Coventry for good, close the curtain behind him and keep driving; but he forced himself to look at Blish's red patch – not her ruby lipstick, her rather frenetic sexiness. No wonder – she and the captain. "When?" he asked.

"Last night, I guess. They found him this morning in his bunk."

"What happened?"

"Just went. Slept away."

"Where is he?"

"They have him in the Sick Room."

Blish threw a thumb in the direction of the nurse's office. The Sick Room was a large supply closet with two bunks, and served as the infirmary.

"What's he doing there?"

"He's being embalmed."

"He's what?"

"Coventry Funeral Home is embalming him gratis because he's a terminal ward of the state or something, and they're even throwing in a cheap coffin. The captain arranged it all. That's why he's so agitated. About Frank. Anyway ..."

"Well, let me get out to my shift."

Cal closed the door behind him and walked into the sergeant's office. He called Rachel. No answer. As he waited to try again, the captain's door opened and closed, then

Blish's door opened and closed. A radio, playing gospel music, came on in Blish's office. Cal thought of his mother. Singing gospel. He called Rachel again and still nothing. Dialed his father. No answer there either. He hit the yard.

Count had cleared. The inmates pounded out of the dorm and the cook shack. Thrake hobbled up to Cal. He wore bedroom slippers, and his face was blotched with a red scaly rash.

"What happened to you?" Cal asked.

"I woke up like this. Feet so swoll I can't get shoes on and I have this other shit all over my body."

"What are you doing here?"

"What do you mean what am I doing here?"

"You look like hell. Go home and go to bed."

"You think I'm going to give that black son of a bitch the satisfaction?"

"What are you talking about?"

"You know what I'm talking about. That goddam spook is witching me."

"C'mon, Sarge. You're probably having an allergic reaction to something you ate."

"I don't eat a damn thing without throwing it up. Is my car having an allergic reaction? Did you see my car?"

"Yeah. What happened?"

"Your boy. That's what happened."

"Look, Thrake, I don't know what you're talking about or who my boy is."

"No? I'll tell you what else. He was clean on that piss test he took yesterday."

"So he was clean."

"How in hell could he've been clean? Tell me that, Gaddy. There is some evil shit going on. I am going to be like a shadow on that son of a bitch. I am going to bust his black ass and I don't care what it takes."

Thrake shook his finger at Cal. His voice had become shrill. Several of the inmates stopped what they were doing and stared. As Cal looked at him, thinking how ridiculous he looked with the rash and the slippers, Thrake's nose began to drip blood, drop by drop, onto his brown moccasin slippers. Thrake put his hand under his nose and caught the drops. He looked into his hands and then at Cal, his eyes wild. Blood ran freely out of Thrake's nose, over his mouth and down his shirt front. He tried to catch it in his red dripping hands as Cal and the gathering inmates and guards simply gaped. Then he took off running across the yard to the gate and stood there bleeding as he fumbled with his keys. Then, leaving a thin trail of blood, across the parking lot into the office.

Cal felt sick. The inmates unglued themselves. "Payback," he heard one of them say. *The hell with Thrake*, he thought. Friend stopped on his way out of his shift.

"What the hell was that all about?" he asked Cal.

"Hell. I don't know."

Friend lit a cigarette. "I don't feel like things are stable here."

"That's no revelation, Friend."

"No. I mean there's some bad shit going down."

Cal knew Friend was stoned. Cal was still stoned himself. He realized that he always felt that way, whether he was or not. A crew of inmates, ramrodded by a couple of guards, Icemorelee and Nightcutt, marched by them. The inmates carried ladders and tools, and towed the garbage scow loaded with bound coils of new concertina, each labeled *Excalibur*. The officers nodded to one another.

"Y'all watch your topknots," Nightcutt said.

"There's some shit going on here, Gaddy," said Friend. "How do you figure Pitch's piss test for negative?"

"I don't know."

"I hate this place."

"Get away from me, Friend."

"What's the matter with you? You need another round for your twenty gauge?" Friend laughed.

"Just get the hell away."

"Alright, partner. Happy trails."

The wire crew had ladders against the fence, gloved inmates on the top rung of each, looping the new concertina around the five strands of horizontal barbed wire already up there. Icemorelee and Nightcutt shouted at the men on ladders. The rest of the crew stood on the ground, looking up at the spinning silver razors tining into the plump blue sky. Guys played basketball on the netless, rusty hoops. Cal walked into the cook-shack.

The TV was on, patched and taped after its run-in with Thrake. A couple flies walked across its face. Inmates could fix anything. Frank had once told Cal that if they had so desired, they could bring a tank into Coventry. Water ran in the latrine. The breakfast cooks were in their bunks. Pitch was absent, his bunk made up perfectly. On it lay a furry dead black bat, wings widespread, face up. Cal's heart thudded so hard, he tasted it. He hurried out the door to the chowhall.

CHAPTER 19

itch, his rock forearms white with flour to the elbow and bones plaited in his hair, baked biscuits. In one corner of the big dining hall, an AA meeting droned. Cal grabbed a cup of coffee, sat at one of the tables and filled out the application for the sergeant's exam. As he did, he periodically lifted his head to study Pitch, whistling something unintelligible, smiling vaguely as he worked the biscuit dough on stainless steel. His upper body was huge, yet Cal had never seen him fool around with weights. It pulsed and corded as he slapped the slab of dough around, pressed it flat with a rolling pin, then with a coffee cup cut out biscuit rounds and laid them on a black baking pan.

Cal wasn't sure why he liked Pitch. Or had liked him. Maybe it was Journey, some sense of shared woe. He certainly liked Pitch better than Thrake. Cal had learned from his father that it was pure folly to care about a convict. He knew it for himself too. But he couldn't help it, and he told himself that it did not stand in the way of his job.

From the back of the chow hall came the somnolent drill of the drunkalogues: that devout confessional tone of sudden light and abstinence. Reformed convict drunks foreswearing the demon as long as the man had a lock on them. They'd tell the world. Cal needed to talk to Rachel. The guilt on him; he just was not worthy. Maybe he should slink on back there with those rummies and trot out his story of no higher power.

The last of the sun coursed sideways into the room. Cal looked out the window. The new concertina was almost up, the men hoisting it opalescent in the light stream. Just above the distant tree line, a bank of packed clouds slid across the sun. Then the cloud departed and the light pressed against his face like a camera suddenly firing, blinding him.

Father Tuesday's pulpit voice, impossible not to hear, came at him from the AA meeting. Short, bearded, bald and spectacled, Father Tuesday wore a black shirt with a little white square affixed to his collar front – the Catholic Roman collar. Like he had a sugar cube stuck to his Adam's apple. Cal couldn't imagine the priest a drunk, raising Cain. But Tuesday had confessed to the men himself: he used to get drunk on sacristy wine. Like a vampire, he asserted, he had swilled the blood of Jesus.

Tuesday confided that he knew all about it. They need not hold back. *You hung a puppy once. You put another man's thing in your mouth. You dug up a grave. You beat an innocent child half to death for her milk money and then bought you a tiny woman-shaped bottle of paregoric and got reposed.* Tuesday didn't care. Tell it, he exhorted. Unburden. He understood. What was worse than what he had done: sucking the blood of Jesus for a buzz.

Yes, they were fallen, and in more noticeable and dramatic ways than most. But who was not? They had lived their lives in the secular sump of flesh and now they were paying for it. Brown suits and uniformed men with guns and chains. History playing itself out.

"Don't just tell me about the shampoo you guzzled or the catnip sandwiches. What have you been pouring into your soul? And what does it look like? The liver is not the only thing liable to cirrhosis. But there's no such thing as a soul transplant. There are no donors. They reside at permanent addresses: heaven or hell. Right now, as I judge it, you're in Purgatory and there's not a thing you can do about it. But I can make you a promise. No. No. Forgive me. Jesus Christ can make you a promise – He as made you a promise – that if you so desire, you can be with Him this day in Paradise."

How? The men wanted to know. "How, Father?"

"You have to be baptized and confess and receive the Eucharist. Enter into a state of sanctifying grace so rarefying that your soul will be white as the wings of the Holy Ghost."

On Sundays, during visiting hours, Tuesday baptized; and, after AA meetings on Fridays, he heard confession in the way of drunkalogues, dispensed a communal absolution; then, swapping his purple stole for a white one, administered communion, offering the men a sacramental vision of their lives, Father left them, each toting the *Big Book* and a *Baltimore Catechism*, in the sober shimmer of sanctifying grace.

"Fellows," Father Tuesday was saying. "If the devil showed up on the porch with his devil suit and a pitchfork, we wouldn't let him in. Would we? We'd say, 'Why, I know you,' and slam the door in his scarlet face. But he appears in disguise. As a banker, a beautiful woman, a new car, a bottle of beer. Whatever it takes to get you in his clutches and then, *blam*, you're up to your eyebrows in it and chained up behind a high wall."

There came few mumbled *Amens*.

"Sooner or later. Sooner or later, you will find yourself on your knees begging for help. Each man has his own time for it. Some of us have great pride and endurance. We can stand years of pain before we cry out. Some it doesn't take so long. But sooner or later, every man-jack of us comes to the same realization that we all have a big hole in us and it can't be filled but by one thing. You can call it what you want. You can call it the sun or the moon or a rock or whatever. But I prefer to call God God. Because that's what works for me."

Another chorus of *Amens*. Tuesday sat utterly composed in a pink plastic chair. His purple confessor's stole hung from his neck. He sipped coffee and smiled. The men sitting in the circle with him ate doughnuts and drank coffee from white Styrofoam cups – the sun now on them.

Cal turned back to what he was doing, signed his name, dated the application and stood. His eye caught Pitch's and they stared at each other for an instant. Each saw in the other's strained face a kind of pain. Then it passed and Pitch said, "A hot biscuit for Mr. Gaddy? Just like mama used to bake."

Cal couldn't help smiling. Pitch pulled from the oven the pan of biscuits, spatulaed one up, laid it on a napkin, then held it out to Calvin.

"Let's see what you're made of, Mr. Gaddy. Can you resist a fresh-baked golden biscuit?"

The bread rested on the white square in Pitch's

outstretched black hand. It was perfect. Pitch smiled broadly. Calvin took the biscuit and bit into it. *Nearer My God to Thee.* Still smiling, Cal heard his mother singing it.

"You can't resist," said Pitch, closing his eyes as if in prayer. "It's everything one imagines life to be."

"You're a deep one, Pitch," said Cal, his mouth full.

"And you've just sold your soul for a biscuit."

This was Pitch's way of talking and Cal knew all about it. Talking shit in the joint was a way of life. But he didn't like what Pitch had said. That business about his soul. It produced in Cal an almost physical sensation. He had the urge to slam his hand into Pitch's smiling face. He set down on the counter what was left of the biscuit.

"How'd you scam that piss test?" he asked.

"No scam."

"We both know better."

"I don't use drugs."

"What's that bat doing on your bunk?"

"He is my deceased pet."

"Well, you better get rid of your deceased pet because your deceased pet is contraband and, if I happen in the cook-shack again and see it there, I will flat write you up. Understood?"

"You are the shackle, Mr. Gaddy, and I am the hand."

"Spare me the poetry. Get rid of the bat."

From the meeting sounded the gibberish of Father Tuesday's Latin absolution as he shuffled among the kneeling men. At each of them, he whispered, "The Son of the last day." And when they whispered in return, "Amen," he laid on their snaked-out tongues the bread of life.

"What's going on with Thrake, Pitch? And don't play dumb with me."

"What is the matter with you, Mr. Gaddy?" His voice sounded baffled, hurt.

"I'm just not in the mood," said Cal. "I don't think I'll ever be in the mood again. What do you know about Thrake?"

"I know he is a pig and he doesn't bathe."

75

"Have I been straight-up with you since you've known me?"

Pitch smiled. "I could ask you the same question. Let's leave it at that."

"Thrake thinks you're witching him."

"I could not do a thing to Sergeant Thrake unless he believed in me. Were you listening to that preacher man back there, Mr. Gaddy? He is laying down the same lick. Sergeant Thrake has faith in me."

Cal smiled. "Get rid of the bat," he said, then walked away, his face down. He didn't want to look in Father Tuesday's reformed drunk's eyes.

CHAPTER 20

Cal recalled his own baptism. At Michelle Baptist, before the entire congregation, in a makeshift pool the deacons had carpentered because the church lacked a real one. His father, in his suit, sat next to his mother in the front pew. Cal had thought, during the second he glanced at them, before the preacher put the cloth over his face and tipped him back and held him down in the water, how fine they looked together. Then he had surfaced, a dripping new spirit girded with the sword and buckler of the savior. His eyes went again instantly to his parents. His mother cried; his father looked away. And Cal had felt no different, just scared that it hadn't worked.

He remembered communion, the loaf bread soggy from dipping into a cup of grape juice, its cloying in his throat, the nauseating feel of it sliding down his gullet into the tomb of his empty stomach.

Cal still had the sensation that he was going to throw up. Three of the inmates who had been working on the fence charged across the yard toward him, two holding up the one in the middle who was bleeding along his collar, blood welling up over it like the rim of a pot boiling over. Nightcutt jogged behind them, yelling, "Hurry it up. Hurry it up."

The man himself, young, spindly, and losing color, wore a cap and had a toothpick stuck to his bottom lip. His eyes were intent on the gate and he added to Thrake's now-black blood-droplets big red coins that fell out of him as he ran.

Cal hustled to him. There was nothing much he could do, but get the gates open. The bleeding man – really a boy – whimpered over and over: "Good Christ, have mercy on me."

The nurse and the captain flew out of the office. Thrake, holding a rag to his face, still in his bedroom slippers, chugged behind them. The three of them half-carried, half-dragged the boy inside.

"What happened?" Cal asked Nightcutt.

"He got trussed up in that wire. I don't even know where it got him."

Inmates milled, their faces galvanic, spooked. Cal felt in them the electricity. Not a word. "Alright," he said, sweeping their faces with a look.

Icemorelee and his people had never stopped working on the fence. The wire curled around the dying sun in the impervious blue.

"Alright," Cal said again, louder.

The massed inmates didn't budge. Nightcutt took a step closer to Cal. Shoulder to shoulder, then back to back as they had been taught. Up in the tower, Ernestine cradled the shotgun loosely, throwing the shadow of a cross on the bloody gravel.

"Alright," Nightcutt ordered. "Go on about your business now."

Here's where Thrake would trump these convicts. Flat spit in their eye and make them like it. He loved to put the dare to them, then watch them back off. Like MacGregor Gaddy. A chain-gang man. But Thrake was wearing bedroom shoes today and it was just Nightcutt and Cal with the sergeant papers in his pocket.

"I'll slap another six months of brown on every son of a bitch who doesn't disperse right goddam now," Cal barked. He felt it in himself. He'd do it and enjoy it in the bargain. Grab up one of them and make an example. He was sick of doing right by them. Wasn't a damn thing to stop him cracking someone's skull.

"Try me," he challenged. "I want you to. Please."

The inmates saw it in him – this new thing – and one by one dropped their eyes and walked off.

CHAPTER 21

Cal threw the application for the sergeant's exam on Blish's desk. The captain's door was closed, but Cal heard Blish in there with him: the sound of things being moved around, chuffing and impatience.

Frank's old partner, the convict Ezekiel, swabbed the cut boy's blood from the hall leading down to the nurse's office. The water in his rinse bucket was pink. A tuft of white curls like a wig sat on top of his big black head. Cal had known him from his father's day at Coventry when Ezekiel had been the old captain's catamite. With Frank dead, he was now the oldest man on the camp. Another lifer-to-die. No one knew what crime he had committed.

At Cal's approach, he took his hat off and, in the feudal manner of the convict addressing the road boss, laid it over his heart, tears in his eyes, blood on the mop hanks as he held it in one hand.

"Old Frank's done gone to the master, Mister Calvin." Ezekiel tried to smile. "He sundowning now. Finally quit this wall."

Cal put his hand on Ezekiel's shoulder. "You're a good man, Ezekiel."

The door to the nurse's office opened and Thrake, cleaned up and wearing shoes, gimped out. The rash on his face was raw red, smeared with salve that made his head gleam.

"Get mopping, Ezekiel," he said.

"Yes, sir," answered Ezekiel, lowering his face to the floor and resuming his mopping.

"Were you two having a nice little cry together?" Thrake asked.

Cal had been prepared to ignore Thrake. He had even begun to feel a little sorry for him. But when he saw him, there welled within him not so much hatred, but weariness. Weariness with himself, what he was about to become.

"I remember when you wore dresses around this camp,

Ezekiel. You like being a woman, don't you?" Thrake went on. "Out here crying like one too."

Ezekiel never looked up, just mopped the same spot over and over.

"Why don't you lay off, Thrake?" said Cal.

"Sergeant Thrake to you."

Cal glared at him.

"Sometimes it's hard to believe you came out of your daddy. MacGregor Gaddy was the ironest man to ever set foot on this camp. I walked the yard under him."

"You can leave my father out of it."

"I know he's proud, what with having you for a son and following so close in his footsteps." Thrake smiled. "You missed a spot," he said to Ezekiel, and pointed to a corner.

Ezekiel, weeping audibly, shuffled over with the mop. A little cry came from the captain's office. As Cal studied Thrake – the sergeant's teeth getting whiter, grin growing, gums seeming to recede and take fire in the middle of his glowing face – he wondered for the first time in his life what his father, now invoked, would do. MacGregor's broad hand coming up over Thrake, staying poised over him, Thrake quaking under it as he might under a cross about to fall on him.

Cal lifted his hand, but only to point a finger at Thrake. There came another cry from the captain's office.

"Get out of my way," said Thrake. "I run this camp." Then he stumped down the hall and out the door.

CHAPTER 22

The nurse, at her desk, ate cottage cheese out of a Styrofoam cup. She wore a nurse's white cap over blonde hair cinched in a bun, and a tight white dress, the bodice of which was splashed with blood. She was plump and pretty, her face heavily made up, bowed cupid lips exaggerated with bright pink lipstick.

"Hello, Calvin," she greeted Cal as he entered her office.

"Hello, Virginia."

"How's Rachel?"

"Pretty good."

"Staying on her left side?"

"All the time."

"How's the pressure?"

"You know. Not bad. She's taking medication for it."

"Has she been checking for protein in her urine?"

"She's very conscientious. She really is."

Virginia smiled. Her lips had flecks of cottage cheese on them. "How's the daddy-to-be?"

"Oh, a little frazzled, I'd say."

"Anything you want to talk about?"

"Just the system."

"Believe me. I understand." She indicated the blood on her breast.

"I came in to see Frank."

She nodded toward the sick room. "He's in there under a sheet."

"How's the boy who got cut?"

"Not as bad as he looked coming in. A couple of neck lacerations. Took a few stitches. My God, how he bled though. He's in there too."

The sick room was dark. Just one barred window that had been painted black. An antiseptic, lurid, half-hospital, half-mortuary smell enveloped Cal as he opened the door. The sound of faint aspiration, a vague sucking, which Cal finally realized was the sedated cut boy's sleep. He mashed in the light button and a swaying dirty bulb spread a silver scrim across the room.

The cut boy, covered with a gray, nappy blanket, lay with his face to the wall, his neck wrapped entirely as if with a white muffler. His long greasy hair was full of lint, his mouth open and blameless, eyes like marbles chasing each other under the papery lids. Suddenly he smiled in his sleep, a wan eerie loser's smile. Pinched, nondescript face, a dagger tattooed to the inside of the wrist that fell from beneath the blanket.

If the boy died, no one would miss him. He was a throwaway: death on the yard, on the fence, in front of a car, self-inflicted. And he smiled. At the head of his cot were metal shelves with bandages and cotton balls, grey skinny towels, a dictionary, a book called *The Stranger*, another called *Smiling Through the Apocalypse* and two sets of leg restraints.

The room's stink had forced its way down Cal's throat and was prying loose his stomach. He felt the sheen of Frank on the other cot, the filmy light on the sheet. He made himself turn: a topography of snow thrown over the map of a body, rills and slopes and roils. Poor old Frank. Dead under a sheet in a chain-gang sick room. Named for a monster when really it was the name of his troubled creator all along the monster bore. The monster himself was not bad at all.

Cal put his hand to the top of the sheet. He aimed to have a look at this Frankenstein, castrated and set afire, now pickled and about to be displayed like the freak he had always been. But he couldn't pull back the sheet. Instead he turned out the light and stood for a moment listening to the sough of the cut boy and wondered why Frank – who would have said that his life had been the only one he was meant to live, that misery is accorded to one man only so another might escape it – had been born. Old Frank. The kind people said would have been better off dead. And here he was dead. And nothing was better off. Just another hole in the void.

CHAPTER 23

Blish stood outside her office. "Rachel called. She wants you to call her right away at your father's."

"What's the matter?"

"She said everything was okay. She sounded fine. Use my phone."

Rachel answered on the first ring.

"What's up?" Cal asked.

"The sheriff is here."

"Is Papa okay?"

"Yes, he's fine. But he's in a little trouble. He vandalized a few of those houses going up in the field."

Pictures of Blish's children sat on her desk: two boys, holding long, curved swords and wearing white masks, dressed as ninjas. The phone Cal held against his face smelled of Blish, sweet, perfumed. He conjured an image of his father vandalizing the flimsy tract homes.

"Calvin," Rachel prompted.

"Yeah. Yeah. I'm here."

"Can you come home right away?"

"Yeah. I'll be right there."

"Okay."

"Rachel?"

"Yes?"

"I love you."

"I love you too."

"I'm sorry."

"That's alright. Hurry home."

Blish had disappeared. Behind the captain's door. No sound for their kind of love: tension, seams about to tear loose. Thinking the office empty, Cal had once walked in on them: Blish sitting nude on the captain's lap, he shirtless. Like startled deer, they had both simply stared at him. Then Blish grabbed the hem of the state flag dangling from its pole behind the captain's desk and held it over herself.

Cal beat hard on the captain's door.

"Come in," said the captain. He was at his desk. Blish stood at the window, light slicing raven hair.

"Rachel called," said Cal. "I need to get home. There's a little situation."

The captain looked startled. He stood. "By all means."

Blish turned, her one eye plaintive, sunlight contained in it.

"Is everything okay with the baby?" she asked, her voice quaking slightly.

"I really don't know what's going on," said Cal. "I'll be back as soon as I can."

"Take your time," said the captain, now looking at Blish and the silver barb cutting out of her eye.

"Call us," she said as Cal closed the door and hurried out to his truck.

He quelled the urge to get stoned on the way home. Instead, he grabbed from under the console the shotgun shell with the remaining joints and threw it out the window. He tried to pray because he knew he needed help. "Help me, God," he said to the windshield.

His voice spilled out in a rasp. There was his mother. Teaching him to drive. Next to him, in a dress, cardigan sweater, and her garden shoes. Smelling of talc and cyclamen, her hand on the shift and Cal's atop it as she guided him through the gearbox and the art of the clutch over the very road he traveled, this time of day, solstice, darkening like a pane of glass darkens from the outside in, the radio turned to a gospel preacher: *He works in us the will and the performance, Be renewed in the spirit of your mind, There is no fear in perfect love.*

His mother – so sparkling clean and secret. Cal would pull into the driveway, she seated next to him. Help her bait the field for geese. They stood in the middle of the thirty acres where the tract homes now wandered. The birds honked down around them, lifted the bait from the stubbly fallow furrows, huge wings beating a wind that blew Elizabeth's long undone hair about her face, until she wrapped the

84

wine-colored sweater around her and smiled at her son as if he were a prince about to sprout wings himself: "Calvin. Calvin, my precious boy. 'Even the night shall be light about me. Darken thy memory.'"

The sun bled behind the trees. The sky broke and dropped into cloud floes of pink and blue, the full moon porous, readying to launch out of the woods and reveal itself. His mother held his hand and picked out angels in the fragmenting cumuli.

Then another truck: his father and Frank. His mother squeezed his hand.

"Don't tell Papa I took you driving."

But Cal was already striding from her, the angels above fragmenting into fiery platelets, his eyes on the tailgate where Frank and his father sat smoking, assembling the trappings for the night's catching: torches, chains, guns and a bottle.

"I'd prefer you didn't go," Cal's mother called to him above the geese lifting off into a V above her. Then to her husband: "I'd prefer, Calvin ... ," her voice trailing off. How many times had Calvin promised her never? Never Coventry.

CHAPTER 24

The sheriff's car sat in the driveway behind Cal's father's truck. Under the carport they stood: the sheriff, then MacGregor Gaddy with Rachel's hand wrapped around his arm. The old man's head was down. He brought up a hand to it intermittently as if shooing gnats. Rachel was talking, looking at the sheriff, a big black-mustached man wearing a cowboy Stetson. His hands were on his hips, in one hand Mac's pistol. He tilted down toward Rachel and nodded his head. May lay on her side at the back door. They turned, the dog too, when they saw Cal's truck.

Rachel walked over to Cal as he stepped from the truck. She looked pretty and tired, her skin in the sun lit against her blue cotton dress. Her hair blew across her face. She pulled it back off her forehead and held a hand up to shield the sun, now breaking through the wafery red clouds behind Cal.

"How did you get up here?" he asked.

"I walked."

"You shouldn't have."

"I know." She took his arm and they strolled toward Mac and the sheriff.

"What's going on here?" Cal asked.

"I don't know. Papa's saying insane things. Talking about devils. He's so upset."

"Hey, Andrew," Cal said when they reached the sheriff.

"Calvin."

They shook hands.

"This man's my father."

Cal went to his father and stood beside him. Mac looked at Cal, then lowered his head again. He was lucid. Cal knew this. But he could be that and crazy too. He had seen it in him all his life. What made him dangerous.

"Yeah. I figured," said the deputy. "Your wife said she called you, so you know what we got here."

"What the hell, Papa," Cal said, looking at his father.

Mac lifted his eyes. "I won't have it, Calvin. It'll be devils living in those houses, tunneling into my garden. More faces. I won't have it."

The deputy looked at Cal. "I don't know what your father is talking about, Calvin. But this is what I do know. The builder called me about four o'clock. Said he'd come by to face off a foundation and found your father tearing apart one of his houses with a sledgehammer. He'd already done for one. When the builder told him to stop, he made for him with the sledgehammer. And that's where I come in."

"I will put up a wall," said Mac.

"Where do we go from here?" asked Cal.

"I don't know. That's up to the builder. When I talked to him, he was right warm over that nine pound steel. You pay for the damages and I reckon he'll forget about things. But I don't know. I don't believe the old man knew what he was doing."

"The hell," Mac snapped. "I can look out into that field and see every sorry thing that'll come out of it. Whole damn cohorts of incubi. Succubi."

"Hush, Papa," said Calvin. "You're talking nonsense."

"They'll get in my barn. In my vegetables."

The deputy studied MacGregor. "You need to think about getting him some help, Calvin," he said. "And he sure as hell shouldn't be fooling around with a gun. As exercised as he is, he might have shot that man. And then what?"

He handed the pistol to Cal. Cal glanced at his father, his head down, his lips moving, the white hair around his mouth dirty. Inside his empty holster, his hand balled in a fist. Rachel stared at Mac, her mouth clamped, eyes wet. The baby arched out of her like a planet.

Cal had seen his mother and father naked in that field. After he and his father had come back late one night. After his father had threatened to literally crucify an escape who claimed on the yard he was the Messiah. Mac went so far as to cut a skein of mock orange and fix to the man's scalp a green thorn crown. Had Cal go to the toolbox and fetch a ballpeen and three ten-pennies. With his bleeding head and scorched eyes, the man had looked just like Jesus. Wouldn't say a word. Would not denounce himself, which was what Mac wanted.

But Cal had taken a kind of fit, keeled over at the bare feet of the man and cried, begging him for something. Mercy? He had not been but twelve. Mac would have done it sure then. Tacked that convict to a post. He would not have false gods. Was Frank stepped in, bent to Cal and gathered him up like a baby, then fixed his burnt-out eyes on Mac.

That night Cal wadded a sheet corner in his mouth, so his mother and father wouldn't hear him cry, and with a Yadkin arrowhead he had found in the field behind the Gaddys gouged at his body. He heard his mother bathing his father. Then later, looking out his window, he had seen them in the field, she bent over a hummock.

"We'll take care of it, Andrew. We appreciate what you've done here for us today."

The two men shook hands again.

"Well, I'm going to get," said Andrew. "I'll let you know what we come up with about damages. Y'all take care."

"Thank you," Rachel said.

"Yes, ma'am."

MacGregor looked at the field. "I'm going to build me a wall," he railed.

"You do that, Papa," said Cal.

"I'll wall these devils out."

"You come on down for supper tonight, Papa," said Rachel. She paced over to Mac and kissed him.

"Thank you, honey. But I would not put you out any more than I have already. I know what y'all think."

"Don't be silly, Papa," Rachel said. "We love you."

Mac raised his hand, turned and started into the house. May staggered up after him.

"Papa," Cal called.

Mac turned.

"Frank died."

"When?"

"Last night."

"What happened?"

"Just went. In his sleep."

"He should have never been born. I'll miss him."

"They're going to lay him out on the yard tomorrow during visiting hours. Then bury him in the quarry graveyard."

"My God," cried Rachel.

"Well, I'm bound to go and pay my respects," said Mac.

"You don't have to go," Cal replied. "But I knew you'd want to know."

"Yes, that's right. I would want to know and I'll be going to see Frank tomorrow."Mac had his hand on the door. May leaned against him. "Old Frank," he said and disappeared along with the dog.

The eastern sky darkened. In the west, clouds, the sun trickling far behind them, were the color of watermelon flesh.

"I have to get back to Coventry," Cal said.

Rachel was exhausted, about to cry. Worried too. It was all in her eyes and mouth, the way she held her hands above her waist as if about to receive something.

"Stay home," she said.

He started to say, *I can't.* "Alright," he said. "I will. I'm off tomorrow, you know. Except for Frank."

Rachel dropped her face into her hands and wept. Mac's satellite dish wiggled and thrummed. The only light in the house was the television. Cal wrapped his arms around his wife.

CHAPTER 25

In his sleep, Cal heard something like a dog. May, he reckoned. Then he was awake, but could not open his eyes or move any part of his body. He was conscious of Rachel next to him, her breathing. They had made love and fallen asleep without their clothes. She lay on her back, her stomach rising and falling slightly with each breath. The flame of the lit candle strobed on its wick, swimming in the melted wax pool dripping onto the table and floor.

The play of the flame stood at the edge of Cal's eye, just on the other side of Rachel. He tried to touch her, to move his hand, to open his mouth. He had to get up, but was paralyzed. Then he felt next to him, on the edge of his side of the bed, the pressure of someone's knee. Panic numbed him. Someone was there and Cal could not move. Someone poised above him with his knee on the bed.

Cal's eyelids finally unglued. The room flickered with the drowning candle. There was no one there. He sat up and looked at Rachel, the plain field of her pregnant body, mysterious, sealed in sleep. He covered her, leaned over and blew out the candle, then turned on a lamp, got out of bed and put on his pants. He walked to the front of the trailer, flicked on the outside light and opened the front door. A copperhead lounged at the bottom of the steps.

Cal did not really mind snakes, and was tempted to let this one go about its business. But there was no telling when and where it might turn up again. Cal eased onto the first flue and grabbed the long-handled spade that leaned against the trailer. At his footfall, the snake lengthened and raised its cordate head. It was the width of an axe handle, as long as any pit viper Cal had ever seen alive. A gun would be better, but would scare Rachel. He had seen his father kill them like a spaniel does. Grab it by the tail and lash it against a tree.

When Cal put his bare foot on the earth, the snake stiffened and seemed to turn its head. Cal was behind it.

He carefully laid the shovel blade six inches down from the tip of the head, pinned it against the dirt and pressed. The snake whip-tailed, but could not get away. Cal choked up on the spade and drove down with all his weight until the snake folded where the shovel held it. The blade cleaved it, a sound like fabric tearing. The dirty hourglasses on its skin kaleidoscoped. Its tail jabbed.

Cal lifted the spade: blood at the neck, the mouth open, eyes bituminous. Then he brought the spade down like a guillotine. Then twice more until the contortrix was in two, each piece escaping the other, the twisting body piling itself against a tree, the head sliding in the dirt toward Calvin, mouth still open, the teeth wet shards of milk-glass. Calvin bashed the head until it was paste, scooped it up and threw it in the brake. Then he went back to bed.

CHAPTER 26

When Cal woke Sunday morning, Rachel was in the bathroom, water running. She was sick. Outside was gray, fog webbed in the hardwoods on the horizon.

"Rachel," he called. "Rachel, are you alright?"

"Yes," she called back. "I'm going to take a bath."

Cal turned up the thermostat, got back into bed and listened to the sound of his wife bathing. It was 9:30. Sunday morning. He and Rachel did not have the habit of church. His father had given it up after Cal's mother died.

On Sundays, as a boy, Cal went into the bathroom after his mother had bathed – the room warm and misty, shrouded with her scent, bath oil and lotion, the towels glistening – and dreamt he floated in a little cloud. A gospel choir trebled from the kitchen radio as she cooked ham and eggs, grits and potatoes, her hands white with flour as she rolled out the biscuit dough, his father already in his suit, seated at the breakfast table, watching her in her jewelry and dressing gown as he sipped coffee.

Cal slipped into the bathtub, the bottom slippery from whatever it was his mother had bathed in, and lie with the hot water to his chin until she called to him that breakfast was ready. He never wanted to leave that room. While in it, he imagined beyond its soft wet walls a perfection shattered the moment he opened the door.

Cal knocked on the bathroom door.

"Yes?" said Rachel.

"Can I come in?"

"Yes."

Rachel lay almost flat in the very full tub, her hair trailing in the water around her shoulders. Her face and breasts and stomach protruded in relief from the water; the porcelain rim framed her. Like a sarcophagus.

"How do you feel?" he asked.

"I feel alright."

"You know, Rachel, you don't have to come today. You could stay at home and rest, take it easy."

"All I do is take it easy. I want to be with you."

"Well, I appreciate that. But you really don't have to come. I'm going to make some breakfast. What would you like?"

"Oh, God. I don't know. I'm so sick of eating."

"You have to eat."

"I know that. Anything."

"French toast?"

"Sure."

"Honey, it's going to be okay. We're almost there."

"I know."

She shut her eyes. Cal bent over, steadied himself by putting one hand in the water and kissed her.

CHAPTER 27

MacGregor Gaddy had not been to Coventry Prison since the day he retired. Cal glanced at his father as they came up on the camp, but he betrayed nothing. He wore his only suit, the brown suit Cal remembered, its three buttons buttoned, the brown necktie having slipped outside the jacket. Hair combed straight back. The beard hung over the tie-knot. His hands held each other in his lap as he stared out the window. Between father and son sat Rachel. She had been having contractions all morning.

Driving along Prison Camp Road, they passed the old falling-down wooden trailers that the twenties and thirties chain-gang guards used to live in. Mac had lived in one for a year before marrying Elizabeth. Long abandoned, tangled in kudzu that rose up around them like dinosaurs, they had become homes for snakes and vermin. The day was grey and dense, the sky the same color as the road, the road the same color as the fence, and the fence the same color as the convicts.

Cal, Rachel and Mac took their places among the visitors straggling onto the yard as visiting day wrenched into its routine of longing and havoc. How a convict might have his frocked woman sit his lap while he clandestinely entered her, the two of them locked thusly, mask to mask until he finished, the dress soiled, lips bleeding. The Quaalude passed in a kiss. The Bible, gutted of its holy writ and wherein, hidden, resides the herb, the blade, the pistol.

Weeping, laughing and arguing, the visitors drank Kool-Aid and ate snow cones hawked by the Jaycees. Children played in the horseshoe pit. Never more conspicuous than on visiting day, the guards drank Kool-Aid and tried to turn away. They nodded at Cal and Rachel, touching hands to hats. No one, however, recognized Mac, shambling along, looking neither left nor right.

Cal hated working visiting day. He couldn't bear these

people coming together at the picnic tables, their brokenness was so obviously laid out under the sky. They could no longer hide in a house, or inside their heads, what it was or was not. Over years of doing time, many of the convicts simply lost their families as one might eventually lose the words to something. Unvisited, they sat alone on Sundays and watched the others.

Frank, rigged in an old blue suit, hands trussed together with a rosary, was laid out in the middle of the basketball court. Metal chairs were situated around the bier. Pasted above his head, inside the coffin lid, was a spray of plastic lilies. Then above it a wooden board with crayoned characters: *Frankenstein about a hundred. When my heart was in anguish, thou hast exalted me on a rock.*

No one sat on the chairs. Just Ezekiel, up against the coffin. He smoked a cigarette and, every so often, put it to Frank's mouth. When Ezekiel saw MacGregor Gaddy, he anchored the burning cigarette between Frank's lips, stood and wept. He put out his hand and Mac took it and they stood for a moment, each man looking into the other's face until Ezekiel said, "Mr. Gaddy" and Mac said "Ezekiel." Then Ezekiel wrapped his arms around Mac and held him until Mac brought his arms up and held Ezekiel.

From the old convict's embrace, Mac peered down on Frank, his closed translucent eyelids beneath which the fixed pupils gaped at the molting clouds and chain of circling vultures. Frank lay there smoking, the cigarette like a little chimney spiking out of his face, the white tight shirt collar bunching his neck into ashen colloidal rings. Yet he appeared to smile, enjoying his last smoke.

Cal, Rachel, and Mac sat with Ezekiel. The two hoops, like halos at either end of the concrete slab, waited for the dead to ascend to them. Occasional inmates filed by and gazed down on Frank; and occasional visitors, mostly women. One, crying, even put her hand on him, but quickly snatched it away.

Frank seemed no less dead than he ever had, only uglier, dearer, essential. The captain had suggested they have him stuffed and posed like a wooden Indian in the office next to his cache of contraband. There was something about Frank that no one wanted to part with. Cal could not believe that Frank was dead. In fact, he was sure that he was in some odd way still alive. But it didn't matter if they put Frank, still alive, into the earth. It would be as right as sticking him in prison. As right to Frank. Frank was death, the crypt. And life too. The same as Jesus. Cal understood this; his father understood it.

Mac sat perfectly composed, staring at Frank. There was nothing about the world that shocked the father. He knew Frank was either a devil or an angel, or both, that in the world he had chosen, one was as good as the other. The same world the son had chosen.

Cal, too, like his father, could be steel. There was no shame in their kind of cruelty. Upon waking, Frank would testify to it. Shame was in being on the wrong end of it. But you could not have one without the other. For the first time in his life, Cal wished he had a drink, and thought with regret of the shotgun shell of reefer he had whipped out the truck window.

Friend loped up from the far corner of the yard. Working conjugal, he led back a pair of lovers, and had come to escort the next pair down to the maintenance shack where a lone cot was stationed. There every Sunday, married convict,s who had earned I,t spent time with their wives. Conjugal was punk duty. Friend smirked. At that instant, Cal decided Friend was a fool, a treacherous, blasphemous fool.

The convict and woman strolled in front of Friend. He was lean and long-haired, his goatee sliced into a V, brown shirt open, tattoos on his dark, coiled chest. He smiled broadly, an arm around a woman in jeans and sweatshirt, long, long blond hair, dark at the roots, chiseled face, unsmiling, nearly frantic. A face that became lovelier and lovelier if one took the time to look at it. This woman and this man. Just up from the maintenance shack. Fifteen minutes on a folding army cot, Friend stationed at the barred door padlocked from the outside.

The man and woman took their places at a picnic table where a little boy and girl sat eating snow cones. Another convict and his woman, toting clean sheets and a pillow slip, fell in behind Friend who retraced his steps to the maintenance shack where he would shake down the man, and Ernestine, who every Sunday worked conjugal, shook down the woman. Then the couple were free to lurch in among the tools and refuse and close their eyes.

Rachel had not said a word the whole afternoon, just mooned over Frank, her eyes limpid, her entire manner of sorrow and skittishness. She had spent her share of time on Coventry's yard, and there were only her pretty clothes to mark her apart from the other women sitting around making, with their husbands, a few hours of their sentences.

"How do you feel?" Cal asked. It was the only thing he felt he ever said to her.

"I'm alright."

"Really?"

"I'm having contractions."

"Let me take you home. You should never have come."

"I'll be okay."

"Come on, Rachel. I'm a fool for letting you come here."

"I'll be alright, Calvin. I'm not leaving."

Cal's father held Rachel's hand. The old man looked at his son. Father Tuesday, wearing a black chasuble, and attended by six AA inmates, walked out of the chow-hall and made straight for the coffin.

"There won't be any trouble here today, Calvin," Mac assured his son.

CHAPTER 28

Father Tuesday closed the coffin lid. The pallbearers heaved up the box and trailed the priest toward the front gate where the captain and Thrake waited. Cal and Rachel and Mac followed, then Ezekiel. Then Pitch, in full chains, including an iron ring around his neck, and escorted by Nightcutt.

Thrake stuck out a trembling hand when he saw Mac and the two shook.

"I do know you, don't I?" Mac inquired.

"Jesse Thrake. You were the big dog here when I first started working the road gangs."

Thrake wore shoes, but his face was red and scrofulous. Beneath the line of his service cap were patches of missing scalp.

"I can't place you," Mac said, "but for a face in a whole book of faces. Are you alright?"

Thrake looked about to say something true, but he just said, "Yes," and doffed his hat at Rachel. He refused Cal. Thrake looked like an old man.

Behind the camp spread a quarry, long abandoned, that had been worked by Coventry's earliest convicts. Now it was just a gouged-out hollow, like a bowl, surrounded by sheer yellow cliff faces covered with runes and scrawls, little painted faces and crude drawings of naked women. Gigantic rocks humped out of the black water at the pit surface. Cal had always heard that this was Coventry's first graveyard – before the cemetery on the quarry's far bank to which they bore Frank. Dead inmates – and some not dead – had been weighted, in the chain-gang days, with granite and dumped in the sump where their bones still ranged like white brittle fish waiting for time to turn them back into free men.

Out of the shallows pushed trash dumped over the years by the county: stoves and refrigerators, exploded trash bags grown exponentially with carbonates and bug larvae. For a time, the county chicken houses used the quarry to jettison dead chickens and bad eggs. For every tray of bad eggs, there was at least one live biddy; hundreds of rats swarmed out of their nests to chase and gobble them. For sport, the guards shot the rats as they chased the biddies. It was there that Cal first learned to shoot, coming down to the quarry with his father and Frank, often just Frank, to pot those brogan-sized rats with a twenty-two rifle. They tied flashlights to their gun barrels and hunted the rats at night.

As the funeral procession made its way down to the boards, which bridged the water and led to the path up to the graveyard, the quarry progeny lounged among the scape of refuse on the water. Half-rat, half-chicken, yellowish-gray with the vestiges of wings, they watched the procession navigate the wobbly bridge and trudge uphill. The quarry reek was horrific. Those who had handkerchiefs put them over their faces. Father Tuesday, who led the procession, swung the smoking censer, perfuming the air with frankincense.

The graveyard was a mosaic of wavy crosses and cenotaphs. No names, merely markers stumping out of the tallow at a tilt. The entire hillside looked about to pitch into the quarry. The tar squad had dug the grave early that morning. Their shovels leaned against a carven slab. Next to the open hole stood three sawhorses. Upon these the bearers set the coffin. Father Tuesday stepped up and reopened the lid. Frank's mouth had come open as well as one eye which raked the assembly situated around his bier, then settled on the buzzards kiting above. Father Tuesday walked twice around the coffin, first sprinkling it with holy water, then incensing it.

"Let us pray," he said. "O Lord, do not bring Frank to trial a second time. For here on this chain-gang earth, in this muted place of earthly corruption, he has suffered fire in your name at the hands of infidels and Philistines. Grant him forgiveness for all his transgressions and let the blighted fabric of his skin become a cerement of glory. May his verdict be 'Not guilty,' his time built here in this Purgatory. I commend him to your custody, O God, this man born dead, his sentence finally punctuated, the walls around him crumbling in the final fire, tempered in this torturous forge, yet now in your love impervious to flame. Beware the keeper. May the winged freedom fighters spirit him into paradise. May the martyred convicts lead him into the holy city, and at their head, leading these minions, the blessed saint and patron of felons and the executed, Our Lord and Savior, Jesus Christ."

Father Tuesday again incensed the coffin, then sprinkled Frank with holy water. Pitch raised his chains above his head and rattled them. Thrake looked about to faint. The slightest mist had begun to fall.

"Eternal rest grant unto him, O Lord," intoned Father Tuesday.

"And let perpetual light shine upon him," responded the bearers.

"May he rest in peace."

"Amen."

"May his soul and all the souls of the faithful departed, through the mercy of God, rest in peace."

"Amen."

The captain spoke: "Come on forward now to pay your last respects."

Pitch came ahead, Nightcutt with him, and looked down into Frank's face. Frank's other eye popped open. In the deceased monster's eyes was the catenation of vultures. Cal stepped up with Rachel, shuddering as she placed her hand on Frank's. Cal peered down at Franks's hairless skull and saw, but faintly – for the first time in all these years – above the right ear a bite scar and above it the blue tattooed words, *The Teeth of Sinners.*

Cal felt Pitch's eyes upon his wife, and turned to see him staring unabashedly at Rachel. Catching Cal watching him, he smiled and Cal knew then that he and Pitch had been enemies all along. As Mac approached the coffin, he saw it all too and involuntarily placed his hand on his son's shoulder. Ezekiel, who had not left Mac's side, fell to moaning and swaying. His voice, subsumed by the rock quarry, echoed out over the escarpment of trash, con-faced fish rising as the mizzle pricked the water fifty feet below.

Right there, Mac would have put an end to Pitch. Shoved him over the brink. Wearing that steel, Pitch would have sunk like a crowbar. Mac looked down at Frank. Nothing strange there to him. Just the hideous face of the man who oddly enough had attached himself to MacGregor Gaddy. Mac's hand was still on Cal's shoulder. It was only when he turned away from Frank, and removed his hand, that Cal pivoted toward his father because he wanted to say something to him. Something. He didn't know what – and ended up saying nothing.

The captain eased down the coffin lid. Father Tuesday bent, scooped a handful of dirt and sprinkled it in the form of a cross on the coffin-breast. In the air before him, he traced another cross; then he walked back down the path, the rain steady. Then the captain, Nightcutt and Pitch, Mac and Ezekiel, Cal with Rachel, his arm tight around her.

Thrake suddenly went to his knees, covered his face and wept. From beneath his fingers ran blood as though he cried red tears; but it was just another of the nosebleeds which he now had several times a day, and for which there seemed no remedy. The captain bent over him. The bearers reached for their spades.

CHAPTER 29

Lemuel. As one not dispossessed of the will to live, but as one already dead, narrating from the grave his life and thus impervious to earthly ruction. It was as if death agreed with him and to its method shaped him. He would die a thousand times if only to spit again and again in the eyes of the living, shamming their faith that men were engendered for some purpose nobler than the shackle. For the shackle was his God, booted in the forge of a five-by-eight stink-pit cell. It was there that he apprenticed in blood, taking the first time a razor and then, after that, anything – hasp, zipper, coffin-bone – to cut himself.

What the prison shrinks called a self-mutilator. Lying in his own blood and excrement, the guards' riot batons flailing him, he listened to the other convicts, in their gunmetal cells, along Coventry's single-cell segregation range, keening, *Lemuel.* Calling the way Luficer might clear his throat: *Lemuel's cut hisself again.* Then the guards pouring into the block in riot gear, cleating the cage bars with their sticks: *You want some of this? You want some of this?*

The whole house erupting in hurled piss and shit. Befouled, disgorging, the guards unlocked the cells one by one, went in and clubbed the convicts down to their skivvies and tick springs until the whole block slept on steel.

Lemuel never spoke, never uttered *Don't* or *I can't*, just took his flogging with the feral satisfaction of a dog that gnaws off its leg to quit the trap. Not even when Thrake emptied over his razor-hacked arms a jar of isopropyl. Lemuel knew his writ had been in blood appointed, that genocide had sprung two-headed from Genesis, that Cain had been nothing more than misunderstood.

They led him out as they led him in: full irons and near naked. It was not far off from Christmas. He was like Santa, plucked and Levitical, red his chains and arms to the elbow and spotting the yard as he dragged bloody through the gate on his way to the county hospital the night of the Christmas program the Church Women United sponsored. Each man was handed a paper bag with an apple, an orange, a tract of Jeremiads and a popcorn ball. They sang the songs, drank punch.

Cal and Icemorelee, both in their first months on the yard, had been given over that December night by the captain to drive Lemuel to the hospital. Both young and shambling, a bit blood-crazed about the mouth and eyes and packing side arms for the trip.

Lemuel stood revenant, skeleform, looking nowhere, blood bubbling from him, impastoed in his shorts and socks. A few of the Church Women entering the camp had to pass Lemuel as he came through the gate. Palled, fit to break apart, they gasped and backed away. Cal and Icemorelee said, *Yes, ma'am* and lowed after Lemuel as after an old horse readied for the abattoir.

Hunched in the caged backseat of the lime-green prison Valiant, Lemuel bled quietly. Like a great gray bird, chest concave, fingernails like talons at the ends of the steel-cuffed hands, the arms that he had cut flayed wings dipped in blood. Pumice-faced. Whited eyes. Cal drove, periodically glancing in the rearview mirror. Lemuel just sitting there. Icemorelee about to cry.

At the hospital Cal slipped into narcosis. The room spun. The smell of astringent. The surreal glow of the brute light on white and metal, Lemuel on a gurney, his arms dripping each one drop, one drop, perfect circles on the white tile. Icemorelee had disappeared. Sick. Cal was sick too. He wanted to run, leave this thing to its bleeding. *A cry for help*, he told himself. What the books said about cutters. *An escape from intolerable conditions. A desire for reclassification.* Not simply one more mutilation.

Without anesthesia, without a word – just a rucking in of his cheeks – Lemuel submitted to the needle and thread. Steel, flesh, steel, the scribbling of black catgut up and down his arms. Small cuts designed to bleed. *A cry for help.*

On the way back to Coventry, before Cal and Icemorelee

could do a thing about it, Lemuel had unwrapped the bandages with his teeth and begun chewing out his sutures. They were on a black winding road. Lemuel flailed his gauze-draped arms, his mouth smeared. Blood through the cage that separated him from the boy officers. All over the car. Nowhere to stop. No way to get at him as he devoured himself. Icemorelee pulled his gun.

"Stop it," he screamed. "Stop it."

Lemuel went on eating, tossing blood.

"Shoot him, Ice," Cal shouted. "Kill his evil ass."

Icemorelee shot through the cage. Once. Twice. Again and again.

Cal woke in utter blackness. He reached for Rachel. He wanted her to hold him. He would tell her he had had a bad dream and she would pull him against her, telling him to hush now, kissing his face. But Rachel was not there. 2:30 on the lit clock face.

"Rachel," he called, bolting up suddenly, unable to catch his breath. "Rachel," he called again and slid out of bed.

She was in the living room, lying fully dressed on her left side on the couch.

"What's the matter?" Cal asked.

"We have to go in."

"Contractions?"

"Uh huh. They're pretty close."

"Why didn't you get me up?"

"It's okay. I wanted you to sleep."

"Should we call the hospital?"

"I already have."

"Rachel. Rachel." He knelt at her side and took her hand. "It'll be okay, honey," he said.

"I know." Her voice quavered, tears in her eyes. "I'm so tired of lying on my left side."

"I know, Sweetheart. Let me get dressed. I'll hurry."

"Calvin," she called after him. "I'm not in any danger of having the baby right here on the couch."

CHAPTER 30

Lights burned in Mac's house. Floodlights shone from the roof eaves. The sweep of Cal's headlights limned the jagged heads of rocks, the first two courses of his father's wall, swelling out of the grass. A wheelbarrow of creek stones stood waiting.

"I think that maniac's working day and night on that damn wall," said Cal. "God, he's crazy."

As they drove along the two-track, on their way to the hospital, Mac emerged from the house with May. He walked to the wheelbarrow, staring after the truck-lights.

"It'll give him something to do," replied Rachel.

"I reckon," Cal said.

CHAPTER 31

Cal and Rachel entered the old, dilapidated county hospital through its vacant emergency room. Nothing much even in the little hours, but trauma. Guns and knives, automobiles. They were escorted up to Maternity and Rachel put in a labor room cut in half by a curtain. On the other side of it was a very young woman – a girl, really – in labor, sobbing to herself, whom they had to pass as they came in.

Rachel's contractions were less than two minutes apart. A wrinkled grey-headed nurse hooked her up to a blood pressure monitor and started an IV of Magnesium Sulfate to stop the contractions.

"Is she okay?" Cal asked.

"Well, she'll be better off if we can keep this baby from coming. This should help," said the nurse without looking up from what she was doing.

"Will she have to stay?" asked Cal.

"I don't know. That pressure's a little high. Once I run this strip on the baby, we'll know a little more."

She wrapped a belt, with what looked like a large stethoscope affixed to it, around Rachel's middle. It hooked into another monitor out of which inched narrow graph paper tracing the topography of the baby's heartbeat. The nurse let the strip run through her hands like a tickertape.

"The baby's fine as fine can be," she declared. "Honey, you just hang in there," she said to the girl, now moaning, as she was leaving. "Everything's going to be okay. I'll be back in a little bit. We're going to move you to a birthing room."

Cal held Rachel's hand and they listened to the girl's crying.

"It hurts," she gasped. "It hurts."

"Jesus," said Cal.

"Poor thing," said Rachel. "She doesn't look like she's more than fifteen."

The girl started screaming. Flat out screaming. Cal

rushed around the curtain. The girl sat up in bed, hands on her stomach, mouth wide, tears streaming down her face. She gaped at him through a weir of torn blond hair.

"You," she screamed. "You did this to me. You dirty dog. You. You did this. I hate you. I hate you."

The grey-headed nurse and another one stormed in. The girl had fallen back in her bed, exhausted, choked with her pain. The sound of a small engine about to give out. The nurses looked at Cal for a second before they unlocked the bed wheels and trundled the girl out of the room.

Rachel was crying softly when Cal stepped back to her. He took her hand. The girl screaming as she was wheeled down the hall: "No. Please. Don't take me. I don't want to die."

"I don't think I can do this," Rachel said. Then she laughed through the tears."What's so funny?" he asked.

"Just what I said," she laughed.

"Are you alright, Rachel?"

"Yes, I'm alright."

She closed her eyes, the pillow couched about her head like a wimple. For a long time Cal watched her sleep, red numbers flashing on the monitors, the baby's heart tatting out its strip of white. Through the window a vague shimmer across the face of St. Joan's County: the sun stalled at the earth's edge.

CHAPTER 32

The electrician checked the leads for the last time. The witnesses were seated. The warden spraddled a stool in the control room and waited for the governor's phone call. Lindrey Vance's last meal had been cooked by his mama: country ham, rice and redeye gravy, green beans, collards, spoonbread and banana pudding. The old lady had delivered it to the death-house in a picnic basket. For a little man, Vance ate a lot. Regaled in white, he looked even younger with his head shaved as he walked out of Deathwatch, a tall, bespectacled preacher in a plaid suit, clutching a Bible, one step behind him. As Vance told it, he was right with the Lord. They all get right with the Lord, MacGregor Gaddy liked to say. Put a man in a hole and he'll find Jesus. Sometimes that's what it takes. Kill him and he will become Jesus.

Every man in the big prison stood as Vance entered the death chamber. A choir of thirteen hundred convicts, steel termites eating the house as the saline crown buckled over Vance's head. The executioner ate an apple. A newspaperman got sick. The leads were strapped to the shaved ovals on Vance's legs, two inch leathers buckled at his ankles, calves, thighs, stomach, chest, wrists and neck. The preacher bent his head to Vance's ear and whispered. The condemned man's lips fidgeted.

The men on the range ceased their dirge: perfect silence as they listened for an epitaph that never arrived. No last words. Then the black hood dropped over Vance's head and he was never seen again.

The phone did not ring with a stay from the governor. The sun came out of its cave. The executioner's hand on the breaker. The two minute cycle began. What went on beneath Vance's hood would remain conjecture. Yet there came the unmistakable sizzle of side-meat in a skillet, bones popping, capillaries bursting. Rising up from Vance, his black shrouded head lolling on his chest, eyes ablaze through his shroud, coiled small sacrifices of smoke. Boiling urine hissed, then bubbled on the floor.

The sun was full up when Cal woke in a chair at Rachel's bedside. The hospital had decided to keep her. She was still sleeping, so Cal slipped out and went straight to the camp. His shift wasn't due to start until two, but he had the sergeant's exam at nine and he did not want to go home. There was something in him too that wanted to be at Coventry and nowhere else. Something to do with Vance who had died – Cal heard it on the truck radio on his way to the camp – at dawn as planned.

But Cal had known he had died, had known it even sleeping in the hospital next to his sleeping wife with that life pounding in her. Their child – who Cal had somehow come to identify with Vance. The execution put him back in that whorehouse motel; and that whore was his wife and his mother, and Vance was their bastard. He drove faster. He had to get to the unit, the one place where he suddenly felt he belonged.

CHAPTER 33

Cal pulled in as the first shift was relieving the third. Thrake stood at the gate supervising the shift change. He had taken to living at Coventry, sleeping in the sick room, showering in the sergeant's office, eating in the chow-hall, but never on Pitch's shift. His prize automobile squatted on flat tires in the parking lot, the bashed windows never repaired, its once perfect interior spattered with the elements and bird droppings, creatures coming and going, carcasses, filth.

Thrake was too scared to stay at home where lights flashed off and on all night, the commode flushed unaccountably, food would not keep even in the refrigerator. Constant voices. Horrible smells. Dead convicts called him on the telephone. His water heater blew up. His bed took fire. His cat was crucified to his front door.

Thrake caught Cal staring at him, and turned full to face him. All of his hair was gone, and most of his teeth. His uniform was three sizes too large for what was left of him. He motioned Cal over. Up close, he did not even look like himself. He had aged thirty years, but he seemed to Cal more powerful than ever.

"Hear you're taking the sergeant's exam today," he sneered.

"That's right."

"Moving up, huh?"

"Trying to."

Thrake's face was fire, his eyes blue as purple. He tried to smile. "I want to tell you something," he said. "That nigger boy of yours. He's at the bottom of this." Thrake gestured to indicate himself. "And you know it."

"Sergeant Thrake, have you been to the doctor?"

"Goddam, I ain't sick. I'm deviled."

"Jesus Christ, Thrake."

"Let me tell you something else, Gaddy. Somebody tampered with that piss test or that nigger witch doctor has two dicks. I know one thing for true: that marijuana that's all over this camp is coming in from one of you."He stabbed Cal in the chest with a sharp hot finger. His breath was horrible. "This is what comes from babying these human pieces of shit. They should have lit up about a hundred of the bastards this morning along with Vance, cooked a whole damn tier. And now we're told to be careful with them this morning. We don't want to upset anybody. It takes a sensitive fellow to work here. Ask your daddy."

Cal looked past Thrake. Not an inmate on the yard. "Where the hell is everybody?" he asked.

"They won't come out of the dorm. The cooks haven't even mustered for morning chow. Brotherton and Ezekiel are doing the cooking in the chow-hall."

"Where's the captain?"

"Shit. He's probably stuck like tar in Blish. He's supposed to be on his way. If you want to bone up on your sergeant's exam, you get into your states and follow me. Or don't. You think whatever you want, but I'm in goddam charge here."

Thrake tottered onto the yard, his officers spilling out ahead of him. Cal hustled into the office and changed from his flannel shirt and jeans into a spare uniform he kept in his locker. As he changed shirts, he noticed a little mark on his chest where Thrake had poked him. Thrake might be hysterical, but he was no bullshitter. Cal thought again of Pitch's drug test and Thrake's take on the reefer. He had to be right. Of course he was right. It was one of them.

"One of us," Cal said to himself, realizing for the first time since he had been wearing a prison guard uniform that Coventry was his temple, and within it was necessary, even righteous, work to do. Never mind that whore in the Heart of Dark who had launched herself over him like an electrocuted woman. Never mind Vance. Never mind the sorry chain-gang Jesuses of the executed. He thought of his mother, of Rachel, maybe at that very moment ... Who knew? He might be a father before the day was out, that baby, like it was in him, stretching its tiny fists up into his gullet and choking him.

That baby. That boy. Cal knew it like his own name. It

was a boy. Not the girl he wanted, whom he could indulge and half ignore. But a boy he knew by sheer blood he would influence. That boy bulging in Rachel. Then he thought of his father. Building course by course a stone wall across his pittance of land.

The dorm was tomb-like. The men lay open-eyed, prone in their bunks. They had linked hands, each holding the hand of the man in the next bunk. Each of the three tiers of bunks holding hands, like paper dolls along the cellblock's perimeter. In the middle of the block stood Thrake, screaming for them to get up and get to chow, threatening them with write-ups and more time. But they did not move, did not inhale or exhale, did not flutter an eyelid. As if rehearsing death. The more Thrake ranted, the smaller he got until he seemed a mere speck on the concrete floor, the inmates levitating off their bunks, hovering above him in three layers.

Thrake vomited. Then he yanked a fire extinguisher from the wall and limped around the block, spraying the men. The chemicals brought them out of their trances. Screaming for Thrake to stop as two other officers grabbed cylinders and did the same, they curled up like slugs anointed with salt. Cal stood at the cell door with a hand on his mace.

The men crabbed out of their bunks, some on their knees in the white foam, gouging at their eyes, tearing at their clothes. Eyes down. One look at Thrake would turn them to stone.

"Now," Thrake went on, "y'all got ten minutes to police this dorm, shower and get to chow. If there's a one of you even a second late, I'll fill the Boot with you and stake the rest out in the stocks naked. Goddam try me."

Thrake stumbled, went down on one knee. A couple of officers went to him, but he waved them away, vomited again, then struggled to his feet and let out a croaking roar. The inmates undressed and stumbled toward the showers.

"Not bad, huh?" said Thrake to Cal as they walked, along with Icemorelee, toward the cook shack. "You taking notes, sergeant-boy? You got to draw a line for these bastards and then dare them to cross it. There is no other way."

CHAPTER 34

The door to the cook shack was locked.

"Open it," Thrake ordered, holding open the screen door. "My keys are in the sergeant's office."

"I don't have a key," Icemorelee replied.

"You two are the damn watch officers of this shift. You are charged to have keys, dammit. Why in the hell don't you have keys? Didn't you read that directive that went out from the captain? Jesus H. Christ. This goddam joint is like Romper Room. Go get a key, Icemorelee."

"I have mine right here," offered Cal, fishing a ring of keys from his pocket.

Suddenly the door swung open, and Friend stood there in front of them.

"What are you doing in there, Friend?" barked Thrake.

"Trying to get these convicts to muster."

Friend refused to look at Thrake, but he caught Cal's eye for a moment.

"By yourself? And you locked yourself in? What the hell, Friend? Are you an idiot?"

"Sergeant," stated Friend, "convicts refusing to muster is a security priority."

"Don't read the rule book to me," said Thrake, dragging himself past Friend.

The cook shack stunk. Pitch's stewpot on the hotplate, the augur sitting next to it, flies walking every surface. On a table was propped a newspaper photograph of Lindrey Vance, the one with the cross around his neck, a popsicle stick picture frame around it. On either side of it flickered candles. No other light. The vague scent of reefer, mixed with the bad breath of backed-up toilets and whatever Pitch had cooking, thirteen cooks prone in their bunks, and foul water slopping in the latrine. The heat of the little building was insufferable, like breathing cotton.

"We'll do this one time, girls," said Thrake. "I'll give you to the count of three to get up and get moving, no hard feelings, because I know you've had a terrible emotional blow what with that murdering, raping piece of shit Vance getting fried this morning. You have my condolences. It upset you, I know. I'm upset about it too. I hope you can tell. How can we be so cruel to one another when we're all brothers under the skin? You know, I witnessed an electrocution once. Sounds like bacon in the pan and stinks to high heaven. That boy smoked like a firecracker before he went up. You could hear the bones popping in his fingers when they turned on the juice. And it only took nine minutes."

The men did not move. The only sounds were the leaking plumbing and the convicts' communal aspiration gathering, along with the water dropping and trickling, into a palpable force. The heat stuffed itself into the room – like it was counting ticks till it blew.

"One, two, three," Thrake said. "Time's up."

Then he kicked over Pitch's pot and with his stick smashed the augur. Pitch, as if spring-released, sat up in his bed and screamed. Thrake hit him with his stick across the forehead. Laid him right back down with his hands to his head, a three inch gash that opened like a mouth above Pitch's eyes, but scarcely bled.

"Hit the lights," Thrake shouted.

Icemorelee switched on the lights. The other men mustered, throwing themselves over the edges of their bunks.

"Get your asses dressed and get to chow," Thrake said. Then he took his stick and smashed the picture of Vance, flies rising off it. One of the candles fell into the broth that had emptied out of Pitch's pot. The puddle flared up like an oracle, then died. Thrake breathed heavily, globules of sweat starting from his face and neck and falling to the floor. He steadied himself on a bunk.

The men filed toward the door, Talfont among them. He had only that morning returned from the Boot where he had been for days and days. He was stick thin and sallow. With his widow's peak, goatee, and sunken skull, he made the perfect caricature of Satan. Thrake had allowed him only a diet of coffee during his Boot stay, though he had gotten so hungry he had started eating the Styrofoam cups it was delivered in. Spastic as he walked, he seemed still wired from the coffee and nearly its same color, though he was a white man.

"Pitch is going to turn your ass into a fucking giraffe," he said to Thrake.

Thrake just smiled. He didn't have but a few rotten stalactites left for teeth.

"Dress Maxwell House here in rubber waders and put him in the stocks," he said to Icemorelee. "Castor oil on the hour. That's a sure fire way to cure the full of shit."

Icemorelee pushed Talfont out ahead of him. The yard swarmed with men on their way to chow. Pitch stood shakily next to his bunk – shrunken, almost submissive. He didn't look at Thrake or Cal as he slid in a pair of shower shoes toward the door, that red mouth Thrake had opened on his forehead gaping at them. He stopped and stared at something on the floor: the eyeball from the augur staring up at him, a fly poised on the white of it. Thrake lifted his shoe and squashed the eyeball. Pitch shuddered. Looked up at Thrake and Cal. Then he walked out with Thrake behind him.

CHAPTER 35

Cal stepped into the latrine, unzipped and stood at the urinal. The whites the cooks had washed by hand, and hung from the ceiling pipes, blew softly in front the duct vents, the heat ungodly. Mold and leaky plumbing. Toilets constantly running.

Watching those whites slowly turn, Cal thought maybe the worst thing about living in a prison was the lack of privacy. One of the shirts, as if to concur, turned and dipped in the heat flow, revealing something suspended by a string from a pipe: the vague semblance of a person. Like a doll. A cheesecloth body with three buttons from a Coventry guard-shirt; an onion for a head; the mouth, real human teeth; the nose and eyes rudely fashioned with fingernails; a fez of human hair at the onion's crest.

The floor slicked out from Cal. The heat threw a bag over his head. His vision narrowed until he was looking through the wrong end of a telescope, all around it blackness, rust in his mouth, electric fear throwing him over in a dead faint. As he fell, there came a huge boom from outside. He opened his eyes: still on his feet, urinating, staring at the little, noosed replica of Thrake. There came another boom. He zipped up and raced onto the yard.

Inmates and officers gathered outside the chowhall. A geyser of black smoke and fire shot out of the parking lot. Isolated from the rest of them, Thrake clung to the fence, face pressed against it as he wept, and witnessed his car burn. There was a pop, then another explosion, larger than the first two. An orange ball of fire gushed out of the car and sat on its roof, crushing it. Thrake wet himself and, then, as his car disintegrated, crumbled and went down against the fence. The men went back into breakfast.

CHAPTER 36

Rachel was still asleep when Cal called the hospital at nine o'clock. She had been moved to her own room, everything stable. No answer at his father's house. Cal knocked on Blish's closed door, and she called him in.

The captain was in there, too, pacing back and forth in front of Blish, sitting at her desk. It was obvious she had been crying. The captain too looked like he had been crying.

"This is terrible business," he said as Cal entered the room.

"Yes, sir," Cal answered, not sure exactly what the captain was talking about.

"Do you believe in the death penalty, Calvin?" asked the captain.

Yes, the captain had been crying. Over what, Cal could not speculate. Vance? Maybe Blish or Thrake. Maybe he cried for his own wife. Jane was her name. Cal had met her once when she delivered to Coventry some discarded books from the local library. A sweet, pretty woman, brown hair beginning to silver, glasses and a pink corduroy dress. Cal had studied her, her head cocked slightly to the side, completely solicitous, as she sat with Blish and listened to the story of her eye, how Blish had been accidentally shot in it with a target arrow by her brother, how she had arrived at the hospital emergency room with the arrow still sticking out of the socket.

The eye had been saved, but it had a hole in it that gradually narrowed from the diameter of an arrow to the diameter of a needle. Of course she lost sight in it. But, because of the minute tunnel through her eye, she had felt like her life, in a fractional beam of light, was seeping out of her, and that's why she'd decided on the patch. Like covering with a robe a naked body.

Cal, of course, knew the story of Blish's eye. Everyone did. She told it often enough. But he had never heard her relate to anyone those intimate details about her life leaking out; and, despite himself, he had never thought of Blish in quite the same way. Now, instead of thinking about the patch when he saw her, he thought about the eye underneath, and its steady exhale of Blish.

Remarkable that Blish had chosen the captain's wife to reveal these things about herself. Cal had decided the captain's wife knew about Blish and her husband. Maybe only after Blish's eye story did it dawn on her. It was the last time Cal saw Jane on the camp, and the captain never referred to her. They had three children.

Cal had never been unfaithful to Rachel. Certainly not with another woman, yet he had had for the past many months the sense that he had been unfaithful. He couldn't pinpoint why he felt this way, however, other than that it had everything to do with Coventry. He was certain that his father had never betrayed his mother with another woman. But MacGregor Gaddy had betrayed her with Coventry. All those years, it had been his whore.

"I don't know" is what Cal replied to the captain's question about the death penalty. The same answer he would have given had he been asked if he believed in God.

"Well, it's a little after nine o'clock," remarked the captain looking at his watch. "You'll want to get started on your exam now."

Cal used every minute of the three hours he was allotted. He did not ponder much the words on the pages in front of him. There was little to the test, actually, and he wondered why more people didn't put in for sergeant. Some of it was know-how. The rest was lying. Which pretty much summed up working in a prison. Knowing the right way to answer the questions no more prepared you to step on the yard as ramrod than childbirth classes prepared you to have a baby.

He and Rachel were due that night at their childbirth class at the hospital. In the dingy basement with its one outmoded elevator, the low ceiling with heat pipes scrolling out of it. Attending the classes filled him with hope and panic at the same time. Along with the other couples, he and Rachel walked in with their air mattress and pillow and took their places on the floor where they studied, then simulated, the various stages of birthing.

Rachel would lie on the air mattress. In his uniform, Cal knelt next to her. His job was to encourage, rub her back, mop her brow, feed her ice chips, breathe with her. The early contractions were like gently sloping hills: a slow crest up, then rounding, then slowly down. Easy does it. Breathe. Then transition, where the contractions turned into jagged peaks and the altitude became dizzying, breathtaking, panic-inducing. This was the stage where the woman might get a little out of her head, want to turn back, lose all sense of modesty. Cuss her husband: he had done it to her, put her up on this cross. Cal imagined a screaming, naked Rachel, in unbearable pain, the whole world there to witness how despicable he was, how he'd find out at the moment of their baby's birth how his wife had never loved him.

Cal dropped the completed exam on Blish's desk. She was nowhere to be seen. He sat in her chair and called the hospital again. Rachel's line was busy. He walked out of the office and got in his truck. What was left of Thrake's car still hissed.

CHAPTER 37

Rachel was sitting up. A bag of clear medication hung to an IV tree at the head of the bed. A tube ran from it to her wrist. She still wore the fetal monitor, the strip charting the baby's heartbeat. A vase of flowers on the night stand. Calvin kissed her for a long time.

"How are you, sweetheart?" he asked, sitting on the bed and taking her hand.

"Oh, Calvin. I'm fine. Just so tired."

"What about the contractions?"

"They've stopped."

"Ah, that's good. When can you come home?"

"I don't know. I think I'll be here for at least a few days. They want to keep an eye on me."

"I want to keep an eye on you too. Is everything okay with the baby?"

"Yes. Really. How was your test? You poor thing – with no sleep."

"It was pretty easy – designed for morons. Where'd the flowers come from?"

"Your father was here."

"You're kidding."

"He's so sweet. He came in here holding them like a little boy. Sat right here and patted my hand and told me everything would be alright."

"How'd he know you were here?"

"I don't know. I didn't ask."

"I called him earlier and there was no answer."

"He was out building the wall, I'm sure. He looked terrible, filthy and bedraggled and covered in clay and dried mud. He told me that the whole time he was working on it, there was a chain-gang of devils wearing stripes, humming an old prison work song for him."

"He's crazy."

Rachel squeezed Calvin's hand. "Calvin," she said.

"They did another ultrasound."

The squeeze of her hand, the tone of her voice. Cal went cold and coppery. *Devils*, he thought. *Goddam devils.*

"The baby's smaller than they originally thought," said Rachel, her voice whispery, breaking.

"What exactly does that mean?"

"We just need to buy a little more time. Even a week, the doctor said."

"Well, we can do that. The contractions have stopped. Right?"

"I know, but ... " Rachel choked on the sentence. "I don't think I'll be able to come home until I have the baby."

Cal got up in the bed and held her. "Honey, it'll be okay. If you have to stay, it's the best place for you. I'll be here every second I can. And Papa too. It'll be alright. The baby'll be fine."

Cal leaned against the headboard, feeling he might cry himself. He was so drowsy. If he could simply close his eyes and stop it all for a moment. Rachel felt like a great weight against him. The big wall clock read 1:30.

CHAPTER 38

Driving the back roads to his shift at Coventry, Cal had the old crave to be stoned, out of things, if but for a moment. Lost in a matrix so ridiculously complicated, he wanted only to escape, park his truck, part the undergrowth and walk into the endless forest. Denounce everything and disappear. He wished again for that discarded shotgun shell of reefer. He pulled out the ashtray and found a roach.

The buzz came so sweetly, centering him in the possibility that everything would be fine: work, his father, Rachel and the baby. The country was beautiful: little green birds dodged the truck, a wild turkey flushed from the gorse, sleeping deer, the biding quietus of the secret land. And Cal, still young, innocent on a blue ribbon of road in his red truck. Things would work out. *Joy comes in the morning*, his mother had always declared..

At the sight of the tower and the quicksilver coiling concertina, the buzz inverted itself. Cal's body temperature climbed; he sweated like a condemned man: aching and spent, irritable, a sick headache. It was the camp doing him this way, yet he knew he could stand it. There was room in him for it.

Friend rooted in his customary spot, the shotgun jutting up at his belt. As Cal walked toward him, he had an inkling that Friend might shoot him. Stoned, afraid, Cal didn't know at that moment who the hell he was. His father had said it: *You're either a convict or a guard, one.*

Cal saw, however, that Friend was also stoned. He thought he had smelled it recently on Icemorelee too. Maybe they were all stoned, inmates and guards. Brothers after all.

"Heard you're looking to make sergeant, Mr. Gaddy," said Friend. He smiled, but Cal knew there was something else behind the sunglasses.

"Yeah," Cal answered. "Let me punch in and I'll relieve you."

"No need, brother," said Friend. "I'm working second too."

Friend smiled even more broadly. Cal recognized the shape of it now. How could he have been so stupid as to accept contraband on the yard from another officer? If Thrake was right about how the reefer was getting into Coventry, it had to be Friend. Maybe a couple of others, too, but Friend, at the point, keeping Pitch supplied and taking whatever cut he had bargained for. He had covered himself nicely by fronting Cal dope, and no telling who else, whenever he wanted it. Hell, Cal owed him money for it.

It stood to reason that Friend must have rigged the piss test. Any heat on Pitch was heat on Friend. If Pitch had come up positive, and his cache turned up – wherever it was – then he would take Friend down and Friend would naturally rat out Cal too. Everyone knew Cal was tight with Pitch. Cal was up to his ears in it without even trying. All a result of Thrake's law and order crusade.

But Thrake was just doing his job. In fact, Thrake was the only one doing his job. Cal had failed to recognize the proper devil. Just as Father Tuesday had warned, he had been hoodwinked by what seemed. Such a thing would never have happened to Cal's father. Maybe Mac Gaddy did burn down that building with that escaped boy in it, but he never swerved. Never confused what he was steeled for doing with how he felt. There was not but one way. All along, leading up to the minute you did whatever you were going to do, there had never been but that one way. Period. No choice. Just the one way. Still and all, Cal at that moment did not know what to do. He cussed himself for getting stoned.

As if he knew Cal was buzzing, Friend smiled and smiled. Of course he knew. The two of them were on the same ride. No difference. Cal would have to wait for it to play out. If Friend could wait, he could wait too. He was done with Friend. And he was done with Pitch. Sorry as it seemed, he found himself in league with Thrake. But Thrake, like Mac, would not let anything go. He would see Cal hellified with the rest of them. It was too late for him and Thrake.

123

The reefer had made Cal sick: stomach pains and nausea. This time he'd shed it for good. Never again. There was also the matter of Pitch's magic.

What had started as a joke – Thrake's easily dismissible paranoia and superstition, that he had made himself a cartoon – was now a haunting, though no one else but Cal seemed to pay it much mind. They chalked up Thrake's disintegration to the pressures that went with his job. A job that tried to put one face on evil and another on good; but each wore a mask and it was beyond human ken to distinguish between the two.

And, hell yes, a man could be haunted. MacGregor Gaddy had devils. It seemed more likely than not to Cal at that moment that near any evil could be smelted out of the prison forge. He should have cut down that little effigy of Thrake, but it had frozen him. Good God, it had in truth entered him.

"Why are you working a double?" Cal asked Friend. "Who are we short?"

"Thrake," said Friend. Then he laughed. The eyes behind the shades.

"What?" asked Cal.

"Thrake's gone."

Cal's first reaction despite himself was relief. "What's up?" he asked.

"Don't know. No details available. Anyway, Mr. Gaddy, you don't need to worry about relieving me because me and this shotgun are staying put until count's cleared."

Cal nodded. "Okay." He headed for the office.

"Happy trails," Friend called after him, laughing, "Sergeant Gaddy."

CHAPTER 39

Blish was the only one in the office.

"Where's Thrake?" Cal asked. He was worried about how things would stand without Thrake. Who would be the iron if something jumped?

"We don't know," said Blish. "He just disappeared. We've looked everywhere for him. I even called him at home, but he didn't have anything to drive home in."

"Where's the captain?"

"On the yard. Something happened in the dorm. I don't know what. He went tearing out of here."

"Let me get down there, then," said Cal.

"Is everything okay with the baby?" asked Blish.

"It looks like they're going to keep Rachel until the baby's born."

Blish brought her hand up to her mouth.

CHAPTER 40

Blish's husband's name was Bob. He managed a grocery store in a town fifty miles from Coventry. That's all the captain knew about him. He and Blish religiously avoided talking to each other about their spouses. When the captain walked out of the dorm and saw a little man in a suit making swiftly toward him across the yard, he somehow knew it was Bob, though it would remain a mystery how, in a cardinal breach of security, he had gained access to the yard in the first place. The captain's first impulse was to shake hands, but he carried in his right hand the bloody crucifix, sharpened to a point at its base, he had just pulled out of an inmate's thigh.

With Thrake gone, he had been summoned to the dorm to help break up a fight; but when he got there, the fight – a chain-gang love triangle – had concluded. The two original lovers, already cuffed, were being nudged toward the Boot by a new officer named Childs. Lolling in each other's arms, a conciliatory embrace of tattoos and broken teeth, they pledged everlasting love, no more cheating.

The cuckold lay in shock on the floor of the cellblock, his thigh a mini-Golgotha, Jesus up to his knees in gore. Seeing the Son of God imbedded in a convict's leg, the captain reflexively yanked out the crucifix. A geyser of blood shot out, then settled back to a burble.

The blood had attracted a swarm of inmates, as well as the few guards on yard duty, so Bob had little trouble making his way to the captain. Bob stopped, regarded him through a gauntlet of inmates and shouted: "You leave your goddam hands off my wife."

Cal, along with Father Tuesday and the nurse, who instantly applied a tourniquet to the bleeding inmate, arrived only in time to hear this and see the captain bring up his bloody hand and hold the crucifix for a searing instant in Bob's face. The smaller man lunged at the captain; and had it not been for the inmates, it seemed the captain would have plunged the crucifix into him. The inmates held the two apart while Bob reiterated, "You leave your goddam hands off my wife."

The captain dropped the crucifix. He didn't say a word. He seemed struck dumb – Blish had suddenly appeared through the gate – as if he had suddenly remembered why he had fallen in love with her – if that's what they called it. Father Tuesday picked up the crucifix.

Blish, whose black hair and baby-blue patch had taken on the sheen of the sky, waited at the gate for Bob as the captain stared after him.

"Okay," said Cal, and the inmates scattered.

Though he could only shake his head at the captain and Blish, Cal was almost comforted by the stabbing in the dorm. Predictable. The way things were supposed to be. On his way to check out the cook-shack, Cal passed the stocks where a holy roller, racked in one of them, tiraded against Philistine chariots, great spoils and Satan rearing up against Israel. Saliva dripped from his chin. And Talfont in the other, now living in the cesspool his castor-oiled intestines had leaked into his waders. Catatonic, his face like a bearded white-brown prune, he smelled like the dead.

As Cal passed him, he rasped, "You're next, mother fucker."

Cal called to Childs: "Hose down this man, Talfont, here. Then get him off this shelf and back to population. The Christer too."

The men lined up for chow. Things had quieted. Cal wondered if it might just blow over. With Thrake gone, maybe he should let things slide, at least for now. But Thrake could be counted on to turn up. He'd never relent. Cal too had to stay in it for the long run. God, he felt sick.

In the cookshack the breakfast crew, including Pitch, slept. TV on. Flies. Heat. The place had been cleaned up. Pitch's pot was nowhere to be seen. Cal walked into the latrine. Looked around through the stalls and dripping shower. *Trink, trink, trink.* But no lynched effigy. Just the heat and smell. The blur.

CHAPTER 41

In the aftermath of Vance's execution, Thrake's disappearance, and the scene on the yard with the Captain and Blish's husband, things at Coventry smoothed out and became in fact terribly placid.

The Captain grew ever introspective, mumbling to himself and spending much more time on the yard. He and Blish avoided each other, but between them smoldered an over-tragic soap opera melancholy. While the Captain all but quit speaking, Blish could not fasten her mouth, as if to stop would let in the silence of what was happening all over Coventry. Whatever it was.

Thrake had evaporated. No sign. The husk of his car was towed off and he was filed with Missing Persons. In one sense, he was forgotten. But everyone still expected him to turn up. Minus Thrake, the rhythm of the camp changed for the better. No one in the stocks or Boot. Things seemed to return to the days before Thrake went after Pitch: chow, lock-down, count, shift change. The tar squad and road crew went out every day. AA meetings met. On Sundays, visiting families straggled onto the yard. New Excalibur concertina now completely encircled the camp; the guard towers had been repainted.

That this surface betrayed nothing unusual did little to pacify Cal. The inner life of a prison is inscrutable as a soul. Cal could no longer be both men he had been before. He made Sergeant, and that carried with it a big rock he could never be unshackled from. Not to mention he had replaced Thrake.

Now he was unquestionably a duty man whose psyche stretched back to the chain=gang. Carved in bedrock. He was, by God, MacGregor Gaddy's son. No going back to that tightrope between custody and getting along. He had made the crossover. Call it what you will. And it was not just the imminent birth of his first child, the fact that he was thirty years old, or the extra $140.00 a sergeant's pay put in his pocket every month. Nor rank. Nor power. Something deeper. Deep as his father beating a man with a live snake or his mother clawing her way out of a locked room to be stabbed by lightning. Or that whore in the Heart of Dark. Cal didn't understand it, but it was the way it was. There could be no turning.

It may have been this stepping over that heightened Cal's instincts, but he didn't believe for a moment that things had blown over. The guards and the convicts regarded him in a new way. They wanted to see what kind of a man wore Thrake's stripes. Cal played it cool. Not much was happening anyway. Friend still smiled and bade him *Happy trails*, like a little bit of blackmail. Cal had no choice but to keep his mouth shut. From his perch, he had much further to topple than Friend, and he half-wished it had been Friend, and not Thrake, who had disappeared.

How much Pitch knew about his and Friend's reefer-relationship, Cal had no idea, but he would be a fool if he didn't assume Friend had covered himself – especially now that Cal was Sergeant. Of course, Pitch knew. In the long ordeal of Thrake's witching, Cal had been seduced by Pitch. Cal knew better, and he wanted it not to be, but Pitch had the power to marshal devils. The more he thought of it, the more he realized this was true. So he tried not to think of Pitch, to just do his job and think only of Rachel and the baby and their lives together in the house they would build now that he had made Sergeant.

But, whenever he saw Pitch, the conjure man smiled at Cal like Friend smiled at him; and Cal reckoned that forehead gash Thrake had left. That gash that refused to heal, that was Pitch's real mouth smiling too. Just a different kind of smile. At those times, Cal felt inside him pieces of icy metal scraping together, small living things swimming among them. He smiled back at Pitch. He greeted the men, gave orders and they all, to a man, convict and guardian, minded him.

Now as ramrod sergeant, Cal worked first shift and on

into the second, sometimes both shifts if necessary. This cut down on Cal's time with Rachel. He swung by the hospital before after his shift and sometimes ducked out of the camp to visit her in between. Rachel always looked fine, sitting up in a white gown with her brown hair splayed on the pillows, Magnesium Sulfate dripping into her arm. Biding time. The baby, its drumming heartbeat ever-monitored, grew ounce by ounce as it drifted inside its mother.

On his way into Rachel's room, Cal usually stopped to look through the nursery window at the newborns. They wore tiny knit caps and bracelets and moved frenetically or in slow motion, their mouths open, always open. He stared and stared at these mysterious little people until he picked up his own reflection in the glass – a man in a prison guard uniform – and then he snapped out of it and hurried into Rachel to kiss her and sit on her beds, hold her hand, and ask over and over the same things about everything being alright. He told her he loved her, and often she cried. He fetched her candy and flowers, and confided nothing about himself and Coventry, how poorly he felt, how a great riptide of fear he was too wrought to battle was spiriting him off.

"One more day," the doctor said every day. "Just another day, Rachel."

They could not be exactly sure how small the baby was, but they knew it was small. It needed one more day.

Sometimes Mac was there when Cal arrived. Besotted from his wall, or with his hair combed and proper clothes, his old chain-gang Stetson in his lap, holding sheepishly a bouquet of flowers he had cut from Elizabeth's beds. Of late he had taken to calling Rachel Elizabeth, but Rachel said nothing, just patted the bed, so Mac could sit and take her hand and fuss in his silent way. Sit for hours with her hand in his. She'd fall asleep and wake to find him still there – Cal gone – like a gargoyle guarding her bedside.

CHAPTER 42

Cal didn't know how to set about asking his father anything, so he just took to being around him more. When he wasn't at the camp or hospital, he wandered up to the old home-place and helped his father build his wall. The last days of spring. The pear tree had tiny pears, the apple tree tiny apples. Had it not been for Cal and Rachel, this fruit would have rotted. Other than the garden he kept through habit, the only notice Mac took of that earth since his wife had died was to hitch up the blade to his old tractor and mow the yard that got smaller and smaller as her lavish undying beds invaded it.

The wheat turned brown. Among it stood orange poppies and blue pin-wheeling cornflowers called Ragged Robins. Untended purple phlox and foxglove, daisies, roses and columbine shimmered against the house. Monkey grass cascaded over the walks and lily of the valley demurred. When the wind blew, and it blew mightily of a spring against that house, more so since Elizabeth's death, the fragrance of spore and flower conjured for Cal his mother. For Mac too, though he would never say.

The wall now spanned a hundred yards along the back of the property and was tall as a baby on his first birthday. Cal no longer saw any harm in the wall. It now struck him as utterly remarkable, and he had come to look forward to working with his father on it. As if it were his, too, something he had always wanted, but had not known until he was in the throes of it. The slow toil. The not talking. The simple weight-bearing task of stone on stone. Building time.

Mac now expected his son's company. All day he barrowed stones from the creek and, when Cal arrived, they built. Cal had squared his father's vandalism with the builder; Mac no longer mentioned the houses in the field. Now ten of them in various stages of completion, five on either side of the blacktop cul de sac. All day, machines made noise and workmen pounded. In the evening, families in automobiles drove by the houses, got out and browsed, no doubt noticing the two men working into the small hours by spotlight – Mac sometimes without ever stopping and on into the next day – on a great stone wall.

One evening, after working together, they sat in the grass resting as the darkness settled. To one side of them trembled what remained of the smoky light. On the other, a proscenium of cobalt clouds. May lay between them. Listless. She wouldn't eat or take much water. Mac had taken to letting her in the house, carrying her in when he retired each night. Mac had his hand on the dog. He moved her water dish to her muzzle.

"Go on now, girl. Take in a drink of this water," he implored.

May didn't move. Her eyes stretched to Cal, then Mac. She was nearly eighteen years old.

CHAPTER 43

When Cal was thirteen, Mac let a family named Driggers drop a trailer in one of the far pastures. The man had recently been paroled from Coventry. Cal didn't know the whole story, just that his father had told the boy, Driggers, offhand-like, that he would let him a piece of land to set a trailer on for as long as he was paroled to Saint Joan's County.

Driggers was not a bad boy, per se, but bad to drink. A drunk. Like clockwork, he caught eighteen months from the judge once a year close to Christmas and end up trailing six months active at Coventry – every day of it – then get out and head for a roadhouse. Last jolt, he had done some fighting behind his drunk and broke a man's pelvis. Caught five years for that, then a few write-ups for mischief on the yard. On and on.

They finally paroled him at thirty months. Mac had promised him a patch, never figuring Driggers had the sand to take him up on it. Richard was his name. A young man with a nice enough face, but enough fight and cut scars, especially around his eyes and mouth, to make him look lost and worn out. And when he got drunk, he got mean and his face turned.

Cal had seen both sides of him and, even as a boy of thirteen, understood that two sides could exist at once in a man. But he didn't like Driggers. Had it not been for Mac, nothing stood in Driggers's way if, on a drunk, he decided to cross the pasture and enter the Gaddy house. But Richard Driggers knew better than to buck MacGregor Gaddy.

Driggers lived with a young woman – he called her his wife – and they had a baby girl and a pregnant German Shepherd. Driggers left the trailer every morning and puttered a moped up into the next county where he had a job picking nectarines.

Mac told Elizabeth not to worry: "He will not be here

long. He can't last a free man more than six months, if that. I pledged him the land. He'll catch himself."

But Elizabeth never worried. Worry was a sin. What had Jesus said about the lilies of the field? She had faith in God and faith in Mac; she was never afraid. She gleamed so that Driggers couldn't even lift his face to hers for fear of blinding. Elizabeth spent time with the woman, a pretty little girl who smoked and watched soap operas on television and waited for Driggers to come home every night so they could carry on.

Elizabeth made curtains for the trailer and invited the woman to church. She carried her pound cake and bought clothes and play-pretties for the baby, always dirty on the trailer floor with the dog. Elizabeth would lift that baby to her and bathe her in the sink, singing and making over her. It was summer, the trailer packed solid with heat. Elizabeth made Mac buy them window fans.

"It's throwing good money away," he said. "I give him another week."

You heard them once the sun went down. Loud music, often shouting. Laughter. Weeping. But never a gunshot or broken glass. And, sure enough, one day Driggers didn't come home from picking nectarines. Left the girl and baby and dog. They stayed on and Elizabeth took them over. Got them connected with the welfare lady and made sure they had groceries and formula. Wednesday nights, she chauffeured the girl and baby to prayer meeting. Mac speculated that might have been the barter all along: groceries for Jesus. *Elizabeth*, he said to himself and nearly smiled.

In two weeks, the woman and her baby got gone. Fled the trailer and most everything else, but what could be carried. Elizabeth cried, but there was nothing Mac could say. None of it had ever had a dead man's chance of working out. He had just given his word. A convict is a convict. The county came to haul off the trailer.

A few days later, Cal and his mother heard whining from the woods. They walked around outside trying to place it. It came from somewhere near where the Driggers' trailer had been. Off in the woods, they found the mama dog, Duchess, chained to a tree. She stood on shaky legs, exaggeratedly long because she was starving, curved ribs in stark relief against her shrinking black coat. Her breath came in heaves, cinching the black coat tighter against bones, her tongue coated red with clay. Distended and purple, her dugs, like 30.06 shells, dragged the ground.

The puppies tried to push up on their back legs to nurse, but they were too young, eyes barely opened. Four of them: blondish-brown and black, white socks and tail tips. They tottered and fell over. Duchess had no milk. She kicked them away and they cried, tiny voices shrill, ceaseless. Two other puppies, black and brown-tipped, lay dead next to each other on the earth floor.

Elizabeth and Cal ran back to the house, returned with water and saucers and a basin of biscuits crumbled in milk. They let the dogs drink first, then spooned onto four saucers milk and biscuits. They gave the basin to Duchess. She went wild, gorging herself in great snarling gulps. The puppies scurried from saucer to saucer, then to their mother and tried to eat from her food. She growled and they tumbled off.

Duchess devoured it all, but too far gone, she couldn't hold it in her. The puppies rushed for what came up. Cal and Elizabeth pulled them away.

"We have to get them out of here, Calvin," said Elizabeth, hiking up her dress. Flies and worms and dog mess. Those dogs had been living there who knew how long. Elizabeth grabbed two puppies and handed them to Calvin, who already had one. Duchess shook. Her eyes were slits, distilling the last bit of what fire she had left. One puppy still tried to eat. Whining, it staggered among its mother's legs.

Duchess let Elizabeth take the puppy. Then she reared and went for the woman: the yellow dress tensed high on her white leg and the dog's exaggerated mouth like a crocodile's clamped around it, the teeth sinking as if in butter, Elizabeth cradling the blonde baby dog.

Cal watched it and watched it and watched, but could not do a thing, but hold to the three squirming pups. His eyes knew to search for a stick or a rock, yet they could not swerve from his mother who kept talking to the mama dog, who dropped the pup in her dress pocket and seized Duchess's muzzle and pried it open from her leg and threw the dog over on her back. And then stood there, didn't hurry. But, backing away, lifted that yipping pup to her face and kissed it, the thigh already blackening and a runnel of blood to the ankle.

Cal cried. Holding three of her children, he screamed at the mother dog. He would kill her, he said. Kill her sure.

"It's alright, Calvin. Alright," his mother soothed, clutching him up against her, she too crying, but for a different reason. The last time she would hold him like this. The last time he ever let her. He was thirteen. The four little puppies pressed between them, crying.

CHAPTER 44

Cal's father had been talking. What was it he'd been saying? Cal had been listening, it seemed, for some time, so he remarked to himself that he must be drunk. Mac's was a measured voice, much softer than one would imagine, yet a voice that carried across a river, almost liquid itself. Elizabeth had ever been after him to sing in the church choir. But he didn't sing. Cal had no recollection of his father singing. Nor humming, nor being part of any tune whatsoever. But the voice itself. It would go on without the man, though liquor usually served to rust shut his mouth.

Later, Cal was sure he had merely imagined his father had told him about the tornado with which Cal's conception had then and forevermore been associated. That night there in the near dark with May's aspiration ticking between them, Cal forgot he was listening to his father while the older did not realize that his thoughts had found a way out of his head.

Any sky can hide it. You look away for an instant. But it's not so much look as feel. Weight and no weight at once. Like it's you spinning off into the firmament, yet railroad spikes through your feet so you can't move. Your mother. It was before I knew enough to lock her in, or try to lock her in. Locking being my business. We'd been married just shy of two years. She was out in it. Second-sensed when it came to a blow, though I would not particularly dub this a gift.

There came an unholy brigade of lightning and hail big as teacups. Could have killed her dead, but there she stood blithe as a fish. I braved a shattered skull. One of those ice balls caught me above the ear and opened my head like a mush melon. And I carried her in. She smiled and sang "Old Rugged Cross." I never quite cared for that hymn. I did not mind church singing, though your mother might tell it different.

The old man paused to drink and pass the jar to Cal. Full dark now and the floodlights not yet on. The new tract houses blacked out. The wall ahead of them like a long night of stone itself. And

May. Ticking.

No, it was never the singing. More the voices, if you take my meaning. I'm bleeding, Calvin, and your mama is chiding me about how hurt I am as I'm hefting her up the back steps. And then the hail and lightning desist and there comes this whoosh and it's like an ocean wave washed across us side-wise. Not rain-wise. Because it traveled exact parallel to the ground. Liquid wind. Not liquid and wind. Then it stops. On a dime, I mean. And the sky gets light and still, goes green, pink, green.

Then you hear it highballing like the Point South & Comfort on rocket gas and banshees. Between a whistle and a blow. So I turn, still holding your mother, her fussing at me about the cut, and there it stood. Like a hangman's knot. Looping in at one hundred and fifteen miles, though seeing it come at a distance, right across the field yonder, it looked slower.

He pointed beyond the invisible houses to where the far end of the field blackened with the tree line.

I knew what it was, but I had never seen one so up close, so big. As it came on, you could see whatever it had already come through churning in its upswell. There was it, and there was a whole world along with it. Chairs and hogs and chickens and rooftops. The field it was coming through was held in tall corn and it fell off like whiskers, the stalks going up, gravity reversed, like they were lodestones. Staring at it, I felt the pull. Your mother was saying, calm-like, "Put me down, MacGregor. I want to witness this." Felt like my face was being ripped right off. Like a mask right off my skull. It was a mighty thing you could not look away from. And your mama was always bad about such.

We got in and shut up in that walk-in cupboard under the staircase. Then. It was leaning on the house, bracing itself for its own impact. As if it knew how to get in a man's house without opening the door. Secret. Spirit. Swelling the house. In and out like a balloon it was fixed to blow in until it busted. Inside. Not outside. Like the movers were there and they didn't care what got broke. The furniture walking all over, bashing itself into walls. Glass and windows crashing. The piano playing a funeral song.

Then we heard this tinkling sound coming down, falling down, all around us. The sound a prism chandelier makes in a wind. Not a window or the plates and goblets, but something else. It was in the walls. We could not figure for it. Black as print in that cupboard. The door bowing and knocking. The smartest thing your mother and me ever did was leave it shut on whatever wanted in. Listening scared is never bad as seeing scared.

The whole time of it, a right smart, me and your mother. That tinkling, shimmering, tiny bell sound ringing around us, and both bloody from my head. She tore off her dress to staunch it. Ever peculiar in her choosing. Anyway.

Come to find that the back porch was sheared clean off. Portions of the roof and one of the chimneys. All the windows and plenty of bust-up. But the house stood it. Took it head-on and weathered. Later, when I patched the roof and looked down between the walls where the joists were bare, I saw what all that tinkling sound had been: bottles and jars shook loose from where they'd been stashed up and down three storeys. Right behind those tongue-in-groove planks. Some call it bead-board. My daddy's bottles. Each one emptied and yet to be emptied into him.

He'd pry open a slab and stash it so Mama wouldn't find it. Full bottles too, I reckon, for the whole mess smelled sweet and I expected the walls to bleed homemade mash. But I left every bit of it, taking as I went what I needed for myself. Your mama wanted me to clear out such "damnation." She said that very word. Closest I ever heard to her cussing. Though she suffered my own "damnation," and would remind me in the way of explanation or rebuke for her own failing, that I was her husband, as if I had not yet inkled this. And that was that. Just so. I was her husband. But I should remove that "damnation." So I turned a verse on her: "Let the dead bury the dead."

The night of that blow. Me and your mother, Elizabeth, in that cupboard. Nine months later to the minute, you were born. I can still put my tongue to those walls and taste it.

CHAPTER 45

One day. More. One day. Less. Cal's body was stone, a great unwieldy machine he had to commandeer. Hoist it out of the bedclothes and into the truck. Lift boot sole upon boot sole over the yard of Coventry. Then in between shifts to the hospital where like as not he slept in a chair next to Rachel's bed. No pain, just a silence coming on: weight, density. If there was a way he could put a word to it: *heaviness* was what.

Cal's father eyed his son's gaunt body, even his clothes gaunt.

"You are falling off, Calvin," he said.

Mac, eating only baby food himself, cooked slabs of beef and potatoes for Calvin. "Wake up and eat this food, boy. You are falling off."

And Calvin ate. Tried to eat. But he couldn't. There was no eat in him, but there was eating in him. He didn't want to think about it. He willed his body to pick up one more stone and soldier it into the wall. He talked to his limbs, cajoling a leg or an arm to mind him.

It might have made another man mean, but Cal it only distanced. Like he was just outside whatever it was, looking on as through an old mirror beginning to dis-silver. Like looking at something there, yet unnatural, and it causes you to rub at your eyes and turn away and you can never get at the thing itself.

The nurse at Coventry offered to take blood from Cal. To see. But he wouldn't hear of it. He couldn't afford to be scared any more than he was. He'd wait, he told himself. Until the baby was born. Another day and another day. Rachel, in white, in bed, the Magnesium Sulfate. Dripping. Slow.

They would do one last ultrasound, the doctor said. Just to make sure. Calvin sat next to Rachel and held her hand. They watched the baby move, its little heart banging up and down like a drill; and, at one point, the baby lounged out of its interrogative ether and stretched.

"Just give me two or three days more, Rachel," said the doctor. "One more day."

CHAPTER 46

Maybe one day later. Maybe more. Not less – because the light was exactly as it had been the night before and it was the exact time when, night after night, Mac brought out the liquor and May lay there on the ground between them, her side clocking. Up. Down. Falling. Falling. One day later because the wall was maybe a course higher.

It stood now sullen against the southern cornice of the plat. A hundred yards and more. Less stones in the creek bed, more in the wall. How does one cipher more from less? A man doing time does one day more and one day less simultaneously, each day somehow negating itself in a straight line stretching off in either direction until the two ends meet and form a circle. No more and no less.

And so the wall went up and Cal opened his eyes each evening and there would be his father and May and they would drink and mostly not talk; and it was one day more or less when he finally asked his father: "What should I do?"

CHAPTER 47

Thrake finally turned up – in the quarry. Brotherton and his kitchen help had been down there dumping spoiled food when Thrake sounded the surface in a great spindrift, then floated in the flat water – a giant blowfish, his trunk three times its size, his limbs stumped and gristled from his sojourn among the convict-faced fish. His head, however, had shrunk and sat shriveled on the atoll of his body. He was naked, though now clotted in lichen and feathers, the protuberance of supernumerary limbs, what everyone would later say were wings, at his shoulder blades.

The inmates refused Brotherton when he ordered them to fetch up Thrake. They wouldn't go near the thing. At the time, they had not known it was Thrake. There were so many stories about inmates cast in there over the years. Brotherton himself had to gaff Thrake with a garden rake and tow him to shore.

Cal knew right away when he was summoned to the quarry that the dead man was Thrake. He didn't have to wait for the Medical Examiner. Had it been up to him, they would have tied it up the carcass with steel and sunk it once and for all. But they all knew the thing's name even if they would not say *Thrake*. The Captain, Father Tuesday, sprinkling it with a stick that sprayed holy water, Icemorelee and Friend. They knew.

They loaded it on the garbage scow and the inmates towed it with ropes back up the hill to the camp where it sat with a tarp over it – like some prehistoric secret, waiting for the meat wagon.

CHAPTER 48

"What should I do?" he asked again because Mac had apparently not heard him. "Papa?"

But Mac had gone into the place where all there was was earth and sky. He studied these two rapidly becoming one in the colorless firmament and mumbled something about shades, "goddam shades."

The very day after Thrake, Cal, on his rounds, had gone into the cook shack latrine and seen it. He realized only then that he had been going in there every day expecting it. He had suffered the new quiet of Coventry long enough: its seeming order, the inmates placid. The more or less of everything. Stepping in for Thrake at Sergeant. And now Thrake come back. Now he had seen it and knew what he had all along known.

Spotted with flies, dangling from the dripping pipe, the water knifing down and splaying out, the little puppet with the onion head twirling on its twine. This one not like Thrake's, but with toothpicks nimbusing its onion head and spent twenty-gauge Federal shot casings for legs.

No doubt now. Pitch had turned it on him. But Cal swore then and there he would not capitulate. He would refuse to believe that Pitch could do it to him. Do it by sheer dint of willing it on him. Will against will, his father had taught him. His father with his eyes and ears full of devils. But his father was not afraid of devils. He would let them come on. He would spit in their eyes.

Cal heard his mother's voice – always there: *Do not be terrified in any way by the adversaries; for this is to them a reason for destruction, but to you for salvation and that from God.* But even if it was not fear – and it was – it was an utter exhaustion so profound that he could barely spit. Crying tired. *There is no fear in love; but perfect love casts out fear, because fear brings punishment. And he who fears is not perfected in love.*

He reached up and yanked the puppet off the pipe, threw it in the commode, flushed and reflushed. The thing swirled in the gorged porcelain. The toilet coughed and sucked. Cal flushed until it went down and disappeared. He flushed again, went to a sink and doused his face with water. When he came out of the latrine, Pitch was sitting at his pot. The familiar reek of it. Heat. Pitch smiling, knowing, the mouth on his forehead still open.

The other men slept, wheezing, in their demonic wet dreams. The TV prognosticated. Flies walked across the man and woman on the couch inside the TV. Snoo smoked a cigar. The man slid his hand under the woman's skirt.

"Blessed Savior, yes," exclaimed Snoo.

Cal left the cook shack. *What can I love that hard?* he thought. *To put a stake in the heart of fear.*

"I love Rachel perfectly," he said, wanting to hear said words and not thought words, since to him it was the noise of words that made them true, the way they took up space outside of him and, how once uttered, he could not foreswear them.

He must have said it aloud because Father Tuesday, walking past the cook-shack as Cal staggered out, said, "Mr. Gaddy?"

CHAPTER 49

Sixty square tables with yellow Formica tops. On each: salt and pepper, ketchup, Texas Pete and hot pepper vinegar. Around each: four plastic chairs of disparate pastel colors. Calming colors like pink and avacado green, powder blue.

The chow hall could feed up to 240 convicts, though the population rarely swelled that high. Right now they were holding at 160, not counting the cooks.

Evening count had just cleared and the 160, in increments of four, pounded into chow. On a stainless steel tray, divvied into squares and triangles, each man received from the serving line the same measured portions: beans, collards, slaw, meatloaf and gravy, bread pudding and a glass of chartreuse bug juice.

On the yellow walls around them hung pictures the men had painted in art class. Pictures of white houses and barns and streams, the ubiquitous, plaintive hand of a woman pushing open the picket gate in welcome. Portraits of women, winsomely sexy, dark swirling impastoed hair and Oriental eyes. Harlots who doubled as virgins.

But, more than anything else, there were Jesuses. Usually sublime and honeyed, with blue eyes and soft hair. And, indeed, as more and more men seated themselves in the chow hall, it was obvious that the artists had in their own incarnations affected Jesus: the shoulder-length hair and beard, the wistful longing in the eyes, the implicit zeal.

But for every sweet Jesus was a black-eyed savage one, nail holes and thorn crowns swirling out of red paint and chains, scars and tattoos. The Second Coming as a jailbreak, a prison riot. There was even a Jesus in brown clothes, hanging from the cross.

The chow-hall was noisy. The men chattered, pathologically dousing their food with condiments. The monumental smell and heat from the ovens and steam table.

A shroud of cigarette smoke hovered each table. At the piano, Snoo beat out *The Midnight Special.*

Drinking chain-gang coffee, Cal and Father Tuesday talked. Father Tuesday had listened well, nodding his head, urging Cal forward, once even stretching his hand across the table to rest it on Cal's. Then, with confessional gravity, he sat silent, his hands lifting several times toward his mouth as if weighing the words he was priming himself to speak. Or perhaps the hands, these same consecrated hands that placed the body and blood of their Savior on the defiled tongues of convicts, were merely going through their own ritual pantomime of lifting shot-glasses.

"Mr. Gaddy," Father Tuesday began.

Cal regretted that he had troubled this priest, this good man.

"I believe in evil, but I do not believe Tarl Benefit killed Sergeant Thrake, directly or indirectly. I do not think either that he is killing you. I do not, I will not, accord him that kind of power. Any man. Once I allow myself such indulgence, I am back in the gutter feeling sorry for myself and preparing for, even welcoming, the ghastly to enter my heart."

"I'm not here about drinking, Father."

"I know you're not, Calvin. What I'm trying to say is that you can choose. To believe in life or death. Period. Not both."

"What happened to Thrake, then?"

"Sergeant Thrake chose to find consolation in fear. And it resulted in his death."

"So you think the whole witching thing is bullshit?"

"I wouldn't call it bullshit. More like a self-fulfilling prophecy. Sergeant Thrake invested Tarl with the power that ultimately killed him."

"What about the nosebleeds and vomiting, the rashes, the car blowing up? Thrake's goddam teeth fell out, Father. Excuse my language, but Jesus Christ."

"Yes."

"What do you mean, 'yes'?"

"Yes. *Jesus Christ.* I'm not saying that there was no

connection between what happened to Sergeant Thrake and whatever it was that Tarl was trying to do to him. What I am saying is that Sergeant Thrake believed that Tarl's deviltry could kill him. Had he chosen Jesus instead of the devil, had he chosen love over fear, then I think he would have been invulnerable to Tarl. Sergeant Thrake had a weakness. Tarl sniffed it out and exploited it."

"Thrake was a pure-T son-of-a-bitch, but he was no weakling."

"No weakling," agreed Tuesday. "Harder than quarry rock. But he had a big spiritual hole in him."

It all made a kind of sense to Cal. He could not help but think of his mother. But he didn't want a shrink and, as it turned out, he guessed he didn't want a priest either.

"What's happening to me then, Father? I can hardly pull myself out of this chair. I can feel my bones grinding together. My wife's about to have a baby."

"I'll tell you this, Calvin. You can't be put in your grave with an onion and a stinking pot of herbs and yard trash. I'm not telling you what to do. I'm just relating what I know to be true and what I believe you have known all along: There is one way only."

Tuesday smiled and said: "All this from someone who's been there. I can still feel the sweet burn of whiskey at the back of my throat."

Cal looked at Tuesday, but looked through him too. Looked at the men with their heads bent to chow. Thought about this business he had chosen. Or had chosen him. In his mind, choice played leapfrog with destiny. He couldn't distinguish between the two, nor get it through his head that a man would choose brown clothes over a set of freeman's. Convict or guard, one, each man-jack born fixed to a mold. It might slumber in you for years or mere minutes. Keep it down or rouse it up. With church or whiskey or silence or secrecy or whatever. But one day, whenness suddens in and you find yourself in the Boot or toting keys, one.

The fact was Cal could not imagine any other life for himself. Or for the men around him eating chain-gang food

- and grateful for the occasion. Cal trusted Tuesday. He was not just some Christer het up with preaching. He was a sufferer. It resided in his nervous hands fretting his face, in his worried lime eyes. He wanted a drink. Bad.

Trouble was that Cal could not readily line up Tuesday as convict or guard. He was something else. Those sad confessor's eyes bearing into him. The Roman collar. Tuesday knew all about Cal. How close he was to breaking. How far.

"Calvin, why don't you let me hear your confession?" suggested Father Tuesday.

Calvin had already looked away, his eye caught by one of the Jesuses on the wall: savagely effete with a bangle earring and snaggled smile clipping out of a bushy beard, His eyes pink geodes. An animal skin thrown slant over his torso. A black sheep slung over his shoulder. Caption: *The Bad Shepherd.*

Calvin heard Father Tuesday's voice coming at him over, actually under, the welter of feeding inmates. Good it sounded to him. To confess. Lay it all out and prostrate himself, declare his terror and powerlessness, be forgiven. Start over. Father Tuesday would guide him. Introduce him to the Roman collar God. Get it all sorted out. *He works in us the will and the performance.*

There came Father Tuesday's hand again. On Cal's. Nervous. Strong. A hand that knew whiskey, and the bread of life. By God, Cal was ready.

Getting religion was the cheapest, vilest, most sentimental play on the yard. Zedda Pate and Lindrey Vance, the good thieves, getting right with God in the eleventh hour. When it came down to it, Cal flat could not abide it. He was a duty man now, like it or not, and he mistrusted prison contrition. His or any other. He was not throwing off Tuesday, and he told the priest as much. He just mistrusted. There was no God in a prison.

"I understand," Father Tuesday said, his hand gone from Cal's and gripping his shaved jaw.

149

CHAPTER 50

I never figured myself for a state man. There was my mother and my father, and I was between paying homage to two different Jesuses, one with a crown of barbed wire and the other with one of lilies.

What I would like to say is I loved them both. Mama, yes. How could I not? But she was hearing something nobody else could. A song off in the distance. Whatever. But I believe now she was never fully with us to start. Like a spirit. Something always gone by the time you turn to it.

And Papa. He wasn't there either. Too hard, too impenetrable, to be a human father. I walked in her spirit world of growing things and I learned hell around the vigil cook-fire on escapes with him and Frank. And I was of both worlds, but mostly of the in-between. Between was nowhere and I wanted nothing. To be neither a builder nor an executioner. Nor even a witness. I wanted in a word to be nothing. When Mama died, I found out nothing became me, that out there was a void and its name was Coventry and that all along I was Papa's truest blood and there is no God in prison.

But I was lonely. So Mama sent me Rachel who saw in me something I have yet to see; and while I was overjoyed that such a pure woman could love me, and consent to be my wife, I was equally terrified that by and by she would see me for what I was – something in between, lukewarm – and leave me. So when she told me she was pregnant, I said to myself, "This is a sign." And, sure enough, things started to go bad. I would not say bad with my mouth because saying bad is making bad. This life unseen living in Rachel, while cause for joyousness, foretold annihilation. For in my mind was the vision of my heir, a little boy, not the girl all the machines predicted was living in Rachel's womb, but a boy who would one day wander into a room – a cellar, really. And imbedded in that cellar's dank ceiling was an axe and beneath the axe was a table with a yellow hoop cheese and when that tiny boy leaned over the table to have his cheese, the axe would fall and kill him.

I could not protect him any better than I can the woman I love who in her pregnancy is being eaten up by this man-child. And it all came from me in a prison and my father before and the devilness of it all coming finally to roost in the jackassery of a dangling jackleg bad luck doll wearing what I took to be my face. I suppose because to me my face had always been back luck. Demons themselves, how like convicts to loose demons on you. They should be absolved, but it is not in men's hearts to forgive.

One afternoon, Papa and Frank and I were out fetching a convict named Tombs. He'd been gone the better part of three hours before we got started after him. Papa was never in a hurry. It was his theory that a run convict wanted catching. All Papa had to do was let him know he was out there in the free world after him and he would be certain to come to Papa. Like the Prodigal. Home is home. If Papa had any religion, it was the belief that there was a single plan. Call it divine. Papa never said it wasn't. But Papa never said. And that all of everything is swept along, however confusedly, toward the fulfillment of that plan. Convicts were just part of the plan and, as such, necessary, as they necessitated prison and hence prison guards and hence Papa and so on. No different from disease and doctors, drought and well diggers. The holes in the handcuffs were meant for hands, bars for people to stand behind. It wasn't so much a hierarchy as a principle, like gravity or combustion.

So Papa needn't feel bad about what he was doing: his job. It was simply his part in the plan's fulfillment. Therefore, the notion of pitying the convict, the notion of mercy, never entered his head. It was upon this principle that Papa chain-ganged: that inevitably the keeper ended with the kept; and the kept ended with the keeper. Part of the plan. So he never hurried, yet he never tarried.

Tombs was one of the ones back then they called a switch-blade. Tall and lanky with a long rat face and the usual facial scars which in his pedigree were almost cosmetic. Thick black hair, Dixie-peached into a swirling do, a duck's ass and a ringlet on his forehead. He tailor-made himself, rolling up the cuffs of his pants and shirt to show off the vernacular tattoos and his weightlifter's veins. A cigarette in his mouth, one behind his ear, a leer rising out of his smoke, he would rather cut a man than shoot him, but this only after he had violated him.

So we're walking. Not fast. Buzzards cutting figure-eights a ways off. Frank, sniffing and twitching like a bird-dog, at the point as usual. A little further, we came onto a terrible smell. Something big rotting. Buzzards keening not far. The smell just unbearable. Papa and I need handkerchiefs. But not Frank. By the time we get to it, we're nauseated sick. A dead angus cow in the middle of a pasture. Bloated obscenity, its legs upspraddled like tent poles and the belly a gaping maw that had been eaten out by vermin and insects and whatnot. The buzzards held aloft by their own updraft. Black garments wafting up and up, but getting lower.

As we got closer I heard the buzz like a 220 current of flies swarming, and under them the kinesis of putrefaction. The cow's eyes were gone, pecked out by crows, which is the order of things. We stood there a little ways off, just looking, before cutting a wide swath around that cow. The buzzards were huge, hellish, to see up close. Papa brought up his shotgun and fired both barrels into them. He had loaded rock salt that day and it did not kill a one. But it sent them out of there, black feathers floating down over that black cow, a black billowing sheet of flies going up and then redraping.

At the shot, a possum scurried out of that carcass and made fast across the pasture. I didn't know a possum could go so fast, since they seem to take their sweet time even with headlights a foot from their snouts. It turned my stomach: seeing that possum shin out of there. I had eaten possum before. Around the fire with Frank and Papa. On other escapes. There is something almost forbidden about meat and the fire and the woods when you are chasing a man you'll kill if you have to. Possum is stringy and nothing greasier.

Skinned out, it's lumpy and yellow-tallowed. But I had eaten it and never thought a thing of it. But after that pasture I never ate possum again, and it took me a sight before I could go back to cow. But, more than all that, it might've been the worst thing I've ever seen. That possum lighting out of there, more embarrassed than anything to have been caught at it.

We were all startled. How unlikely that one creature would emerge full-blown from another. Horrible, really. Like a matinee in the darkened, crumbling Victorian theatre when you are too young to be there, egged in by the older boys. And something so hideous and unimaginable gouges out from a hidden place and it's your nightmare forevermore. That possum. That cow and its open belly.

And then. Out of it crawled Tombs. The three of us just dazed. Even Papa who could stand to see anything. And Frank who had been set fire to. Tombs crawled with the offal of that carrion, dripping like he had been remanded to the sea slime from whence humans first issued. Papa's first reflex was to shoot him – he brought the shotgun up and we wouldn't have been surprised – just so we could be shed of him.

He said: "I ought to put you out of your misery, boy. I don't know to who it's the biggest desecration. You, the cow, or the possum. But you sure aren't riding back to the camp in my truck."

Then we all fell out laughing. Laughing and laughing. Frank with that high-pitched yip of his. And my father. The first and last time I can remember him flat letting go like he was really enjoying himself. Tombs laughed loudest and longest. Like if he stopped, everybody else would too and he'd go back to being a convict and we'd be who we were. I imagined that possum was off somewhere grinning. Even the buzzards kited back from the edge of the woods where they'd been roosting in a stand of dead sweetgums.

I laughed with the rest of them, laughed because they laughed. I didn't think it was funny, but I wanted it to be and not what I knew it was when I first saw that possum come out of that putrefied cow. And then a man. I pitied him. I

153

half-liked Tombs – and he was the type to strangle his own mother for a cigarette – standing there, the cow behind him, as if he had been turned inside out, literally, laughing until he finally made himself sick.

CHAPTER 51

Mac: Catatonic. Prelapsarian. Stone-crazed. His head hung over the jar of whiskey, scraggly, white strands of his hair playing around its mouth.

"Do?" he murmured. "Do?"

"Yes," said Cal. "What in hell should I do?"

"Are you bound to it?" asked Mac.

"What?"

"That jail. Coventry. Are you bound to it?"

"It's my job."

"It's not a job. It's a calling. Is it your calling?"

"You talk about it like it's being a preacher."

"Put whatever handle on it you like. You been on the yard long enough to know what I'm talking about."

"I been on the yard all my life, Papa."

"And I would not blame you for chiding me for that fact. Nor blame your mother for taking me to task. It would've more than broke her heart. And I reckon, Calvin, she knows all about it."

The two sat there, not looking at each other. Mac passed the jar. The satellite dish quivered. A star fired down, shone in May's left eye, unblinking, and then her right. But neither of the men saw it. Cal thought about the shackle and scourge as a calling.

"If it's not your calling," advised Mac, "then you should let it go."

"It's not my calling."

"Only you can answer that. But if you can't help it, if it's a calling, do it with all your heart. But if you can stand to do something else, there is no reason on this earth for a man to do what I did for forty-five some years. And what you are doing right now. It is caution and devotion forever. And a great portion of pure hell. But with it, there are sometimes moments when a man has such control over his heart that he does not care if he lives or dies. If you have no choice, do it.

I had no choice. It was a calling and maybe it was worth it. I don't know."

"I want to stay with it," Cal said.

"Leave it now. Walk away from it this minute, Calvin. Denounce it. Shoot it in the head. Kill it."

"I can't, Papa."

"Alright, then," said the father. "You run it to the ground and take what comes. God help you."

Cal drank deeply and handed the jar back to his father who then drank too. There was no moon yet. Just stars. In May's eyes. She refused to drink from the water dish next to her muzzle. A light breeze ruffled her long blonde hair.

Cal said it: "I got an inmate trying to witch me, I think. I figure it's what drove Thrake to death and now he's turned it on me. You see what I've come to. Can't sleep. Can't eat. Can hardly move hand to mouth sometimes. The only gumption I have is for this wall, and I do my job out of shear meanness. I found a little doll made up to be a likeness of me in the cook-shack."

"Is this conjure man white or black?" Mac asked.

"Black."

"Hmmm."

"What?"

"Black's the only ones who know how to do it proper. Whites try it from time to time, but there's a suffering that goes with it that they don't have the hang of. Frank knew all about it. If he had a pain, he'd put a knife under his mattress to take it away. Drink his own piss. Turn around so many times in a circle if someone said a certain word around him. He would fix a doll on a man every now and again."

"Can it be done?" Cal asked. "Can a man put something like that on another man?"

"A convict can. The curse is the oldest thing on record. You had a sight of Bible from your mother. That whole book is filled with one curse and then another. You don't have to read but a few pages before Cain kills his brother and God places a mark on him. Your mother would read that book and see saints and angels, glory and more glory. I see it as a rule book. Chain and whip and curse."

"Do you believe a man can be witched?"

"I have to believe what I see and hear. I been hearing about witchings and spells and bodement since I first came on the state. I can't deny these devils bearing down on me, sure enough. But it's got so I hardly mind them. I do to them what I did to a convict that got in my way. I took him to task one way or another, and he always knew I could sound my music louder than his. These devils come at you, trying to make you regret. But I don't have an ounce of regret in me. I hoe them out of the plow-soles and go on and, if they can sit and hush, I don't mind them. I reckon I deviled enough of them in my day. Now it's all coming back on me and, if it is God's will, I'll be back to haunt them after I'm gone. But it was my calling, and about what I bargained for."

"So it can happen?" Cal asked. "A man can be witched?"

"Calvin, look in your own heart. Some things I can tell you and some I can't. But I'll lay this much: once you walk on a prison yard, you may as well check your sanehood with your valuables. Because anything can happen. Anything. Curses. Witchfare. Miracles. Convicts and a prison itself have pomps. They surely do. Rule number one is never be surprised."

"What about Thrake then?"

"Don't know. When I knew him, he was as tough as they come. But this other one, this black boy, he must've gotten into Thrake. Must've made him doubt. Made him scared. It doesn't take but one time to look away. One minute of inattention. And then."

A moon tried to come up. Like it had been lying on the ground. Full. Just its dome sounded above the trees. Looking at it, Cal felt almost strong. The way things had stopped. He thought of Rachel. Then he thought of the story about the axe in the ceiling, and suddenly he was able to place it: a story his mother had read to him when he was a little boy. About a very young man and woman just married who go to the cellar to cut cheese and see an axe hoved into the ceiling above the table upon which the big wheel of cheese sits. They throw themselves into each other's arms and weep because they know that the boychild they are destined to have will one day come down to the cellar; and, while he is helping himself to the cheese, the axe will mysteriously dislodge and kill him. This dear, doomed child. They are inconsolable. Their hearts are shattered. They cry and cry.

Finally the old grandfather of the house comes down into the cellar and asks why they are crying. When they tell him, he laughs. Then he walks over to the table, steps up on it and removes the axe from the ceiling. The new husband and wife are overjoyed.

"What should I do?" asked Cal.

Mac shifted his whole body so he could look at Cal. He held out his hand and touched his son as if to make sure he was still there.

"You start with you are right and he is wrong. Make him a sight more uncomfortable than he makes you. Expect no pleasure and have no mercy. They've already had their trial by the time they get to the jailhouse. And remember. This conjure man. You do for him before he does for you. God'll forgive you. If you believe that way, you're already forgiven. But if you're not up to putting that black hood over his head, get out of it. It's not your calling. I give you my blessing. Now I will say no more on it."

Saying this, Mac held up his hand. His seal. To put an end to it. His hand as if resisting the moon now sitting on his son's head. Now in May's cold eye the moon, a dab of whitewash on the lusterless pupil.

CHAPTER 52

Maybe an hour or two more they worked. In silence. Sizing, lifting, canting, biasing, mortaring and pointing. Floodlights bathed the yard. The wall nearly to Cal's buckle. The moon, big and white, straight up with the faintest writing on it, but neither man could make it out.

Still early. Cal figured bed, and be at the hospital before his shift, just to look in on Rachel. She'd be sleeping. Those little babies behind the nursery window. That little chorus calling out to him as he passed. For now he just wanted sleep and felt empty enough to close his eyes and lie there alone in the empty trailer nearly frantic for Rachel. Not asleep. Not awake. In between.

He made for his truck – he no longer walked to and from his father's – as Mac gathered up May to carry her in. The father said her name: verbal auxiliary, imprecation, maiden, a simple syllable increased because it bore a name. Cal had never heard such an inflection issue from his father. He hadn't been there that day his mother swallowed lightning to hear how, and even if, his father had called her name. Never had he heard his father inflect sorrow; and he reminded himself that there was nothing about MacGregor Gaddy familiar to him. Hearing his father say May's name with the only sound that, ever since Cal had known him, betrayed what might be in his heart – a single syllable, *May* – Cal then knew May was dead.

What he did not think of first was his own sorrow, but going to his father and comforting him. But there was no precedent, so Cal merely walked to where his father knelt, the old man's ear on the dog's flank, his hand held up to Cal as if to hush him. The moon filled the old dog's eyes with cotton.

"Papa," Cal said.

"She's dead, Calvin. She's dead."

Calvin sunk to his knees beside his father, and one of the

men – it couldn't have mattered whom – said, *Oh, no.* Mac reached down to close her eyes, but they would not close.

The old man rose with the dog in his arms. Limp and warm, for all appearances asleep. But the eyes. There was a little arbor of loblollies in a patch Mac had cleared thirty years earlier, planting the spindling seedlings and ripping up with his bare hands poison ivy so dense it grew in a weir, rooted on thick stalks wrapped with brown hairy filaments. Among the baby trees, Elizabeth had planted Vinca Major. Now the last of its full four-petal purple crept along the ground. The new houses reappeared in the moonlight.

Between two of the loblollies, three stories grown, Mac laid May, and began on his hands and knees pulling at the Vinca engrafted into the rocky tallow. It would tear, but he could not disroot it. It had to be hacked out with a mattock; and so too the hole for May, the spade used only to scrape or scoop what he unclodded.

He cursed the ground again and again. Harder than him. Filled with quartzite and hiddenite, hardscrabble Piedmont. He cursed it because it was harder than him in his grief. And then his son cursed it, as the father rested, chopping the grave finally with an axe, after spading down on tree roots, the steel head sparking and devoting – the father finally with a shotgun detonating both barrels of twelve gauge at point range, grave and spark, to dig what the blade would not penetrate, Calvin's and Mac's mouths filling with blasted dirt and nothing to show for it, but pocked gouges and a single stunning blue marble they found as they dug. The blue Cal remembered of his mother's eyes. Tanager blue. And so they went about it until they had a semblance of a place, but not a proper grave. What the earth allowed. No more.

Favoring no cerement, but the moon, Mac laid her gently in the concavity and stood quietly as if about to say words. Then of a sudden he fell on May and wrested her up, holding her to him.

"Calvin," he cried. "She's breathing. I swear she moved." Like a child, he gazed up at Cal.

"She's dead, Papa."

"She's dead," said Mac, then relowered the dog and scraped the earth in on her with his hands. Wanting shed of it, Cal took up the shovel.

"Wait," insisted Mac. "I won't have her trapped in there by herself with these devils."

He picked up the shotgun and ran into the house. Shortly there came a boom from inside. Just one barrel. Cal stood there staring at May, dirt on her coat. He knew he should go into the house and investigate, but he didn't move. The moon had a ring around it. It had not had it before, but now it did. As if it made a difference.

When Mac returned he had clutched in his hand a sheet of paper: a page torn from Elizabeth's Bible. The only Bible in the house, the family Bible. Filled with pressed flowers and names of the family dead, it resided on the night stand next to the marriage bed in the locked room Mac had blown open with his shotgun. This page Mac placed in the grave and then they covered May and Cal beat down the dirt with the spade.

Then they filled a barrow of stones and spread them carefully over the grave face. When they finished, Mac lifted over his head an obelisk-shaped chunk of sandstone that would have taken two right-minded men to budge and stood with it, poised like Moses. Then brought it down with an oath, driving it into the earth at May's head. Then to his knees, and cried, a deep gathering fluid cry that he had built over the years, stone, by stone, without realizing it . His hands in his face, strands of beard leaking through them, the hank of raggedy white scalp thatching down over the hands. Hunched over in brown clothes under the moon.

Calvin stood over him, not wanting to cry. Not feeling led that way at all until his father, whom he had never seen cry, with tears streaming down his cheeks into his beard, gazed childlike up at him again. And Cal remembered his mother telling him that Peter, after denying Jesus for the third time, and realizing the enormity of what he had done and how it had been foretold, had cried bitterly, incessantly, for all of his life. That the tears had worn gutters in his cheeks. Cal could have stood it until that moment his father looked up at him, the wet moon gleaming in his tears, and said: "She was a good woman, Calvin. I will ever miss her. I have always loved her." It was not until then. But Calvin still did not cry. He sunk to his knees and took up his father.

CHAPTER 53

The last thing Mac said before falling asleep on the sofa was, "Don't tell Elizabeth." But he meant Rachel. About May, Cal surmised. But maybe it was about something else. Missing Rachel and all he couldn't tell her welled up so suddenly he sat in a chair and buried his face in his hands.

How long had this been going on? His parents' living room was a travesty. Jars and jars of baby food on the coffee table. Empty whiskey masons. The remote lying sprung on the floor among newspapers. A valence listing from its traverse rod. Piano stacked with clothes. The TV, coated with dust, glowered from its stand. Smell of urine: from the fireplace where his father nightly had a fire, regardless of the heat outside, then put it out by pissing on his devils. Cal asked himself again how long this had been going on.

Cal didn't even know how old his father was. But in repose he looked aged and puny – frail white hair and beard shrouding his face. Cal took the afghan off the floor and covered him.

In the kitchen was a pot of stew beef and potatoes Mac had cooked for Cal. He stood and ate from it with his hands. Walked down the hall to his parents' bedroom. The room that before this night had been locked twelve years. The door flayed wide, lock and doorknob and part of the frame gone and a good bit of the rest splintered from the shotgun. Pellets stood out on the door like sequins. The lamp was on.

Twelve years since he had entered. The room to which he would run as a little boy after nightmare, to his mother's side of the bed. And she would lift him in and he'd sleep between the walls his parents' bodies made. In the huge chestnut bed with the ceiling-high headboard, scroll-worked and carven with angels. The bed where MacGregor Gaddy was birthed. A relic. One of the last beds made before the chestnut blight. Worth a fortune, as were the other pieces of the suite: a dresser with enormous mirror; washstand; and bedside table draped with a doily, on it the lit lamp next to the Bible still split at the page Mac had ripped out for May's grave. Ecclesiastes: *He that toucheth pitch, shall be defiled with it ...* The rest of the scripture departed. In the earth with May.

Cal closed the book and laid down. Chintz spread. Damask curtains. Scent of his mother. The room was immaculate, as if it had been kept up these twelve years. But his father had locked it from the inside, climbed through a sash, and nailed shut the windows.

Cal shouldn't have laid down. He tried to get up, but it was as if he were chained, his body weighted. He sunk into the bed, into a sleep like child-sleep. Seamless, motionless, even dreamless except for the dream that was his life. Someone turned off the lamp.

Elizabeth had told Cal the story of his birth. How he had come on so sudden, catching her unaware. how she and Mac arrived at the hospital at the last minute. No time to even anesthetize her. While Mac huffed cigarettes in the lobby, she was rushed into the delivery room. The doctor asked if she would like to see her baby born. He stationed at her feet a giant mirror; and it was out of it, as if surfacing from a vertical pool of crystalline water, that Cal emerged in the predawn hours of a steamy summer morning –

the time of day when most people are born, the time of day also when most die. And, if Cal had been asked, he would have said he remembered hurtling out of that mirror into his mother's keep.

The phone. The phone was *ringing. Ringing.* Cal reached for it. *Ringing.* Knocked over a candlestick. *Ringing.* He opened his eyes. Not at home. Didn't know where he was. Not yet full daylight. The *ringing.* Then he smelled his mother, saw the chestnut and remembered.

The phone had stopped ringing. Cal barged into the hall where his father stood with the telephone at his ear. The old man looked surprised. Sheepish. Unrecollected. He said into the phone, "He's right here," and held the phone

164

out to Cal.

It was Rachel. "Where have you been, Calvin?"

"I've been here."

"I called and called. Home and your father's."

What with May, Cal had forgotten to call the hospital, which he always did on the nights he stayed up late with the wall.

"I'm sorry, honey. What's wrong?"

"Where were you?"

"We were outside for a long time."

Now she was crying.

"What's wrong, Rachel? What is it?"

"My water broke. Last night."

"Oh God."

"They got me up to go to the bathroom and it just gushed out."

Cal's father stood there. The two men gazed at each other as if trying to remember how they were connected. Cal looked at his father and thought: *Other men have done this. Seen a wife through birthing a baby into the world. Men despite themselves. One day later. A duty man. There is no fear in perfect love.* Cal and his father regarded each other. Each terrified at the other. One day later.

"Calvin."

"Yes. Yes, honey. It's okay. I'll be right there."

"Calvin. They've taken away the Magnesium Sulfate. If I don't go into labor myself in the next twenty-four hours, they'll induce."

"Don't be afraid. Don't cry."

"I'm not afraid. I just want you here."

"Yes, Baby. Yes. I'll be right there. I'm on my way."

"I love you, Calvin."

"I love you too."

Cal handed his father the phone. Mac took it, studied at it as if it were a sacred object, replaced it in its cradle, then looked back at his son.

"Rachel's water broke," Cal said.

Mac, as if in the throes of revelation, was working

165

himself up to something. Words to impart. He brought up his hand, but something stopped it before it could light on his son's shoulder.

"Well," he said.

CHAPTER 54

The sun seemed coming out of the earth, not sitting still all those millions of miles off, waiting for the much smaller ball to turn on its invisible skewer and receive its ration of fifteen, maybe sixteen, hours light.

It was close to the solstice, the longest day. The farmers were taking the wheat. A combine, its lights drilling the still-dark morning, lumbered noisily through the crop, gleaning and threshing. Another idling combine sidled up to a huge, square grain truck. Like a yellow waterfall, two tons of saved-out grain prilled out of the tall tube-like auger into the dump truck bed. Half the field was already harvested. The sun nudged against it, jagged like half a buzz-saw, the wheat shimmering, rising in the illusion of the cupped, streaming light. The wheat almost white in the dawn and roiling like water. June 19th.

In his uniform, Cal sped along. In every field, it was the same. Where the wheat had been, in another month would flower soybeans. And he would be a father. He wished he could keep driving. For a month, the baby a month old. Things at Coventry would be settled, his father's wall complete.

By now, at Coventry, they were pushing the men through breakfast. Pitch's shift. Friend's. Not Thrake's. Grits and eggs, biscuits, livermush, redeye gravy. Cal had left the message about Rachel with the Captain who now never left the camp, sleeping in the sick room, eating his meals in the chow-hall. Even as Cal rushed to Rachel, he pondered how to resolve his business at Coventry.

Rachel had been moved to a birthing room. She wore instead of her own gown a paisley hospital shift. The Magnesium Sulfate was gone. Just the blood pressure and baby monitors. Fretful, her eyes wide and tear-rimmed. Cal tasted medicine when he kissed her.

"It's alright, angel," he said.

"I don't think I'm ready for this," she said.

"Shall we just go home?"

"As long as you're here, why don't you stay?" said the nurse.

Her name was Jackie and she had been with Rachel all night. Rachel's age, very small, blunt-featured and tired. Curly black hair. Blue scrubs and a stethoscope.

"How are we looking?" Calvin asked Jackie.

She smiled. "Good. The baby's fine. The mama's fine. The minute we took away the Mag Sulfate, her contractions started, which is exactly what we wanted. Her pressure's a little high, but we're watching it. Once the water breaks, we have twenty-four, thirty-six, hours, at best. I'd say, right now, everything's on schedule."

Cal knew everything Jackie had told him. Learned it at childbirth classes or had read it. Throughout her pregnancy, Rachel had pored through books on childbirth, breast-feeding, child development. Cal had early on resolved to read everything that Rachel read. But he hadn't. It had all gone too fast. From the day he heard the news – he had been unspeakably happy – to this moment when he stood helplessly, feeling dread. He wasn't ready either.

"How soon?" Cal asked.

"Judging by her contractions, some time this evening," said Jackie. "But there's no real way to pinpoint it. Nothing is going to happen for a while. But you'll be a father before the day's out."

"If I had to run back to work for a little bit?"

"That would be fine," said Jackie.

"Just a few minutes. I need to run by the camp," he said to Rachel.

"I'll be fine, Calvin. You go on."

"Are they bad, honey?"

"No. They're not. I might try to sleep." Eyes half-closed. Jackie looked at him as if to say, "It's alright. Go on."

"I'll be right back, angel," he whispered. He leaned down and kissed her forehead.

"Give me a real kiss," Rachel murmured. She was asleep.

CHAPTER 55

It was lunch time when Calvin made it to the camp, so he went right to the chow- hall. He was weak and to the point of being unable to stand. Not hungry, but he thought maybe some food might help. Sleep too, but that would have to wait.

Blish, smoking a cigarette, sat at a table with the Captain and Brotherton. When she saw Cal, she waved and motioned him over to the table. She and the Captain had taken up again, with more ardor and devil-may-care than ever. Like an escape caught in the wire: the more he struggles, the worse it cuts him.

Blish and the Captain. Cal wasn't even disgusted anymore. They were making it. Like the inmates. Shutting up and not asking questions. Letting time pass. Cal felt something else now. Only five minutes before, stepping out of his truck, he had felt this new thing: when his boot fell on Coventry and he had seen Friend standing there with his shotgun and smirk. Cal was primed for meanness. Not just writing somebody up or throwing him in the Boot, but cutting off his ears or branding him. And justifying it. He sat down at the table with the others.

"Are you a daddy yet?" Blish gushed.

The Captain and Brotherton smiled. Snoo played the piano. A tune Cal didn't recognize. Inmates, in fours, shuffled in through the thwacking screen door. Friend stood behind it with the shotgun.

"No," he said. "Not yet."

"When?" asked Blish. "How's Rachel? What are you doing here?"

"I just came to look in. Nothing is really happening with Rachel right now. They figure the baby will come some time this evening. I'm going to eat a little something and head right back there."

"That's exactly what you should do," agreed the Captain.

Brotherton boomed at the steam line: "One of y'all bring Sergeant Gaddy a tray."

A he-she cook named Ben-Hur brought over a tray. He wore a hairnet and his eyes were made up. "I hope you enjoy it, Sergeant Gaddy," he said as he placed it in front of Cal. Something called a chuckwagon sandwich. A breaded square piece of deep-fried meat on a bun. With it were two identical white scoops of slaw and potato salad. A wedge of sweet potato pie and a cup of coffee.

Cal drenched the sandwich in Texas Pete and started eating.

"They made a positive identification on what we fished out of the quarry," said the Captain. "It was Sergeant Thrake. Cause of death was drowning."

Cal left it at that. He had known all along it was Thrake. And he did not care what they said was the cause of death. It didn't matter much now anyhow. The food agreed with him. It was the best thing he had eaten in a long time. "Blish, can I have a cigarette?" he asked.

"You don't smoke."

"I just want one."

Blish lit a cigarette off hers and handed it to Cal. He inhaled deeply twice, holding it down as if it were smoking reefer. He smoked and sipped coffee. When the cigarette went out, he stood, and said, "I got to go."

Then he saw Pitch. In the kitchen cooking. Pitch turning slowly, smiling, as Cal, suddenly sick at his stomach, let out the smoke hidden in his lungs. Pitch who should have been sound asleep after getting up in the middle of the night and cooking with the breakfast shift. But there he was where he should not have been, smiling at Cal, holding up a spatula in greeting, the second mouth on his forehead now like a third eye, Cyclopean, all-knowing. Everything in Cal loosened.

Cal was stretched on the sick room bunk where Frank had been embalmed, a dirty thirty watt lightbulb dangling above his head. He was dying for a cigarette. A smoke would choke back the nausea. He could not let himself be sick anymore. That son-of-a-bitch, Pitch, had switched shifts, or worked both, just so he could poison Cal. Friend was the watch officer; he would have had a hand in it.

Cal had to get to the hospital to see Rachel, but he needed a smoke first. The bunk next to him was piled with the captain's belongings: toiletries and clothes. And tangled in with them were women's things, shimmering and sweet-scented. He smelled Blish's heavy perfume. And formaldehyde. She and the captain had to have been shacking up there – in the sick room, on the bed where he lay. He spied a pack of cigarettes poking out of a paper sack. Got up and lit one, took in the smoke. In and in. That was better. He laid back down – to think. There was Pitch and there was Friend: they were trying to kill him. The way they did Thrake. He lit another cigarette. What had his father said to him? "Do for him before he does for you. God'll forgive you."

The door opened and in pranced Blish, her black hair swooped up and the patch, black today. And a black, sleeveless dress that stuck to and curved about her like blacktop. She closed the door behind her.

"Calvin," she said, smiling. "You gave us a turn." Calvin braced himself up on his elbows. "You lie back and rest. You're just all worn out. Aren't you? Just all worn out." Cal wanted to tell her about worn out. "Aren't you?" she repeated, sitting on the side of the cot, her hand against his face.

"Yes," he admitted. "Yes."

"You go on and tell me all about it. I can be your girl too."

"Yes," he said again.

She stood up, pulled the dress over her head and laid against him on the cot.

Her mouth tasted like butterscotch. And her perfume. But there was also the formaldehyde and he couldn't help but think of Frank even as he kissed her. Frank lying dead where they now lay. He had to get out of there. He told Rachel he would be right back. Rachel – maybe fighting for her life, and the baby's, wondering where he was.

"Hasn't there always been something between us, Calvin?" she said, kissing him, ripping at him. "You're so tired."

"I am," he said, reaching at her with his stone limbs as

she positioned herself over him and whispered something he couldn't quite hear; yet it fell on his ear, a drop of fire, and purled its way clear to his eye, stirring the vision he kept there like an icon of the whore in The Heart of Dark.

"Do you want me?" she asked.

Cal knew not to want her. He knew all about her, what her name would be if she had a name. But he said it anyway, sold it off that quick with his "Yes."

Blish reached up and undid the patch – the way one might the last vestige of modesty, a revelation beyond mere nudity. With her uncovered onyx eye, out of which leaked her life in a steady bead of white light, she looked down upon him splayed out, waiting.

There was a knock on the door and the nurse walked in. Cal opened his eyes. It was the smell first. Then he remembered. He was in the sick room. He tasted cigarettes and nearly gagged.

"How do you feel?" asked the nurse.

"I don't know. I'm okay. What happened?"

"You fainted."

Pitch. Cal saw his leering face, his two mouths, his third eye. He remembered the chow-hall.

"How long have I been out?"

"About forty minutes."

"I got to go. Rachel's in labor." He swung his feet around and sat on the side of the cot.

"Do you need some help?" asked the nurse.

"No thanks. I'm alright. Just a little tired."

"You check out alright, Calvin. All your vitals. Even your blood. I took the liberty and labbed it myself right here. But you can't run yourself like this. Whatever it is."

"I know. But I have to go. Tell the Captain I'll be back when I can. I'll call. And thanks for everything. For your concern."

"Let us know about Rachel, and you take care of yourself."

CHAPTER 56

The day had turned hot and cloudy. The wheat fields now brushed clean. Miles of blonde chaff on either side of the road. Cal was frantic that the baby might have been born without him, and would be behind the window wearing his toboggan with the rest of them and he, his father, would not even know him.

But when he got to the hospital, Rachel was dilated only two centimeters. Jackie was on one side of the bed, studying a strip of paper feeding out of a machine, and Cal's father on the other, holding Rachel's hand.

Cal nodded at his father and kissed Rachel. "I'm sorry. I got hung up."

"I was getting worried," Rachel said, her voice strained.

"How we looking here?" Cal asked.

"The contractions are picking up," Jackie said. She showed Cal the strip. On it were jagged peaks of varying altitudes.

"Are they bad, honey?" Cal asked.

"Not too bad."

"I'll be back," Jackie said. "I've got two other women in labor. You know what to do, Dad. I've been helping her with the breathing. You just coach her right through it."

Rachel stiffened and started sipping air as they had been taught.

"Easy," Cal said. "Easy." He breathed with her. Deeper. "Easy."

It went on a long time. Cal could almost feel Rachel's hand squeezing his father's. She sweated, the hair around her face damp, eyes closed, breathing. They were on the hospital's top floor. The dense gray day sat on the sill and looked in as Rachel panted and gave just the least cry, Cal breathing with her, and then the pain began its backwash and she slid back down the side of it, relieved, but already girding for the next.

173

"Is it bad, honey?" Cal said.

"That one was a little bad. Don't leave me again, Calvin."

"I won't. I won't. I promise."

Mac fetched a Styrofoam cup with a straw from the bedside tray and held it for Rachel to drink. When she leaned forward, sweat ran out of her hair. Cal took up a cloth and ran it across her brow.

Not less, but one hour more. Sweat standing out on Rachel's forehead. On the clock was *only*. Not *more*. The way she gripped Cal's hand when the contractions came on, lasting longer each time. Her eyes lidded. Behind them just she and the baby locked in the word, *contraction*, and outside of which was nothing. No analogous word to say – especially for the baby – this is the word. The word commanding you to leave this place you'll spend all of your days trying to return to.

The baby knew only the sweetness of its mother, her inscrutable warm geography; the sadness of parting, its tongue already whetted with her blood. But no word for any of it. Just this force. This inevitable. What Rachel was wrought up in, bartering at each peak with God, with the baby, for more *only*. Less *more*. Her mouth now saying, *Oh*. An astonished *Oh* that she was a self in the world and this was her. What the baby was saying with no words. Unsaying. *Oh*.

Then Rachel would come back to them, her eyes open, the shades coming up on the same day, gray and threatening, Cal breathing with her, looking down upon her, the thing in her hand his hand. He said the same thing over and over: comfort words that had long ago ceased to matter because he did not have the words. If she did not have the words, and the baby did not, how could he – on the other side of her veiled eyes?

He mopped her brow. He spooned ice chips into her mouth. By now, beyond these ministrations, she found it all reproachful – especially the old man, something ancient, who sat in a chair and called her Elizabeth, astonished at everything but the pain. She wanted to come back from behind her lids, but the contractions were ceaseless. There was nothing else.

"Is it getting bad?" Calvin asked.

"It's alright." Her voice a sough.

"We can get you some help, sweetie," Jackie said.

"Are you ready, honey? It's okay, you know," said Calvin.

"I'm alright."

"Well, you just let me know," soothed Jackie. "I'm going to go ahead anyhow and order an epidural. We probably won't even need it. But if you decide. Okay?"

Rachel nodded, her eyes closed. It was on her again. The baby too closed its eyes, opened them. Jackie studied the blood pressure monitor. Red integers twitched up and up.

"Let me measure again," said Jackie.

The old man got up to leave.

"Stay, Papa," Rachel said.

Mac ambled over to the window and looked out. Jackie pulled on a glove and examined Rachel. "Four centimeters," she announced.

Rachel didn't cry. She closed her eyes.

CHAPTER 57

After church they piled into the old Galaxy. It had a three-speed on the column and Rachel's mother hated it. Hated it because ramming that stick through the gearbox was hard and unladylike. Especially of a Sunday. White gloves and the children. Hated it because a man should drive. But there was no man. He cut right o'way for the State with a prison bush-axe and lived in another county most of a day's drive away along roads that ran between water and teeming sawgrass swamps where turtles sunned on cypress logs and the last of the red wolves lived.

Rachel's father's name was Daddy. He lived in a camp with men dressed identically and slept in the same immense cellar-like room. Sunday was visiting day: when Rachel, who was the baby, and her brother and sister arrived disheveled after the long drive, not looking anything like the family they really were, and her mother cried.

What Daddy had done didn't matter, Rachel's mother had told the children, told them as their preacher had told her. A rangy, handsome blonde man, Daddy smiled all day Sundays. Bought them peach ice cream made right there in the camp kitchen. Rachel never again bringing herself to put ice cream in her mouth, once she found out years later, after her parents were dead, the truth about her father.

Behind the camp ran a stream. Along with her brother and sister and the other Sunday children, Rachel crouched along its banks, launching sticks, gathering rose quartz and moonstone that studded its walls, lifting the wide, flat bedrocks for crayfish and salamanders.

She hadn't known that yellow jackets made their homes underground. So thinking *bees* when the first prick came, she glanced up and saw only sky – bright, seductive silver coils of concertina. lashed against it along the camp fence. No bees. The pain on her thigh was a fire, then pricks all over like brads hammered into her. Still she looked up. Until her voice found itself, and she screamed and flailed, and happened to look down and see ejecting from a tiny hole in the creek bank the queue of yellow jackets. As if calibrated: one, then one, then one. The tiny striped bodies like struck matches. Her brother beat them off her and rolled her in the creek. The other children ran off, shouting.

The uproar brought a band of the identically dressed men, her father among them. He scooped her up. She wrapped around him her arms and legs, buried her face in his neck; she knew she was going to die. Her mother had taught her that death could come at you like this. A hole might open in the earth: there it would be and the fault would be all yours.

"What, honey? What?" her father kept asking. And the men around him. All at a jog back to the camp. Cooing at her, telling her it would be alright.

Sorry. *Sorry* was what she had been saying. It was her fault. Born with fault, then it creeps out of a hole to find you at play, and kindles inside you a fire.

There was her mother's voice, then her father laid her down in his bed, another bed above it, in the big room of stacked little beds exactly alike. Her father's bed smelled of sweat and night and regret. But it was her father's bed, and he and her mother and brother and sister hovered above her, loving her, telling her it would be alright. Her mother and father together above her bed at night before the lights were turned out.

An ancient man came to the bedside, mad-looking, with two different colored eyes and rotten teeth, wattled throat. colossal ears.

"What's your name?" he asked her.

She told him though her lips were stiff and swollen, her tongue like a dry ball choking her. The old man smiled and packed each of the twenty-three stings with wettened tobacco. She laid there that way a long time, watching her mother and father the way they were with each other that day at the camp on Sunday because she was dying. It seemed easy, even though her mother had always warned that dying is not that easy. She was glad for her death if this is what it meant: her mother and father at her bedside, those men gathered like angels above her.

Her ache mounted, bigger than anything she'd ever imagined. Like a baby. Like the baby she would have with Calvin, her husband, whom she would meet on a prison yard. The man who would put his arms around her and tell her it was alright, who knew all about having a father in prison.

CHAPTER 58

Now. An hour later. A minute later. It didn't matter. The pain: a swarm of yellow jackets that would not cease stinging. The contractions, the pressure, were crushing Rachel. She could barely suck in a breath. Sweat drenched her reddened face.

"I don't know," she cried, her voice wild, desperate.

The old man was on his feet, confused and ready. Like he might fling himself through the window. The blood pressure monitor blinked red.

"It's too much," Cal implored. "It's too much now."

Jackie, slipping on a glove, stood between Rachel's legs.

"You can get some relief now, honey," Cal coaxed. "You don't have to hurt like this. Let them give you the epidural."

He sponged her forehead. Her eyes sat on her face. Blue. Maybe bluer as they raked him like an animal who simply wants it to stop.

"Let me get them to bring it, Rachel. Yes?"

Mac brought his hands up to his head. Saying something, his lips moving. But no sound. Over and over. Rachel, weeping out of sheer outrage at the pain, watched him. He said, "Elizabeth. Elizabeth."

"Can I tell them to bring it, sweetheart? Please?"

"Yes." Finally.

"Okay," said Cal. "Okay. Jackie, can we get her the epidural now?"

Jackie peeked over the crest of Rachel's stomach. "It's too late for that," she said, smiling. "This lady's about to have a baby. Right away. She's dilated ten centimeters. I'm going to page the doctor. I'll be right back. Whatever you do, don't start pushing yet."

Jackie rushed back with Doctor Craddock, a burly man in blue scrubs with hairy arms and dark hair curling out of his collar.

Dr. Craddock patted Rachel's hand. "Easy, Rachel," he

said. "Slow the breathing. Slow the breathing. We don't want you to hyperventilate. And don't start pushing yet. I know you want to, but wait for me to tell you."

"Sips," Jackie coached. "Sips. Breathe with me. Dad, we need you up at Mom's head," she reminded Cal.

Dr. Craddock examined Rachel. "We're talking minutes here. The baby's crowning."

Rachel paid out a long delirious gasp.

"Come and see this, Calvin," said Dr. Craddock.

Cal looked into the V of Rachel's legs. Visible, pushing against the dilated cervix, was a patch of flesh, not Rachel, covered with thick dark hair.

"That's your baby, Calvin," said the doctor.

"Did you see it?" asked Rachel.

Calvin welled up and held it there. "Right in front of me. Knocking on the door." Then returned to Rachel and leaned over her, facing the doctor seated on a stool between her legs.

"At the next contraction, Rachel, I want you to push," Dr. Craddock said.

"You two fellows need to get into gowns too," Jackie said.

She tossed one to Cal, then helped MacGregor into one. He fumbled his hands together as she tied it off at the neck. Dr. Craddock lathered Rachel's perineum with a rust-colored liquid. Cal looked down at her face. Upside down. Marshaling for it.

"Now push," commanded the doctor.

Rachel grunted and bore down, holding her breath, her face bright red.

"Breathe," said Jackie. "Help her, Dad."

"Breathe, honey," said Cal. He breathed. "Breathe with me."

Trying to get her into the rhythm. She seemed to nod, like *Yes, breathe*, and she breathed, like clearing her throat, stertorous, atavistic. The blood pressure reading blurred red, numbers piling on one another.

"Now, relax," said Dr. Craddock as the contraction

cleared off. "And get ready. Here we go."

In it again. Rachel. Pushing. Growling. One contraction more. One more push. The numbers red dizzy and the welling in Cal. Mac on his feet, mumbling, "Elizabeth," and "Girl," standing behind Dr. Craddock who said, "Okay. A little more. One big push."

Jackie inserted Brahms in the tape deck.

Hearing the lullaby, Cal looked out the window and saw the clouds cleave and uncleave, and out of them the sun. The entire room leavened. Then in stormed the neonatology team.

The day, the hour, the minute, the very second: one day later, June 19th, 4:09 p.m. The day they took the wheat. That Rachel heaved and spent that one last push and cry, and there hurtled out of her what had been there all along, yet the most unlikely thing imaginable.

A boychild. Who Dr. Craddock held up in the stream of Brahms and sunlight. Who cried and batted the air with little fists. The awestruck sigh that breached out of Cal and Rachel simultaneously. And then Cal's whispered pronouncement, "A boy," Mac falling back into a chair, hand over his heart, finally broken, his uttering, "Well."

Dr. Craddock laid the baby on his mother's breast; then said, "Just a little tear," and quickly sutured, though no one heard him nor saw him anymore. Rachel wept, Cal wondering when he could weep. He looked at his father and he knew that, whatever, both loved the other. Finally. But this little boy. He was the one.

CHAPTER 59

Along with Childs, who cradled a shotgun taller than himself, Cal stood at the door of the white transfer bus as the men fresh from Central Prison in Raleigh, in full irons, clinked down the four stairs to their new jolt at Coventry. They already wore brown and their skin had that porous, shadowy cast that men too often indoors take on. More than anything, they were shocked and tongue-tied. They had lost their souls back behind the big walls.

Calvin was so tired. Every minute he was not at the camp, he was at the hospital where the baby was still in neonatal intensive care. He had been much bigger than they had expected. Four pounds, eleven ounces. But, even so, tiny. Cal and Rachel had had him only a few minutes before he was dashed off to ICU.

They had been so blithe and happy there alone in the birthing room: the Brahms playing, Rachel's placenta, a little bloody tree on a steel tray, the sunlight on it, Mac finally in the elevator on his way to his truck.

After the birth, Rachel was almost instantly herself. She sat up, her eyes and mouth for the first time in months unburdened. She was hungry and, after she ate and rested, Cal helped her into a wheelchair and they went to visit their son.

Neonatal intensive care was a huge open room lined with bassinets, each equipped with myriad machines, buzzers, alarms, lights – and a corps of nurses hovering over the babies. Babies, some of whom were merely small; some minute, less than two pounds, the size of a gourd; others with unnamable afflictions, sutured and splinted and spliced into wires that nourished them and kept their bodies going and registered it all in flashing numbers above their heads, just below their nameplates. A place of light and clamor. Like Limbo: angels incubating.

Cal strolled Rachel through the racks of babies. There

was nothing they could do until they came to the name-plate: *Gaddy, Boy*. Because they had not yet named him, both then and there resolved for him a name - *Eli* - for his being nameless was the first sorrow.

Lying naked on his back, wearing a baby-blue toboggan and oxygen hood, splayed out like a frog. A tube inserted through his navel. Every joint, every appendage, wired and connected to electric boxes ringing his bassinet. Cal and Rachel would have never known him, but he was theirs. This Boy Gaddy: Eli. They could not touch him. Could not get to him. Only stand beyond his bubble and gape.

Every day Rachel and Cal, at the side of their son, asked the nurses minute to minute how he was, getting repeatedly the same patient assurances. Each day, Eli's lungs took over a bit more, less oxygen from the machines, his furzy little body moving ever so slightly.

This was how the days rolled over each other at the side of their son, now on his stomach under the bili lights because he was jaundiced, a little mask to protect his eyes and a green and white seersucker diaper.

Cal dozed on a stool beside him at 4 a.m. – before his shift at Coventry – starting, his heart hammering when a buzzer went off, because his own uniform startled him, because it was always full shimmering white dawn in this baby room.

If not Cal, then Rachel. Or both. Finally the grandfather with a white stuffed bear and a baseball which the nurses placed in the bassinet. And after that, the old man came every day and sat silently in a chair at the feet of his grandson.

CHAPTER 60

The last man off the bus was just a boy. Too pretty. Sandy, shaggy hair. Along his soft jaw and chin circled his first wispy beard. Terrified, darting ice blue eyes. A mouth about to cave in on itself. Cal had seen this boy a thousand times. He had already been done in at Central, his spirit jack-knifed out of him. Wore his lostness the same way he wore his browns and chains.

These things registered in Cal only remotely, a moment of lucidity after surfacing from a sleep-drug, then drifting back under. Not simply that he was exhausted and sleepless. It was a weariness beyond anything physical. As if his soul were tired and he would have to lie down a long, long time apart from the dream of life.

And it could have been a dream. Eli hurtling out of Rachel. How moments after Rachel had passed the vine of afterbirth, Jackie had taken both her palms and heaved down on Rachel's now slack belly. How another small river of thick blood had washed out, and Rachel's moan. Another nurse then brought a warm blanket and covered her and she slept smiling for almost an hour while Cal stared happily into the sunlight flecked with her blood.

The other parents in ICU, with stretched, yellow skin under the fluorescence, guarding their helpless, sometimes dying infants, faces past crying, incredulous at the swaddled few pounds they had made. Day after day, night after day – as if there were day or night.

On the sixth day, they removed the oxygen and Eli did just fine. That evening, Cal and Rachel were allowed to hold him for the first time. Rachel cried as the nurse handed him to her. The baby remained oblivious, still trussed in a dozen monitor wires, but no longer the feeding tubes – in his own dream of consciousness. No language, just life on earth. *How strange*, Cal thought as he accepted for the first time his son from Rachel –like he might a vase of nitroglycerine – and held him determinedly close against his uniform shirt.

When Cal first handed Eli to MacGregor Gaddy, the resemblance between grandfather and grandson was so apparent that everyone who passed commented upon it. The mouth and ears, the deep, brooding cast of the eyes. Rachel said it first, laughing. Cal, envisioning his father as an infant, smiled while the old man, imperceptibly rocking, sat silently staring into the baby's eyes, then brought him up and kissed his forehead, just beneath his little hat.

Two days later, a nurse, carrying Eli, escorted Rachel and Cal to a small room with a love seat and easy chair. She seated Rachel in the chair, handed her the baby and left them alone. Rachel folded the blanket back from Eli's face. He lay in the perpetual dreamy doze of the premature. But at the sound of his parents' voices softly calling to him, his lids slid open. His blue eyes fixed on his mother's face, his father an out-of-focus light blue backdrop behind him. His gaze wandered lazily over the topography of the mother's countenance until quite accidentally the blue of his eyes spilled into the blue of hers and he saw himself mirrored in them. He still was unaware that he had a life apart from her. He closed his eyes again.

"Now, honey, don't go to sleep," Rachel said. She jostled him gently, opened her robe and unbuttoned the first three buttons of her gown. She had been expressing milk all along. The nurses kept the milk in a freezer and used it for the baby's bottle feedings.

"Wake up, Eli," Rachel urged.

"Wake up, Eli," Cal said. "Come on, buddy. Wake up." He put an arm around Rachel.

The baby's eyelids fluttered. Rachel pressed his face to her breast, guided the nipple into his mouth. His lips curled around it for a split instant before he again fell off to sleep.

Cal felt like he should tiptoe out of the room. He had no mother. As if only then, for the first time, he had realized it.

CHAPTER 61

The image of Rachel proffering her breast and his innocent, overwhelmed baby boy taking it lodged in Cal's mind along with the involuntary spasm of whatever it was that rent him when he saw it. *Loss.* But it wasn't loss.

He gaped with the same wonder and loss at the boy coming off the transfer bus. Recognition, yet loss. And love. So that when the boy took off running, Cal needed a moment to work his way from the side of his wife and son back to Coventry where he stood on the macadam watching a scared boy convict toddle off in chains.

There was nowhere for the boy to go. The entire compound, parking lot and all, was surrounded by a twenty foot fence. The only opening, now locked, was for vehicles to come and go. Everyone stopped to watch him make for the entrance. Ernestine, in the tower, hit the alarm. Icemorelee and Nightcutt bounded out of the office.

"Everybody back on the bus," Cal ordered.

The transfer inmates climbed back up into the bus, then craned their heads out the windows to watch the boy.

"He's escaping," Childs said.

"No shit," Cal responded.

Childs raised his shotgun.

"Put the gun down, you idiot," Cal said.

"He's escaping."

"Where the hell do you think he's going to go with those irons and that fence? Stay here with these men."

Cal trotted off after the boy, who hadn't gotten fifty yards. Running hunchbacked and swagging pigeon-toed from side to side, his chains ringing, he looked like an old man. Cal wanted to let the boy go, just let him keep on running.

"Hey," Cal called as he chased. "Stop."

Coming from the boy was something like chanting, the sound of his chains making music. Behind Cal came the slap of Icemorelee and Nightcutt gaining on them.

Cal reached out and grabbed the boy's collar. The boy froze. He was crying. Cal let go of him, and the boy turned. He looked like he had just awakened from a bad dream, his light, ample hair tousled, his beautiful face streaked with tears. Slight and a head shorter than Cal, not more than eighteen, if that, his browns hung on him as if they were the boy's father's clothes. Behind him, encircling all of them, the concertina twinkled. Beyond it the deep black green woods. And beyond the woods, if one ran long and fast enough, hid a planet of light and forgetfulness, and finally endless water.

The boy threw himself on Cal with such force that it almost knocked Cal over. He dug his hands in Cal's sides and held on, his sobbing buried in Cal's chest. Cal held him and his chains there as he quaked and jangled. The boy was fear – fear dressed in brown fatigues. He smelled the way Cal remembered the big prison in Raleigh smelled. Like the dead sweating. Cal's first impulse was to hurl the boy away, turn the tables and escape from him.

Looking down into the boy's matted hair, Cal saw death training in his skull, getting bigger and stronger every day. Cal recoiled, but the boy held tighter; then Cal remembered Eli, only ten days old – who had only begun breathing on his own four days earlier, how he had been flung into the world, helpless. Then he thought of his mother and he kissed the top of the boy's head, held tightly to him and whispered, "It's okay."

Icemorelee and Nightcutt shouted. Cal turned his head toward them for the first time. Icemorelee had his stick raised. Cal let go of the boy, held up his hand and yelled, "No."

"You little son-of-a-bitch," Icemorelee roared and blackjacked the boy alongside his neck.

Cal lunged at Icemorelee, grabbed the stick and flung it. "Goddam you," he yelled in Icemorelee's face, and then advanced on him.

Nightcutt, still holding his own stick, lunged between them. The whimpering prisoner hunched on the blacktop, his arms folded around his head.

"What the hell's wrong with you?" Icemorelee said to Cal.

"Why the fuck did you hit him?"

"I thought he was on you, Cal. Jesus Christ."

"Godammit, I had him. Why'd you hit him?"

Nightcutt bent over the boy. "Get up, son," he said. Then to Icemorelee: "C'mon, Ice. Let's get him to the Boot."

"Just back off. I'll take care of him," said Cal.

"Suit yourself, Cal. Just suit your goddam self," snarled Icemorelee, as he walked off to retrieve his stick.

"We thought you were in trouble," Nightcutt said to Cal, then took off after Icemorelee.

Cal got the kid to his feet, took his arm, and led him out of the lot into the camp. Crying softly, the boy's head hung, his hair cascaded onto his sunken chest. The men on the bus sat there, gaping. A few of them laughed as Cal and the boy passed.

Childs smiled. He held the big, heavy shotgun loosely in front of him, across his body. He looked like a schoolboy dressed in guard's clothes.

"Where the hell did he think he was going?" he asked.

"Just get these men off the bus and processed, Childs," said Cal. "Get Ice or Nightcutt to help you."

"They don't know when they got it good," quipped Childs.

"Shut up," said Cal. "And don't point that gun at me. You know how to hold one of those, boy?"

Childs quickly shifted the gun toward the clouds. "I wasn't pointing it at you," he said.

"Just shut up and do your job, Childs."

The chained boy never lifted his head.

CHAPTER 62

The Boot at Coventry was a freestanding building. An eight by eight pillbox with a five foot ceiling. A solid steel door that was opened twice: when a man went in and when he was let out. The one meal per day – water, grits, beans, streak o'lean and a hoe cake – was lowered through a slot in the ceiling, opened at night, closed in the day. Sometimes the opposite.

The walls were concrete, pocked with teeth and fingernail marks, imprinted with skin and tongue and long epistles crayoned in blood and excrement and whatever its occupants could manifest to hack with. Love letters and derogations; poems; confessions; prayers; maps; pornography; the etched figure of a whore Madonna, the archetypal chaingang pinup. A palimpsest of solitary. But, because no true light was permitted in the Boot, it remained invisible.

The smell was of caged men, at once familiar, no longer shocking, to those who lived with it. Shit, piss, blood, semen, sweat, fear. The cement floor had sharpened staddles spiking out of it – Mac Gaddy's inspiration – so a man could not lie down; but, if he was not too big, could sometimes wedge himself into a corner and sit. No one could stand – only hunch. No mattress nor bunk. In the middle was a hole for a bathroom that would occasionally back up and drown the Boot in half a foot of septic. Little brown bats roosted from the ceiling, came and went through the roof slot.

The key to the Boot weighed a pound. Cal jammed it in and turned. The door swung in of its own volition; the stink rolled out in a hot sheet. On the floor was a parallelogram of light from the roof slot, staddle shadows skewering it. Even with the light from Coventry yard dribbling in, it was too dark to see.

The boy had done enough time at Central to know he had to walk in the door, but he didn't budge. He finally lifted his pretty tear-stained face to Cal who said, "There's nothing

I can do about this. Find a corner and don't move around too much. Try not to touch anything. There's a hole in the middle to do your business."

The boy, it seemed, was trying to say, *Please*, but "Thank you" is what he said in a whispered voice. A raped voice. From I and J block. Cal remembered.

"There's nothing for it," Cal said. "It won't have to be for long."

Cal nudged him. He just wanted to shut the door now. He couldn't look at the boy anymore. The boy did resist, but he stalled there in the lintel.

"Go on," Cal nudged again, this time harder and with more of his father in his voice than he had ever given credence. The boy went in hard against a staddle and disappeared in the darkness. Cal heard him slide to his haunches against a wall and weep. He hefted shut the steel door and locked it, then went into the office to file the write-up.

CHAPTER 63

The Quakers believed that if you locked a man up by himself in a black pit with just bread and water and the Bible, he would sooner or later come around to the word of God and be regenerated. Most men, by degrees, went mad. More than a few died. But most dangerous of all – and unaccounted for by the original architects of prison – there sometimes emerged from the dark onliness a prophet.

Tarl Benefit was such a one. He did his first stretch in the hole at Osteen Farms on the coastal plain – below sea level, so that the hole, called Alone, tended to fill with swamp water; and, even though there was no light, the sawgrass and yaupon spikes wormed through, and the palmetto bugs would eat the stripes right off a fledgling convict.

Tarl was only fifteen, doing his first time for killing two dogs. He told the shrinks that voices had led him to it, but he had done it for revenge. One day, he had climbed over a fence into an orchard to steal peaches. On the other side had been two German Shepherds, and they had chewed up his legs before he could scramble back up over the fence.

The next day he had gone back, limping on bandaged legs, and killed them with a pitchfork. He was sent to the youth camp at Osteen. He was a good reader and knew all about voices. So when he was asked *why* about anything, he answered *voices*; and every time he did, the captain, Boss David, who carried a riding crop he used to spank the boys blue and bloody, threw him in Alone. Boss David claimed he would cure that bughouse Benefit with a little quiet.

Tarl had never been afraid of the dark. He had never clearly been afraid, but he did worry about whether or not he would go to heaven or hell. So he got into the habit of telling himself stories in which God sided with him – where God would look down and say: *Go ahead, Tarl, drive a nail into that man, set that one afire, but be this one's friend, don't borrow from this one, be long suffering and patient in your quest for immortality for it shall come.*

Somewhere along the line, while Tarl was in Alone, God took over. It was as much Bible believer's faith as anything, and only a fool would turn away from the word of God when it manifests in one's own head. After a while, it was God telling the stories. Not the devil. It had never been the devil. Tarl knew his scripture. From his mama. All good things come from God. Not the devil, but God Almighty, got Tarl through that hole time. He could not have made it on his own. He talked and someone talked back. Voices issuing from the deepest love, and he knew from his mother that there is no fear in perfect love.

God and Tarl in Alone: four inches of Atlantic Ocean backwater, his feet like pig-hocks from squatting in it, teeth chipped from eating raw blue crab and periwinkle snails. Then after so long – he'd lose count of the days – Boss David would swing back the door and Tarl staggered out and rejoined the population, and the voices kept on until it got so that he relied on them for everything, from how much shortening for the cornbread – he was apprenticing as a cook at Osteen – to whether or not to shank a boy who had cut his eyes at him funny.

CHAPTER 64

Boss David was a big fat man. Shirt so tight on his belly – like the skin of a bloated turkey. Red, whiskey face, one cheek wadded with Bull Durham, cowboy hat, jeans, and cowboy boots. He liked to hang around the kitchen. Every so often he'd waddle in and single out Tarl to fix him something. Sausage gravy or salmon cakes, fried chicken and deviled eggs.

"Bake me a chocolate cake, Pitchfork" – what he had taken to calling Tarl and had been picked up by the other boys. Boss David lounged there and watched Tarl prepare the food, his eyes side-longing into him, a cross between want and madding hate. When Tarl brought the food out, Boss David had him sit at the table with him as he ate: four dozen chicken livers, gravy, black-eyed peas, chow-chow, pickled peaches, biscuits and a pan of Apple Betty. The whole time, Boss David complimented the food, and told Tarl the same story, occasionally reaching over to squeeze him behind the neck, less and less gently, as he allowed how good it all was, squeezing Tarl's neck till the pain was excruciating, daring him to bring up a hand so he could drop his fork for the riding crop stationed at his plate-side.

The same story about a boy just like Tarl who had gone into a man's pasture and shot the eyes out of a Tennessee Walker with a BB gun. How that boy had come to Osteen. How the other boys there had hated him so dear, because a horse is a gentle creature – anybody who would do that – that Boss David kept that other boy, for his own protection, in Alone.

This boy tinkered with poetry. A real he-she, and there was more to blinding the horse than what it looked like on the psychiatrist's clip-board. Some crimes are bigger than they seem and some smaller. Not just head doctor stuff. It was obvious the boy was disturbed. Boss David knew that. Not something worse necessarily. You can always find worse in a prison. Just something more. It was only a matter of time before what the boy was really sent to do, something ingeniously apocalyptic, came to pass. So Boss David, in what he felt was his duty to the citizens of the North Carolina, just forgot about him. Left him in Alone and never went back for him. Just never went back. And as he said to Tarl, as he threshed through his food, "That boy, I can't even remember his name, he just disappeared. Because you know what, son? He wasn't never here to begin with."

CHAPTER 65

There was no one in the building. Cal went to the sergeant's office and grabbed down an infraction form and sat drowsily at the desk. The radio in Blish's office was tuned to the Christian station: a preacher recounted a story about going to visit a family and finding a diapered baby in a crib.

As he edged up to the crib, the preacher noticed that the baby had a beard; and, as he peered closer, he saw that the baby was covered in hair, that it was not a baby at all. It was a man who had never grown. And it occurred to this preacher that many a Christian was like this man-baby. They did not want to grow; they wanted to remain perpetually in a baby-like state and be washed and diapered and burped. The preacher went on to contemplate what might issue from the mouths of these kinds of man-baby Christians were they burped.

"You burp'em," he shouted, "and out comes *Playboy* magazine. You burp'em and out comes a bottle of liquor. You burp'em and out comes a X-rated movie."

Cal wrote: *The boy didn't look old enough to be on an adult camp. He was barely shaving. He looked like a girl – long blond hair, blues eyes and pretty, already punked a hundred times. I don't know what he had done to get here, but he was scared, smart too. He had read too much all his life and now he was stuck in a book. I haven't really slept in weeks, so when this boy came tearing off the transfer bus with nowhere to go, it struck me as funny. At first, I just watched him try to navigate across the lot in chains. It was funny and pathetic. He was surrounded by fence. I thought I might be dreaming. But there was something in me that wanted him to get away. All I think about is sleep. I guess I came to when I heard the alarm. I secured the men on the bus and left Officer Childs with them. Then I started after the boy. He hadn't gotten far at all. There was nowhere he could go.*

From the radio came a wild piano rendition of *Just a*

Closer Walk with Thee. Cal's mother walked into the sergeant's office. She took off her white gloves and, before skimming off the purple tam o'shanter she sometimes wore cocked on her head to church, removed a hatpin and set it on the desk in front of Cal. Then she sat in the chair next to the desk and sang a speeded up, madcap version of the song playing on the radio, smiling the while and staring out the window above Cal's head at the concertina. When the song was over, she looked at her son and said: "I wonder if Jesus ever regretted giving up carpentry for the pulpit?" Among her fingers shot tiny sparks, and smoke seeped out of her.

Cal shook himself out of a doze, and tried to refocus on his wiry penmanship. The radio preacher announced he had a small child named Little Hattie right there in the studio with him. Little Hattie had come back to life on a morgue table.

"How long were you dead, little lady?"

"I was dead two days, almost."

"What was it like being dead?"

"It was like being under water, but you could breathe and every little bit another person would float by, sometimes two and three. Everybody still had their clothes on."

"And when you come out of it, you could speak in tongues?"

"Yes, sir. I am certified in tongues."

"It's a miracle."

"Yes, sir. I believe it is."

Officers Nightcutt and Icemorelee had come out and were running after him too. I reached him first and he didn't put up the least fuss. When he turned, I saw it was me, if that makes any sense. I stared at him like I was looking in a mirror. He was shook like a dog, his chains clinking. I wanted to let him go, get him up over that fence and into the woods. I wanted to go with him, leave it all myself, but I have Rachel and Eli ever burning in my head.

As I stared at him, stared by God at myself, he grabbed hold of me. My first reaction was to hit him, get him off me, shoot him, kill him, anything – he's a convict – but I heard him crying and realized he was just holding onto me. But he

*and his fear were choking me too. I couldn't breathe, like I
was going to black out, but he held tighter and tighter until
I was powerless.*

*I've felt so weak lately. I suddenly thought of Eli – and I
don't know why – but I kissed the boy and let him hold on to
me. I put my arms around him. I know now that Icemorelee
hit the boy because he thought he was attacking me, but I
just could not stand for that boy to be blackjacked. I cussed
Icemorelee. The boy was on the ground, holding his head.
Officer Nightcutt offered to take him to the Boot, but I waved
him and Icemorelee off. They were both angry and, I must
admit, with provocation. But I had had the situation in hand
from the beginning. I got the boy up and led him off. He
was still crying and, as we passed the bus, some of the men
laughed.*

*I ordered Childs to finish processing the transfers and I
escorted the boy to the Boot. When we got there, he didn't
want to go in. None of them do. It's like climbing in a coffin
full of shit and then having the lid screwed down.*

*I tried to be gentle with him, but my own revulsion at the
opened Boot door, the smell, the ghosts. It was all too much.
My father invented the damn place. I wanted the boy in there
and that door closed and I wanted him to mind me and I
wanted shed of it. I was tired. I haven't slept. I told him what
was what, gentle, no chain-gang to me. Again, this boy lifted
his face, my face, to me and spoke for the first time. He said
"Thank you." I could have taken just about anything else
out of him at the time. "Go on," I told him, still gentle, but I
wasn't far from cracking.*

*He rooted right there, panicked in the doorway. "Go
on," I said again, giving him a little push. But he stayed,
and then I reckon I threw him in there pretty good, because
I heard him hit and go down against one of those pointed
stobs Papa planted in there, then his whimpering again. I
locked the door and nearly ran off myself.*

Cal signed his name and let the pen fall from his hand.
Then he noticed a gold hatpin with a mother-of-pearl head
lying on the desk.

CHAPTER 66

The story about the boy who just disappeared became a parable Pitch never forgot. What he found in Alone was that he was suited to the dark, that he could take the torture and disappear impervious into his skull. Boss David's spankings and advances were nothing to him. He left his body and watched the big, fat man fumble over him in the locked office; then served him a vat of persimmon pudding and accepted his caresses. Pitch simply was not there. Sometimes, he'd be in the cellblock, in plain sight, and a guard would fail to count him. There were nights when the other boys, because they could not see him lying in his bunk, thought that he had finally turned rabbit. But, even gone, he watched them.

Cook School graduation at Osteen was a big event. The boys fixed a banquet: fried chicken, country ham and redeye gravy, country-fried steak, rice and gravy, chicken and dumplings, salt and pepper catfish and hushpuppies, candied sweet potatoes, stewed tomatoes, fried okra, green beans, succotash, corn, squash casserole, cornbread, cathead biscuits, pies and cakes and cookies. The chow-hall tables were decorated with table cloths and bud-vases of plastic jonquils. Prison big-shots from all over the state showed up to make speeches, pass out certificates and eat.

On the serving table, rising up over the platters of food, loomed an enormous ice sculpture likeness of Boss David that Pitch had carved. Everyone was astonished. They declared Pitch was a genius, what a future he had ahead of him. Boss David was thrilled with the sculpture. He, more than anyone, praised Pitch. Smiling until he sweated, squeezing Pitch's neck, he swore he had known all along the boy was something special.

Boss David was so taken with the sculpture that he ordered it stored in the walk-in freezer. He never wanted to part with it. But finally, after the yearly slaughter of the cows raised on the farm for beef, the sculpture had to be removed so the meat could be hung. Boss David had his likeness carried to his office and placed standing in a washtub. It weighed as much as him. He kept the air conditioner on full blast, but every day the tub had to be bailed of melted water.

As the sculpture grew smaller, so did Boss David. He spent whole days in the dining hall, eating foods and pastries he had Pitch prepare for him. He locked Pitch in his office with him, his ice twin overseeing his grunting and prodding. The more he ate, the more he fed off Pitch. The more buckets of melted ice hauled out of his office, the smaller he got. Smaller and smaller until one day in the dining hall, squeezing Pitch's neck as he finished off with soda crackers a quart of potted meat, he fell over dead.

CHAPTER 67

I spread spotted beans out on the big steel counter and pick out each bad one, each bit of gravel and dirt that made it into the picking. I make note of their configuration, count two hundred beans per convict, three hundred beans per guard, ten hundred for the captain, a few extra for God. Fifty thousand beans I dump into a boiling vat of brine big enough to cook a man, add six ham-hocks, spit in it and stir.

Boss David loved pinto beans. Eat five thousand himself, chopped onions, chow-chow, hoecakes the size of barn shingles slopped with fresh butter, whole pots of sweetened tea. Grunting and chewing with his mouth open and talking shit to me the whole time: "Pitch, you some boy, some badass boy, Pitch," the inside of his mouth like a cud, up and down, spewing, his hand on my neck until I was near paralyzed and him guiding me down, down, and shoveling it in. If he found a piece of gravel in his beans, he'd wear me out me with that crop and then have me hogtied and thrown in Alone.

I could tell you the story of Jesus and his love and it would be no different than the one I first told the shrink after those dogs chewed me up: My daddy saw his own daddy killed in front of him before I was born. My granddaddy was a little biddy man, a good man by all accounts, churchgoing and all; but if he tipped the jug, he turned devil.

After church, one Sunday lunch, granddaddy sunk into the jug, getting meaner and meaner, and for no reason reached across the table and slapped my mama, his son's wife, still to this day a gentle woman.

Everything stopped. My grandmother, a churchwoman if ever there was one, was cutting tomatoes with one of those old locus- handled knives and she just turned at the sink and stabbed granddaddy in the heart. Killed him on the spot. She didn't even know what she was doing. Law never did find against her. But to hear it told, it was bad – blood and everyone fixing to lose their minds, my mother with her *stinging cheek and daddy still rooted in his chair, that knife handle sticking out of his chest.*

I don't know if he held his daddy's death against my mama, or what she did to earn that slap in the first place, but Daddy picked up drinking, started hitting on Mama. He was okay when he was sober, but a devil like his own daddy otherwise. Beat me too. One day, early in the morning – he wasn't drunk, he wasn't anything – he came out to get in his truck and go to work. My mama was gone off to my old aunt's. I had found this ruined bicycle on someone's trash pile and I was working on it with a screwdriver and wrench, trying to fix it up for myself. Daddy asked me why I was using his tools without permission and who the hell did I think I was and then he worked himself up and punched me.

I knew right away my nose was broken. Crunched like an ear of corn snapped in half. Blood like a river. When I went down he kicked me like a dog, just kicked the fire out of me. Curled up with my hands around my head, I pleaded: "Daddy, please stop. You're killing me. Please, Daddy." Blood all in my mouth. Puking. I knew he'd kill me, but finally he stopped, then got in his truck and went to work. I couldn't move; I hurt all over. My nose and ribs were broken. One arm broken. I dragged myself two miles to my aunt's house. My mother swore she'd kill Daddy. My aunt swore she would if Mama didn't.

But it all blew over. Mama wouldn't even take me to a doctor because she didn't want anyone nosing around. So we went home. When daddy came home was as if nothing had happened. While I healed, he beat my mother until I was well enough to stand whipping again. But he never again beat me like that. One day I climbed a fence because I liked the taste of white peaches. How could a man do his own son like that? My daddy's pitchfork killed those dogs and fetched me three years at Osteen Farms. I never found out who snitched.

They say "Tell your story," the shrinks do, then shy from it like they would the devil. All those days and days and days in Alone, I told God my story and He didn't turn from it. He loved me for my story. I learned in there with God that

201

people hurt people when they are afraid of them, that it is not even, so much, hate; it could even be love, but it's mainly fear.

"Does it make sense," I asked God, "that my father loved my mother and that's why he beat her?"

"Yes," God said. "Fashion a likeness out of your enemies' fear and put it back on them. Feed it to them. They will devour it like a dog his own excrement."

I didn't do anything to Boss David he didn't want me to do. He supplied me with his own undoing. I made a statue of him with ice and, when it melted, he was dead. No one said Conjure Man then, but I knew from then on I had power over the other boys. At Osteen, I made the augur. It started as a joke: a mason jar of ditch water, a chicken thigh bone, dandelion greens and a dead dog's eye I cut out of a rotting carcass with a paring knife. I didn't name it augur. *Just laid it on my bunk one day. Their eyes, convict and guard alike, told me what it meant and, from then on, I was in the spell business.*

I left Osteen a gangster and went to work for my daddy running reefer out to the boonies. I was nothing but a delivery boy and the money was good. Daddy was the same bastard drunk and hit Mama whenever he was so-minded. I was too big for him to hit on, but still it got next to me when I was straight enough to notice what he was doing. "Mama," I'd say. "Get out. What's wrong with you? Leave him."

I stayed fucked up. First on reefer, then cocaine, then running Heroin up and down my arms. I'd drive a truckload of dope down to Columbia, meet an army man at Fort Jackson and get back in the car with eight thousand dollars cash. I bought a .44 Magnum pistol, blue steel, cold, mysterious, beautiful.

One night, I staggered into my aunt's house and saw mama all banged up, puffed lips, eyes punched and weepy. I went crazy, got in my car and floored it all the way to the front door, hanging wide. He was sitting, no shirt, fat belly and a tall Malt, in a big stuffed chair, watching TV.

I came right in on him and jammed that steel under

his eye and pulled the trigger over and over. Or at least I thought I did. I told him that if he ever laid a finger on my mama again, he was dead. I don't know how it was I didn't kill him. That had been my intention. He never said a word, just dropped the beer can.

I ran to the car, hit up and peeled out of there and didn't stop until the all-night Fast Fare parking lot at the corner of Mount Berry-Salvation Hill Road. Just past midnight. An old orange-headed, bearded, mumbling lady was working the counter, no one else there. I hauled out that .44 and put it on her and told her I wanted what was in the register. She just crumbled, sat back on a stool behind the counter and took a fit. I reached around, cracked the register and split with thirty-seven dollars in paper. Left the change. I had twelve hundred dollars in my wallet when I walked in.

I didn't get half a mile before a roadblock. A big yellow county cruiser had been sitting in plain sight just across the road in the Tastee Freeze lot, but I hadn't see him. The deputy watched the whole thing and radioed for backup. I didn't see the roadblock either until I was on them, shotguns braced over their car hoods, the deputy from the Tastee Freeze hemming me in from behind, blue lights unraveling into the night like, Praise God, the second coming: Jesus in a gunfight.

I reached for my piece. It weighed as much as a newborn baby, same blood density, as if inside it pulsed a life. But I was so wasted, I couldn't find it. I busted out of the car like a silent movie gangster, my empty hands machine-gunning the infidels with sooth. Pulsars of fire. "Rat-a-tat-tat," I whooped. And they in turn let go: the shotguns and revolvers, bullets whumping into my car, scattering the windshield across my face, over the blacktop, each tire suspiring as it died with a hissing whish.

I crouched and rolled and fought them with nothing but a child's apocalyptic finger until I took a round high in my stomach. Like a vexed mule had kicked me in the solar plexus. I sat down, leaning against the killed car, and still they shot, ceasing only when a gentle rain began to fall. Then silence.

203

The crickets and that eternal Piedmont summer heat. And the rain, the drops like off a hot skillet dancing back into the sky in curlicues of smoke. The lump of steel in me finally pulled me earthward, my face against the sweating asphalt. Rain splashed into my mouth. Smell of charged gunpowder. The click of their creeping toward me. The throaty banter of their radios. Then their shoes. Identical. Black. Shiny as snake eyes. Creaturely. More and more of the hunchbacked shoes until I was ringed, and still they came. To eat me alive as I lay there bleeding, Glory be at the crossroads.

So it came to pass that I did not die, and the judge dropped half a lifetime on me. I wound up at Coventry where I became a devil, an honest devil, I might add. Folks gravitate toward fear, especially the men in prison who carry keys. Would you be undone by the sight of a kewpie doll with your state nameplate on it? Could a gold hatpin through its groin cripple you? Did I have the power to blow up Sergeant Thrake's car, to give him nightmares in his own bed far away from this place? Yes? No? Yes? After that night with my gun in his face, my father never took a drink again. He began treating my mother with respect. Sent her flowers and took her to restaurants. Bastard. Dead now. And I miss him.

Along the way I sired Journey, my baby boy, with a woman I have totally forgotten. I was the father to him my father had never been with me. Journey lived with his mother, but whenever I was able, I went for him. On this particular day I ended up in a house on Howe Street, set down at the end of a little brick alley where one could cop and sell.

Scaggy whores ran wild and pimps circled the blocks in El Dorados. But I was down with all of it. Making those runs for my daddy twice a week. My britches bulged with jack. I drove up Howe in my ice-blue Buick Deuce and a Quarter, just checking things out, sailing, so flush; and with that beautiful boy of mine I was an ongoing entity in a paltry universe. Immortal. Ten minutes on Howe Street, I figured, put a little head on, maybe rum over ice or something sweet. A free man can act on temptation.

Shara was smoking a joint and ironing socks and the

204

rest sat around the kitchen table. J'Quail was tying off and fixing, and in the middle of the table was a bale of yellow fuzzy reefer that St. Thomas, one doubting mother fucker, was carding like wool and shucking off into quart baggies that Soledad held open for him. I sat down and took my turn on this righteous hookah my inventor brother St. Thomas had contrived. It looked like a fountain with big black rubber hoses spaying out of it and, on its top floor, a bowl filled with keef and opiated hash. I mean. Chaka Khan on the stereo: "Tell me something good. Tell me that you like it, yeah."

Journey toddled around – he had just started walking – stepping to the music, dancing, just digging it. I was happy. Everyone watched him and smiled, something very right happening at that moment. Quail nodding and kind of clapped his hands.

Soledad said about Journey, "Look, he's fucked up too," and we all laughed.

Shara had this high laugh like broken glass. Journey just looked at her and laughed and we all laughed some more.

"C'mere and gimme some sugar, little man," she said. Journey weaved off toward her, started to go right down, caught himself with his two hands on the floor, then staggered to Shara who gave him a big kiss.

Let's get married," she said to him. "I'm waiting on you because your daddy is so full of shit."

The baby plopped down on his bottom under the ironing board. Everyone laughed. I was feeling fine, high as Saturn. In a family way. None of that drugged Gangster mope.

"Girl, what you doing ironing socks? " I asked, and she let go another laugh, a picture window in a condemned house shattering.

"What you want to drink?" she asked.

"Southern Comfort on the rocks," I told her, and she sashayed over to the refrigerator and opened the freezer and took out an ice tray. I kept my eyes on her. I knew she knew I was watching. Why not Shara? I pondered.

I liked her kitchen. I liked the way she talked, the way her dresses plastered against her like wet leaves when she walked, and I have always had the craving for red women. I heard her kids playing in the backyard where she kept a garden. She had an old scar from her children's daddy under her right eye. She poured the Southern Comfort into the glass of ice and placed it before me, then handed me a joint. I sucked deep and held it, took a sip of my drink – tasted like a peach, like I knew Shara tasted – then I blew out the smoke in a gust that shrouded the room.

I have tried to imagine what my son was thinking when he pulled on the cord of the iron he sat beneath, that perhaps it was a beanstalk and he a giant killer locked in some fable where nothing bad could ever happen. When I picked him up, I could've been cradling in my arms my own dead soul.

As for the noble Mr. Gaddy, I don't know what moved me to tell him the story of my dead baby child, but when his wife became pregnant, I set my curse upon him. An eye for an eye, according to Christian and penitentiary doctrine. Sergeant Thrake smashed the augur. But I don't need an augur. A pot of beans will do.

CHAPTER 68

The cook-shack had no memory of being built, no memory of being new or uninhabited, merely a sudden consciousness of its sprouting on the landscape, its thingness. It was old, sick and blind. But it no longer needed eyes to see. It just *was* – in the omniscient manner of God being *is* – having grown into a most perfect nothing. Yet, unlike God, it had control over nothing that happened within its cruel, moldering walls, no feelings or sentiment whatsoever about cruelty.

Sweating day and night, the repository of convict shit and piss, spit and semen, the soured-over demonic wet dreams of imprisoned cooks, it had seen so much that its eyes had burnt out the way television tubes burn out, yet still it witnessed everything –this being its curse and, little by little, it ceased to know things in terms of good or evil. This became a blessing, another way of not caring. Amnesia.

Occasionally it sensed that it had had once a flesh and blood life – and glimpsed in routines of shaving, voiding and fornicating, even laughter and pornography, something familiar, recognize in an inmate, even a guard, something of itself. What irreparable sin it had committed to be the object of this sentence – the curse of a haunted house built with convict labor, its penance simply to witness for eternity the noisy hell of men, levied by what court and judge – had long been forgotten. It was hell itself, yet it liked to conceive of itself as a little church, squat, four-walled, four-square, impregnable, concrete belted in steel.

As it settled further into senescence and chronic pain, it exerted upon its captives the pressure of regret – for even the unremembered and they, in turn, crawled in its steely, brindle hair and toothless mouth and slept on its tongue and in its cortex – and it slowly went mad, like all the buildings of Coventry, each with its own story, some smaller, some larger than the cook-shack's.

Sometimes, at night, in the little hours of the new day, when the men were most like children in their unguarded baby talk and nightmare, it felt like it was on the verge of recovering its story. But if it strained too much, a seam in its walls opened, a stud split, the rusted pipes coughed and erupted, the jerry-rigged wiring fizzed and shorted. Catastrophe attended its every attempt at recollection.

It was sure it had imagined the men in it. If it could just have its blind eyes puttied, they would go away like apparitions. The plumbing dripped and the flies sucked at its abscessed skin. Its bowels went bad. Even TV no longer interested it.

In its madness, it singled out Pitch as fire – the cook-shack had seen him hover above his bunk like a spirit – because there was something about fire and conjuring stirred into the aggregate of its walls. Suicide and Arson. The cook-shack knew – the way cave-rock knows – that it had been a bad man.

It was the hour of the wolf, four o'clock in the morning or thereabouts, at the verge of night becoming day, or even the reverse as time in prison is spatial, not chronological. The exact moment when most people heave last breaths, lunge out of their mothers' wombs, when souls transmigrate, become metempsychotic, when curses take hold in the synchroflash of the beholder's eye.

The mewling of a restive convict, twisted up in grey blankets, nudged the cook-shack out of its swoon of forgetfulness and into the tangle of its blocked synapses. It had a tendency to panic when it found itself more than a mere exterior, and its reflex was to try and dredge up memory – which always resulted in disaster. Perhaps it was the TV which had been left on, no sound, its flat distorted black and white screen the only light in the black, barred and locked room. On it played a Mephistophelian cartoon devil with a tail, Van Dyke, and horns. Out of its pitchfork gouted fire, and more fire until the screen danced with it and the room began to fill.

CHAPTER 69

Even asleep, Pitch had a preternatural sense of whenness: he knew it was time to bail. In his bunk, at the last second of the wolfing hour, he attempted in his dream to trade places with Calvin Gaddy. To literally exchange bodies, the molecular transposition of flesh, so that when his eyes opened on the morning, he would be in bed beside Rachel and, between them, their baby boy.

And Sergeant Gaddy, in turn, would wake in the predawn stench of the cook-shack, stumble to a shit-jacket, don his whites and wait for the jangle of second shift keys so he could head for the kitchen and start the grits. It could be done. Pitch had read about it in *The Book of Ceremonial Magic*. He had conjure enough left to engineer this one last spell.

Back and forth through the candle flame he passed the corn-shuck doll of Sergeant Gaddy. Back and forth in his dream of gibberish in the mouth of the cook-shack – which itself was seized in its own memory of fire: cement glue oozing out of its tube, the tinny click of the Zippo flicking open and the ancient smell of flint as the flywheel chafed it, the face of that sweet capon boy he was in love with lifting up in immolation like a bouquet of yellow roses.

Pitch whimpered, and broke through his caul into Cal's omnipresent dream of a wall, thudding up course by course around him. In his sleep, Pitch smiled and reached to snatch Sergeant Gaddy out of his wife's arms, then take his place beside her, but he could not undo her grip. It was Rachel all along he had underestimated. All he could manage was to kiss the mouth of Sergeant Gaddy before the recollective fire of the cook-shack ruptured like an aneurism and spilled over the men.

CHAPTER 70

Something bleating, gargling. A little clapper pinging like a time-clock. Heart hammering, Cal broke out of the dream and sat up, sweating, breathing hard. He ran the back of his palm across his mouth, once, twice. Rancid. Next to him, Rachel lay asleep with her white gown open, Eli nursing solemnly, silent, his dark thatch of hair glistening in the first light leaking into the trailer.

What? he thought. *What? What?*

That's how long it took. The space of three *whats* for Cal to place the bleat outside himself. At first he was relieved to realize it was just the phone that had woke him, but the red, illuminated face of the bedside clock wore numbers that meant trouble. Then he remembered the dream – Pitch breaking into the trailer – tasted it again, and raced to answer the telephone.

On the line was Shoble, an old, thirty-year man at Coventrywho had been working third-shift since Cal was a little boy.

"Better get down here, Sergeant Gaddy."

"What's up?"

"Something in the cook-shack."

"What do you mean, 'something in the cookshack'?"

"I don't know. Singing."

"Singing?"

"That's what it sounds like. Or crying, one. Like a baby."

"You want me to come down there on my day off because someone is singing in the cook-shack?"

"I believe there's more to it than that."

"Shoble, just go in there and see what's what."

"We can't."

"What are you talking about, 'you can't'? I'm telling you to get in there right now and find out what's going on."

"There's no key, and it smells like something's burning."

"No key," Cal said, more to himself than Shoble. Then:

"You beat that goddam door down if you have to, call the fire department immediately, then get on the phone to the Captain. I'm on my way."

Rachel stood behind him, holding the baby, swaying and patting his back.

"What is it, Calvin?"

"That idiot Shoble says something's burning in the cook-shack and they don't have a key. No key. Jesus Christ. I have to go."

He didn't even bother with his uniform, hurriedly kissed Rachel and Eli and raced out the door.

It had not come light yet, but Cal made out the silhouette of his father on a stepladder, crowning the wall with another course of stones. The nearly finished, invisible tract houses sulked in the field beyond. Deer and geese, and most of the birds, had gone away. Rats had invaded the Gaddy property. The exterminator's pellet trays sat in corners of the outbuildings and the house's crawl space. Soon the families would come.

Cal thought of stopping and having counsel with his father. He was unsure of what he'd walk into once he got to the camp, or how he would handle it. The old man had the pure instinct to squelch a riot, turn a tide of murderous convicts in their tracks. It was a gift. Like a man has a gift for drawing pictures or running swiftly. He wished he could load Mac in the truck and have him there to direct him. He turned into the road and sped toward Coventry.

CHAPTER 71

Once Rachel and the baby came home, everything had about it the dreamy, dozy silence a newborn engenders. Whispering, they muffled the phones in towels and walked on tiptoe. Because he was premature, the baby had to eat every three hours. Cal and Rachel slept in alternate three hour shifts, staggering in to relieve the other, handing the oblivious child back and forth by candlelight, smiling, passing benediction over one another as the days clicked by.

Eli fit like a football in the space between Cal's palm and the crook of his elbow. There was a photograph of him when he was but three days old: Cal holding him in one hand and in the other a black state boot well bigger than the tiny infant. So tiny that Cal clutched him two-handed, close to his chest lest he drop him. He could feel in his son the thrum of narration, an entirely new story being told. Not in baby talk. Not in talk at all. Something before language, what his mother would have called *spirit talk*. Soul talk.

So powerful was the pull of the baby on him, he forgot for the moment about Coventry out there cooking in the Saint Joan's County heat. He loved Eli, but he feared him too, his little coughs and spasms, the milk he would spit back up, the aspiration so imperceptible that Cal often held a mirror to his mouth to make sure he still breathed. At times, he fell asleep with Eli in his arms and came to in a blind panic, so fearful the baby had stopped breathing that he deliberately woke him. He felt he could never leave the trailer, that Eli had to be guarded from every danger forever. How could he keep this child alive?

Rachel handled Eli with expert ease, bathing and changing him, tending to the black stub of the cord, the red, raw bud of his newly circumcised penis, unbuttoning the top three buttons of her gown, already wet at the bodice from bursting milk, guiding his little mouth to her swollen, painful breasts. Each day. One day more. Now on the other side of the womb.

MacGregor Gaddy took a break every day from his wall to shamble down to see his grandson – Queen Anne's lace and sprigs of goldenrod in his hand, tomatoes and cantaloupes from the garden. He came mumbling, his prison browns plastered to his body with sweat. He loved the heat. At one hundred degrees, he still built a fire each night, sweating out his devils. He about had them bested, he told Cal, his wall near done.

Mac doted on Eli, sitting like a warder at his bassinet, humming chain-gang work songs as he slept. When Rachel nursed him, Mac averted his eyes or left the room. After, he'd take the baby from her and walk him about the trailer, whispering in the baby's ear. It was Elizabeth this and Elizabeth that.

"I wish your mama could see this boy," he'd say to Cal. "Elizabeth would pure delight in this child."

"Elizabeth," Mac would whisper, starting up from his nap beside the bassinet, having sung himself to sleep. "Elizabeth."

He still used his wife's name interchangeably with Rachel's.

"He's crazy," Cal contended. "He makes me nervous."

"He so loves the baby, Calvin."

"This is a precious boy," the old man would say.

Calvin had never heard his father say the word, *precious*, but there he'd be at the door with a scraggly bouquet, two, three times a day.

"You all are my family," Mac reminded them, Cal anxious that they were marshaling, all of them, for one last stand against devils.

"Yes, we are, Papa," Rachel assured him, she and Mac holding hands, the baby asleep under the trestle their linked arms made above his bassinet. The old man had even gone so far as to have a flower shop in the county seat plant in front of the trailer a giant blue stork that dangled a sign from its bill proclaiming, *It's a boy.*

"He's crazy, Rachel," Cal said. "I know for sure now."

"He's just being sweet, Calvin. Can't you let up on him? Can't you be happy that he's happy?"

But Cal worried that he would never be able to protect the child and, in his confusion, he offered his father a bottle. They sat and drank, matching fiery shots. Rachel, this Elizabeth, gushing hot milk, lay with Eli outside in the hammock tied between two hemlocks.

Sometimes she said to Cal, after the old man had kissed the baby goodbye and slumped back to his wall, "Maybe, he's just being sorry for everything."

Sorry is a fine word, thought Cal, watching the baby suckle. Sorry was how he felt. He missed his own mother. Sorry. How he ended up at Coventry.

CHAPTER 72

The baby had no language. He clung to the memory of the fluid silence and solitude of the amnion where he had first begun to hear the whispers of the outside world. Little by little he recognized his mother's and father's voices. Hers, one of gentleness and measure. His father's – childlike, of the abyss. Then his grandfather's – rocky and sorrowful, but without regret or mercy. Occasionally, Eli caught the strains of his grandmother Elizabeth's smoky voice, closer to song as it penetrated his serous fortress.

Being born was like a jailbreak; he was hesitant, but really had no choice. The world of light and racket would not have been his first choice. He knew he liked songbirds, the voiceful scent of his mother, the same without as within, and he knew he was loved. Knew these things without language. Words were like stones, sentences like concertina that pent people up in prisons.

His thoughts were *thisness* and *immediacy, anonymity*. It was only on the morning when he looked into the pale blue pools of his mother's eyes and saw himself that it occurred to him that he was separate from her. Even this did not alarm him. Not in this world where four ton pieces of steel rolled over the earth with men inside them thinking of murder, where a black greasy stick could blow a hole in a man, where blessed milk flowed fountain-like from his mother, where one box sang and another bigger box that his grandfather sat in front of night after night locked people down inside itself like in a cellblock. He learned immediately never to be surprised. Not if the furniture walked. Nor his grandfather spat toads from his grizzled mouth. What could be more surprising than the fact that people lived inside one another?

He shifted in the bassinet, stretched out of his reflexive fetal coil and yelped. His grandfather hurried to him and lifted him, held him to his chest and hummed. Against Mac Gaddy, the baby felt the rumbling, heard the trapped, querulous voices beneath the grill of old ribs.

CHAPTER 73

The earliest timbers of Coventry Prison had been sunk by Kilpatrick's Yankee marauders when they swept through Saint Joan's County with orders from Sherman to torch everything. Having rounded up a few hundred starving, routed, Confederate soldiers, they built a prison on a rise that dipped to a swamp out of which rose jagged walls of granite. Nearly as many Union soldiers, tending the prison and bivouacked around it, died at Coventry as Confederate inmates; and sometime in the summer of 1864, Kilpatrick burned the place down, corpses and all, throwing the ones still living, who had scratched their ways out, into the swamp where a purported school of devilfish devoured them.

Before the Civil War there were no state penitentiaries in North Carolina. The citizens could have had them, but they voted them down. Some territories had jails, but not many. Justice was meted out swiftly and with great formality: the whipping post, pillory and branding iron. There were also a number of homemade punishments that various counties employed: dismemberment, castration, scalping. You could pour boiling tallow into an offender's ears, stuff his nose with camphor, punch out his teeth with a chisel, wreath him naked with poison ivy and tie him to a tree. You could kill him if you were so-minded. Thirty-two offenses called for execution; methods varied from hanging to sewing up an offender's mouth with water moccasin eggs inside it.

After the war, crime flourished. It could be argued that a war that ends up slaughtering over a half million citizens of the same country to no obvious end is a fitting and logical prelude to a crime spree. But this, too, like every record retained and not retained about Coventry, could be apocryphal. At any rate, the good folks of the commonwealth decided they needed a more civilized and efficient means of controlling criminals and so the state prison was instituted. Out of this well-meant initiative designed to "reclaim lives" metastasized county chain-gangs, one of which was located outside the incorporated town limits of Coventry.

Coventry's first prisoners were housed in two makeshift, movable shacks on wheels, similar to railroad cars, though not so large. The roof and floor were constructed of wood, and the sides and front and back were vertical steel bars, floor to ceiling. They were simply called cages because of their resemblance to the cages of wild animals that rolled into towns with the circus.

In extreme weather, tarps were lowered over the bars for protection, leaving the prisoners in utter blackness. Each cage was equipped with a small tin woodstove, a kerosene lantern, water trough and dipper, and ten triple-decker bunks jammed together along the walls, with maybe a foot and a half walkway down the center. Two tiny holes, no bigger than a man's fist, were cut into the floor for the men to void into the three foot crawl space beneath – which was also where the cage was entered and exited through a padlocked, steel slab door hewn into the floorboards.

The guards never went into the cages. Never. If a man were sick or refused to rouse for the dawn work detail, they pelted him through the cage bars with gravel or stabbed him with long, sharpened sticks. Even if a man died, the other prisoners had to drag him out.

The cages were trucked from Coventry out to work-sites by dray horses and left there with a complement of guards to work the convicts until the job was done. Chow was brought to the site first thing in the morning in three-tiered pails called bean-cans – a tier for each meal of the day – because lunch and supper were always beans, frequently wormy and sometimes soured from being left out in the hot.

Sundays, their only days off, whether they were out in the county or parked back at Coventry, the men were confined to their cages. With thirty of them to a cage, they could not do anything but hunker in their bunks where there was not even room to sit. They wore horizontally striped, black and white trousers and blouses, and whatever hat, frequently made of magnolia leaves, they could rig. A chain circled the waist of each man and fastened to a steel cuff at his ankle. They worked buckled together in complements of five. At lights out, dusk, when the tarp was lowered over the cages, they were chained to their bunks.

Fire was a constant hazard. The chimney pipe poking out of the wooden ceiling eventually rusted, then pocked. Sparks tended to leak out and lay on the roof. A fouled wick might ignite the kerosene reservoir. A cadged cigarette butt. A convict out of his head. Spontaneous combustion. Lightning. The cages had ways of taking fire and, if they did, no one ever made it out alive.

As more and more men were assigned to Coventry, the state appropriated money to build a permanent prison on the site of Kilpatrick's death camp and hired an architect named Franklin McDowell. He had designed the Saint Joan's County Courthouse in Dawson, on the very ground upon which Major General Stoneman had camped during his famous raid: a huge three-storied antebellum monument with Ionian columns, and loggias on its front and rear – the entire monstrosity whitewashed so ostentatiously that it spiked out of the center of the county seat like a monolithic gibbet.

On a grey carven plinth – next to the flagpole and forget-me-not planters – its lone centinel, the ubiquitous granite confederate infantryman at parade rest, his musket well taller than he, arched his back and pushed out his tunic buttons. At the building's crest, dead center, rose a glassed cupola like a whale eye from which one could see the entire county. Where Franklin McDowell hanged himself, without explanation, after returning from World War I, but not before honoring his contract to build the prison –

with native quarry stone and convict labor just outside the almost nonexistent town of Coventry – which became known itself as Coventry.

The prison's original cornerstones were still visible – the jagged, charred remnants of those heart-pine timbers staking out the four corners of the civil war camp, still smoldering went the story, as if the penitentiary had sunk, not burned, and convict soldiers were still doing subterranean time down there. There were rumors of a tunnel. Again, more apocryphal. But what is true is that they built one prison atop the other. On the last Sunday in June, 1911, Coventry Prison was dedicated.

Nobody knew when the cook-shack was constructed, but it had been there a long while by the time Mac Gaddy came to Coventry as a green road man, married not even a year, during the Depression. Like the rest of the camp, it had been built with convict labor, not with quarry rock, but rather by pouring concrete into a wooden skeleton, then roughing it in with another layer of concrete.

Its windows were barred. There was only one entrance and exit, double-doored. A screen-door, then a wooden door – a house-door, really – that could be locked and unlocked from the inside and outside with a regular key, but was also padlocked on the outside at night. The cooks came and went at odd hours, so they were never locked down fast except for count and shakedowns. But between nine at night, when the last of the baking was completed for the next day, and four in the morning, when the breakfast shift was rousted out, the building was padlocked.

The night of the fire in the cook-shack, a man named Elton Shoble had the watch. Friend was on duty and so was Childs. Ernestine was in the tower. Shoble preferred working third shift, ten p.m. till six in the morning, because nothing much ever happened. Between those hours, the cookshack and both wings of the dormitory were locked down; and, for the most part, the men slept. If there was a fuss, short of bloodshed, Shoble refused to enter the cell-block. There were things at night he simply chose not to see nor hear. He had no imagination whatsoever, so if it was not spelled out to him in bold letters, he figured everything was alright until morning. Third shift, there was no one to tell you what to do. He pulled his time drinking coffee, sitting in the Sergeant's office, listening to the radio and making his rounds on the hour.

He had never successfully adjusted to the change from his old feudal chain-gang days to more modern times where convicts had to be treated a certain way, more humanely – at least on the surface. Short and big-headed, teeth brown from snuff juice, a little trickle of it slapping out of his mouth-corner, tugging his mouth down into a grimace, he wore the state uniform now instead of the jeans, cowboy hat and boots and the colt he had sported on his hip in the old days.

Barely literate, he tended the paperwork best he could, watched the Captain baby the population, and he conformed, again as best he was able, because he had never really cared enough not to. This was his job. He had feelings about it – mainly that convicts were a kind of curse, period – but nothing worth dying over or, for that matter, being uncomfortable on account of. Until his retirement, which could be any day he said – he already had thirty years in – he aimed to do his time with a minimum of upset. He was not about to let things get to him like Thrake.

Shoble was making a round when he heard the singing coming from the cook-shack. Not exactly singing, but he didn't know what else to call it. It sounded like an old bluesy, prison work song. That high, whistling *please* gathering force. Sheer desire. Shoble stood out in the yard and listened. He couldn't quite peg it for anything in particular.

Let them sing, he said to himself. *I ain't going in there.*

Then he smelled smoke. He thought first to fetch someone and find out what to do, but he remembered he was in charge, that it was his call. He stood there another moment listening to the singing, its pitch heightening moment to moment like a kettle throttling on a burner.

That ain't no fire, he thought. *Son-of-a-bitches are trying to put one over on me. All I got to do is open that door and out they'll come.*

He was a custody man, first and last. Thirty years, no convict ever got gone on his watch. Smoke seeped out around the doorjamb. Shoble wore a little wreath of it on his head. You could smell it good now. He looked up in the tower: Ernestine slumped over, holding that shotgun, like she was asleep. Looked like smoke twirling in the perimeter lights. Probably fog. This close to daylight. He put his hand

220

on the old wooden door. It was cool. The singing like a choir now, revving up to shake the church. *Please*, it called. *Help.* Sweetly. Powerfully. Shoble could have listened to it forever. He called Childs over from the front gate.

"That's smoke," Childs said.

"I know that," shot Shoble. "Where's Friend?"

"I ain't seen him since we clocked in. What's that noise?"

"What do you reckon it is?"

"It sounds like singing, but I don't know. What should we do?"

"I ain't opening this door. That's for sure," declared Shoble. "You hunt up Friend and get back here."

Shoble stood on Coventry yard, silent except for that nearly imperceptible song sneaking out of the building with the foul-smelling smoke. Like hair burning. The lightening sky was rain grey, still night, but starting to pencil in the camp. The live oak in its middle, where the picnic tables sat, the tower, the concertina saw-toothing into the striving morning, a mop and slop bucket next to the door Shoble leaned against.

There would be no sun, just that dead light all day, and no rain either, though Saint Joan's County was locked again in its usual solstice drought. Shoble felt that unlight carving him out of the yard, and knew this time he'd have to acknowledge that something was bad wrong. That singing. Was it singing? Crying? It was a baby. That is what the hell it was. There was a baby in there. Shoble whipped out his keys and shoved one into the padlock, but it wouldn't turn. He tried another and another, but none of them would undo the lock. Maybe he didn't have the right key.

Childs jogged up.

"Where's Friend?" Shoble asked.

"I still can't find him."

"Goddam. Well, open this door. My key don't work."

Childs' keys wouldn't turn in the lock either.

"I'm going to call Gaddy," Shoble said. "You keep looking for Friend."

CHAPTER 74

A long with the oncoming sirens, Cal heard the boom of Shoble's axe as he raced across the yard, sniffing the smoky air, the sky smoke-colored, the morning a dirty shroud over Coventry. He heard the singing too, the not-exactly-singing. Weeping, maybe. A chorus of angry infant orphans louder the longer you listened, till it was a flat unbroken keen which might have been the sound of the asthmatic fire snorting up the oxygen when the door fell in and the barred windows blew. Taking it way down into its lungs and holding it like a dope hit, then expelling it in a roaring, screaming huff that knocked Cal and Shoble off their feet.

Thick, stinking smoke rolled out, blinding and choking them. Creosote smelling, threatening to push out their eyeballs. Coughing, gasping for air, they leapt up and ran from the smoke's reach. It billowed out and up, completely enveloping the cook-shack. What had never been singing was now plain: flame sucking oxygen through a drinking straw, lungs expanding exponentially as fumes from the polyurethane mattresses blew them up like poison balloons, then popped them in mid-word: *Help, please –*

over and over – that old chain-gang refrain. Call it singing. *Mercy* is what it sounds like when you're asphyxiating and on fire in a lockbox – what comes out of you when you try to say what it is.

The cook-shack was a cauldron bubbling smoke and screams. Cal couldn't make out anything inside, except the glow of flame crawling along the back wall. Brotherton ran out of the kitchen with two fire extinguishers and handed one to Cal.

"Shoble, you get down to the cellblock with Childs and keep those men calm, and keep them locked down," shouted Cal. "Ernestine," he yelled up to the tower where Ernestine now rocked, wild-eyed, fingering her shotgun. "Get on the phone and get everyone in here." "Where in goddam hell is

222

the Captain?" he screamed.

Cal and Brotherton made pass after pass at the cook-shack entry, gunning in the foam, then retreating. Smoke filled the entire yard, hung in the trees and dipped into the quarry, pouring out of the cook-shack along with the men's howls – no matter how much foam they launched into it, until the canisters were spent and Childs ran more up from the cellblock, and Ernestine connected the garden hose to the canteen's spigot and pointed a thin jet through the door.

Finally, the fire department arrived in volunteer trickles from all over the county. Mostly boys driving pickups and El Caminos, red hazards plugged into cigarette lighters whirling on their dashes. Then the antique pumper from Dawson with turnout gear and air packs for only three men – and the county ambulance with two EMTs.

Brotherton had collapsed, and sat in the doorway of the canteen, his face blackened, his breath coming in hoarse fits. Cal went to one knee, and keeled over himself as the pumper's hose angled over the concertina a veil of silver water.

The three outfitted firefighters manned another big hose they had connected to the yard hydrant and charged the cook-shack. The singing had ceased. Cal picked himself up and staggered out of the smoke. An EMT bent over Brotherton, and strapped an oxygen mask to his face.

Another ambulance arrived, then another fire truck. Smoke continued to billow out of the blackened mouth of the cook-shack. You couldn't see the firefighters, then one came stumbling out of the cloud, fell on his hands and knees, and was helped off by a couple of boys in T-shirts and baseball caps that had *Saint Joan's County VFD* printed on them. Water slopped over the doorsill. Black and oily, it carried with it bits of brown cloth and flesh annealed to flesh, a little green testament, a roll of toilet paper, teeth, pencils, a chess rook.

The taut, rock-hard fire hose, disappeared into the interior of the cook-shack, pulsed like a python digesting live prey. The smoke began to abate, turn from black to grey. White wisps of it stuck like tissue in the concertina. The firefighters pounded the cook-shack with water for another few minutes. The two firefighters still standing stole into the building. Cal edged as close as he could, made out only the black-caped backs of the two firefighters and the smoke, now like fog, hanging about them.

Father Tuesday had arrived and stood next to Cal. He carried a zippered black pouch and wore around his neck a crucifix. The Captain was there too. And Blish. They knelt over Brotherton, who was beginning to come around. A trail of ambulances, sirens wailing, skidded into the parking lot.

The firefighters, like they had weathered a sentence in Purgatory, emerged from the cook-shack and stood silently in front of everyone.

"Tell them to turn off the sirens," said one as he tore off his headgear. "No hurry. Those boys are gone."

Behind the ambulances veering into the parking lot came other cars, some of the inmates' families who had picked up the news on their scanners. And the Press.

CHAPTER 75

The black and white photograph on the front page of *The St. Joan's County Record* was the same one smeared across the front page of *The Charlotte Observer*: a door thrown wide, then a telescoping view of the devastated innards of the cook-shack at Coventry Prison. Not a thing was recognizable. No bodies. Just the sooty waterlogged tangle of what had not burned nor melted. All of it, the effects of thirteen men, reduced to several dozen wheelbarrows of trash heaved into a dumpster.

The building itself was unharmed, testimony to its original craft. But, in the days following the fire, a story would surface, then eventually be remanded to the mere anecdotal, then be denied and forgotten: On the back wall of the cook-shack, the one facing the door, were inexplicably traced shadowgraphs, like those left behind by the vaporized Japanese at Hiroshima, of convicts pulling their last seconds of time. Like praise – hands uplifted at odd angles like the wings of careening angels.

One could almost hear the singing. On one outline in particular was what could have been a nimbus or horns, it was hard to say, but in all likelihood were dreadlocks, like the ones Pitch favored, standing out in relief against the wall. This phenomenon was visible in the newspaper photo, but barely, and so ambiguous in the grainy newsprint that it could have been anything.

When the firefighters had announced that everyone was dead, Father Tuesday had rushed into the cook-shack, still wreathed in smoke, yet beginning to dissipate. Cal clambered in behind him, and found the priest on his knees in the muck, weeping in front of the wall of picture negatives. On either side of him, the men who had not been incinerated, smoldered, some mere ash in their melted bunks, the incense of their bodies strong as wild meat. Cal fell to his knees beside the priest, and tried to remember the prayers his mother had taught him, but simply couldn't. Then they were overcome and had to crawl out.

CHAPTER 76

The newspapers began their stories by describing the inconsolable convict families gathered in the emergency room at St. Joan's County Hospital, receiving the news that their husbands, sons, brothers, fathers and, in two cases, grandfathers had perished in the fire, the cause of which still remained unknown. It was suspicioned, however, that all thirteen men, one of whom was a guard at Coventry, named Vernon Friend, had died not from the fire itself, but from breathing in deadly fumes from the polyurethane foam with which their mattresses were stuffed – even though the prison system was required under state law to supply flame-proof mattresses.

The quoted families were indignant and mistrustful. They felt authorities were holding back information. They wanted to know why those men had not been let out of the burning cook-shack. They wanted answers. Local clergy at the scene urged prayer.

An investigation was immediately launched. Though problems with the ancient wiring had not been ruled out, prison officials were sure that it had not been "spontaneous combustion." It was theorized that the fire was set by inmates, perhaps inadvertently. Although they were forbidden to smoke in bed, many of them did nonetheless.

Coventry Prison's Captain requested a State Bureau of Investigation arson unit visit the scene. He was advised by a state attorney to refuse to answer questions posed to him by the Press. Prison officials in Raleigh expressed remorse and assured victims' families that they would get to the bottom of things, and announced plans to completely rebuild the cook-shack with strict adherence to the latest safety features. What's more, the entire unit at Coventry would be renovated according to the same specifications.

There were no extant records that Coventry had had the mandatory fire inspection required by the state prison system or even by the county Fire Marshall. Not only that, the cook-shack had not been equipped with smoke detectors or fire alarms, and had no fire extinguishers. An unidentified spokesperson for the Department of Correction had responded to this by saying, "There's not a damn thing you can do about fires and convicts. It's the nature of the beast."

There was also the controversy surrounding the padlock on the cook-shack door that officers on duty the night of the fire were unable to open, either because the lock itself was faulty or the officers literally did not have the appropriate key. Not the first instance of problems with "key control" at Coventry. The door had to be eventually beaten in with an axe, but there remained the question of why officers, when they realized they could not open the door, did not act with more dispatch.

A few of the victims' families were preparing lawsuits. The NAACP had sent a representative to St. Joan's County. The bodies had been shipped to Chapel Hill for autopsies, and samples of the debris sent to the SBI lab in Raleigh. Although the state was being petitioned by the families, as well as clergy and local politicians, to pay funeral expenses for the victims, its attorneys pointed out that under law it was not obliged to bear such expenses unless found liable in the prisoners' deaths.

A sidebar featured the names of the twelve deceased inmates, one of whom was Snoo, whose given name was Clarence Hightower. There was a high school picture of him in football pads and uniform. He looked young and completely innocent. His mother said he was a good boy, and she didn't know how she would go on from here. She said there was nothing for it now, but the Lord.

There were similar photographs and remembrances from the widows and mothers, all of whom remembered the dead convicts as boys and men who had mysteriously once owned lives apart from Coventry Prison.

The name Tarl Benefit, however, was not listed among the dead. The newspaper slapped Pitch's picture to the same page, alongside his dead brother cooks – smiling and rather beautiful, his hair snapped up in rows of lavishly beaded braids, movie star teeth, arms folded across the powerful chest. Neither among the dead nor living. *At large and very dangerous.* They synopsized his life as a criminal: state-raised, a rap sheet as long as Independence Boulevard.

In an adjacent sidebar was a short article and a photograph of Friend under the heading: *Officer Gives Life Trying to Save Inmates.* Vernon Friend was a St. Joan's County native who had graduated from St. Joan's County High where he had played baseball. He had never married, and had lived with his mother. A Coventry employee for eleven years, he had been, according to the Captain, "a dependable and steady presence on the yard." Unhesitatingly, Officer Friend had run into the lethal cook-shack once the door had been beaten down, and had perished with the men he had been trying to save.

CHAPTER 77

After reading about Friend, Cal folded the newspaper, tossed it to the foot of the bed, and stared at the ceiling. His face was scorched pink, his eyebrows and eyelashes seared off. His hands and forearms were the same color and hairless too. Pain was not what he felt, though it would have been a relief, something tangible to focus on as he sorted out what had actually happened and, more importantly, what the next course of action should be. Beside him, Rachel lay napping, while Eli slept in his bassinet.

That Friend was being held up as a hero suited Cal perfectly. In some measure, he felt true sorrow that Friend had died, but Friend had become a terrific liability, a backstabbing, lying contrabander who at any moment could have dragged Cal into his play with Pitch. Then what? But Friend had been anything but a hero. He had not rushed into the deathtrap like the papers reported. Friend would have been the last person to do that. Yes, he was on duty that night, but nobody had known where he was until he was carried out of the cook-shack. He had been locked in there with the rest of them. What had Friend been doing in there in the first place? Who locked him in, and how did the fire start?

The answer seemed obvious to Cal. On both counts. It had to have been Pitch, who had not shown up among the dead, or anywhere in Coventry. Officially listed as *escaped*, Pitch had simply disappeared, like the day Cal and Thrake had searched the countryside for him. But how? And how did he get the drop on Friend? How did he get his hands on the lock? Cal had seen enough to believe that Pitch really was a conjure man. Let him have his freedom, he thought. Just so he stays away, but already he felt haunted by him. Haunted by what he saw as those men were brought out, stretcher by stretcher – smoking slabs of blackened rags, sometimes nothing but a bone, or an effect, anointed by Father Tuesday, still weeping, gagging out his benediction as he signed them

229

with chrism before they were loaded into the ambulances and spirited off. The last out of the building had been Friend, his face near intact, surprised and blackened, but the rest of him charred and his prison badge melted to his exposed breastbone.

He would go along with Friend as hero. He had no choice, and so far no one else had stepped up to say anything different. Not Shoble nor Childs who had been the only others there on yard duty that night. Perhaps they too were mystified or too indifferent to question anything. They just wanted it all to die down since their judgement and behavior would come into question during the investigation.

With Friend and Pitch, and Thrake, for that matter, all gone, Cal could never be implicated in any type of wrongdoing. And just what had he done? Bought a little reefer off a fellow guard. A handful of joints here and there. A stupid, stupid thing to do for a duty man. He knew that now, and he should have known it then. But. *Go ahead and crucify me for that*, he thought. He had had no idea that Friend and Pitch were in cahoots. Cal was innocent. But who would ever believe him? No. He would let the dead bury the dead on this one, and if ever he did see Pitch again, he would take MacGregor Gaddy's advice and put him out of his misery, no different than driving a stake through the heart of the devil. He'd forge ahead and make the best of things. He had Rachel and the baby to think of.

The rest he'd wipe out of his head. And if he could not scour it out, let it live there in its own compound, doing life to die. But then the shadowy mural of the dead men on the cook-shack wall that only he and Father Tuesday had seen stood out in relief on the walls of his brain. Those men in that insane death dance, the one in the middle, Pitch, the one with the horns – dancing off to martyred glory. Cal told himself he had not done anything wrong. He said it again and again. He bolted up, embraced and pounded himself, insisting, "I did not do anything wrong." Then: "Did I? Jesus. Did I?"

Rachel woke and pulled him back down to her. "Hush, Calvin. You were dreaming. It was just a bad dream. Hush.

It's alright." The baby wailed from his bassinet.

He didn't tell Rachel that he hadn't been dreaming. He didn't tell her any of it. He kissed her forehead, then got up and brought the baby to her. With devils, this was how it began. He was wide awake. Time to go to work, but first he had to see his father.

CHAPTER 78

The wall was maybe two days from finished. Mac Gaddy was mixing with a hoe a batch of mortar in a wheelbarrow when Cal drove up on his way to Coventry. The old man didn't look up. Rachel believed he was losing his hearing.

"Papa," Calvin barked, when he was still a distance away. He had never liked to come up suddenly on his father.

Mac lifted his head from the mortar, and shaded his eyes. Cal came out of the August sun, now about two feet above the horizon and already warm.

"Calvin" was all he said, then leaned on the hoe until Cal got to him.

He had never before wanted so much to be near his father. It was all he could do not to throw himself into his arms. "Papa," he said again.

Mac looked him a long time. Calvin in his state uniform. Mac Gaddy's son.

"You have got you some troubles," the old man pronounced.

"Yes, troubles."

They took seats on the ground and watched the sun swell. Cal had contemplated baring it all to Father Tuesday. He liked and trusted the priest, and Lord knew the priest had heard everything, but he didn't want to get him involved. What he wanted was absolution. He had never thought of his father as his confessor, but there was no one else to turn to. No one else who would understand, or have quite the ruthless eye and judgement to settle things.

Cal started slowly, purposely leaving out that he had never wanted to set foot on Coventry yard. Nor did he mention the whore the night of Zedda Pate's execution, or how he missed his mother or the thrill and terror of tracking convicts with his father and Frank. For talk, these things were gone. Absorbed by him. Things that, as a man, as a father himself, he could no longer talk about. He and his father had a pact, an unwritten, unspoken blood pact, that these things were in the grave. Not that they might not beat at the walls of the coffin. But that they were interred. And Cal did not mention love or its absence. He stuck to what he thought might be the story of what had truly happened, what he had not told his father when he first mentioned Pitch's conjuring, what he had been too ashamed to say.

But now he confessed. How he had become friendly with Pitch, and had listened and felt badly when Pitch told him about his dead little boy, how he had accepted marijuana, contraband, on the yard from another guard, Friend. That Pitch and Friend had been in business together. And now that guard, Friend, was dead, burned up in the fire, and Pitch was vanished. Like a ghost. And that picture the fire had left in the cook-shack, and all that had happened to Thrake.

The father listened, the white wispy hair and whiskers launched about his head turning gossamer as the sun came on, his eyes creasing to slits.

"Explanations I don't have, Calvin. What you done, you done, and much of it has been pure foolish and you know better. Or should. Consorting with a convict. Consorting with another guard for that matter. It's putting the knot around your own neck. But let's be quit of that and figure dead men tell no tales, and hope this witch don't show again."

Calvin had left out that he was afraid. "I don't want to lie, Papa. What if he does show back up? They're out looking for him now. He's an escape."

"Then don't lie. What happened with you and this dead man, Friend, is settled, and the settling was not your doing. Fire is natural to convicts. This will blow over. There'll be an investigation and there'll be a passel of new rules, and then little by little it'll be back to the guards and convicts. Period. Between you and this witch is something else. It's your word against his. And you got to remember – I have told you this again and again – you are right because you carry the keys, and he is wrong because he wears the stripes. You go messing with the order of that in jail and you might as well peel off your britches and bend over. Goddam, Calvin. You will yourself right. And right is not a lie."

Calvin let this wash over him like the morning sunlight, and he took a kind of comfort in it.

"I can tell you this much, boy, without a shred of doubt. It is past too late for walking away. You have crossed over."

This was the truest thing his father said, and maybe he had to hear it this way. He had been thinking of quitting. After all that had gone on, maybe no one would blame him for giving it up, especially Rachel. But he had known all along he couldn't, wouldn't quit; he had just craved hearing it out of Mac Gaddy's mouth. *Will yourself right*. He turned this over a time or two in his head. It made the only sense he could live with. If it came down to it, he would have to lie. He would live with it until it became his truth, and then it would no longer be a lie. Like the prison itself.

He knew he wouldn't have to search for Pitch, that the conjure man would always be with him. He wouldn't burden his father with that part just yet. The old man had his own devils.

"Well, I best be on my way," said Cal getting up, then reaching down a hand to hoist Mac to his feet. The sun loomed between them.

"Another thing," cautioned Mac. "Keep it to yourself. Women can't protect you from this."

CHAPTER 79

The Captain had resigned and Blish was pregnant. Not necessarily that the two revelations, which Cal heard from the nurse the instant he walked into the Sergeant's office, were linked. But.

Cal laughed. He couldn't quite help himself. "At least it's an exciting place to work," he quipped.

"That you can laugh at all is proof enough you need a vacation," replied the nurse.

"So who's in charge?"

"Shoble has seniority, but you outrank him. In fact, you outrank everyone. The call already came in from Raleigh that, until a new captain is in place here, you are to assume command. I think I'm quoting almost verbatim."

"I know you're kidding."

"They were going to try you at home, but must have missed you. I was instructed to inform you immediately of this development. And here again I quote."

"Maybe I should start planning that vacation."

He didn't want to appear worried, but this was one thing he had not counted on.

Patting his arm, the nurse said, "Look, everyone's behind you. It'll be alright. You can handle it."

"Yeah. I'll keep telling myself that. Where's Blish?"

"She called in sick. I'm doubling as secretary too.

Cal laughed again. "Congratulations."

"And to you."

"Who went out after Benefit?"

"Icemorelee and Childs. County deputies and the state patrol are looking for him too."

"What about Nightcutt?"

"He's here, on the yard or in the cellblock. He refused to go. Said he was afraid of Benefit signing over him. Something like that."

Now she laughed, but Cal was already out the door.

"Jesus Christ," he said as he hit the yard.

The whole place stunk of fire. Fire gone but a day, and the already fetid, charred remnants of it in the air. The clouds with that burnt out sootiness to them, heavy, low.

"Well, glory be," said Shoble when he saw Cal. "I reckon I can surrender this night club to you, boy wonder. It has been one long shift."

"Go on home, Shoble. This light is pure hell on vampires."

"I believe I will."

As Shoble came abreast of Cal, he hesitated. He was going to say something. He was sweating, shaking. He smelled of smoke. Cal wanted to put his hand on Shoble's shoulder, some gesture of consolation, but his hand could only clench itself into a fist, and it remained like that, immovable, at his side. "Just go home," he repeated, and Shoble ambled off toward the parking lot, bowlegged, crimped, old.

Cal walked down to the dormitory where the men were still locked down, eighty in each of the two cellblocks separated by a concrete slab where Nightcutt, along with Cheatham and Quick, two new officers, paced one end to another. The slab was fouled with cigarette butts, wads of wet toilet paper, razor blades, feces and urine. This building too reeked of stale fire, the stench tamped into the men as well. They yelled when Cal walked in, then grumbled and stomped about, keeping their distance from the bars. Someone threw a nine volt battery that nicked off the steel and landed at Cal's feet. He merely glanced up, then turned to Nightcutt. "What's going on?"

"They fixing to buck is what's going on."

The two new guards looked scared. Cheatham was middle-aged, with the raw, angular look of a farmer fallen on bad times. Quick didn't look old enough to shave. Blond bangs fell out of his hat onto his forehead; his cheeks looked rouged.

"I'm sorry about not going out after Pitch, Calvin, but he's got next to me," said Nightcutt. "In a big dog way. I'll lay down my hat and badge right now if you want me to."

"Forget about that," Cal said. "When did these men eat

last?"

"Been almost a day now. The cooks all burnt up in the fire. Brotherton's up in the kitchen getting something together."

"Why the hell didn't you get a few men out of here to go up and help him. No wonder they're pissed, if they haven't been fed."

"I'll tell you what, boss man, straight up. I was too goddammed scared to open up them bars. I didn't know what would happen the way they been carrying on."

Nightcutt was about to buck too. "It's okay," Cal said quietly to him. "We'll handle it." Cal turned to Quick: "Go on up and tell Brotherton to pull out those steaks he was holding for Christmas and get them defrosted. We're going to have a nice, big supper for these boys. Baked potatoes. Whatever else he fixes for Christmas. Tell him not to spare the horses, and stay up there and help him."

The three guards just stared at him.

"Are you deaf?" Cal said.

"No, sir," squeaked Quick.

"Then get moving. Open up the cellblocks, Mr. Nightcutt."

"Calvin?"

"It's alright."

"Black suffering Jesus, damn," exclaimed Nightcutt. He fit the giant key first into the massive barred door of the east wing block, turned it till it clicked, and tumbled open. Then he opened the west wing. "Calvin, you are crazier than Thrake," he sighed.

The three state men stood there in the gauntlet with nothing between them and a hundred and sixty convicts. Calvin held up a hand and turned, faced one side and then the other, eyeing the whole slew and seeing not fury at all, but fear, as they looked into his fiery face, a visible declension in their bearing. He kept raised his blistered hand and spoke as loudly as he could without betraying the least emotion.

"Ezekiel, I want you and unit maintenance to police this area between the blocks. Each man police his own space.

Full yard privileges. No restrictions whatsoever. Business as usual. Chow will be served promptly at five. Christmas dinner with all the trimmings, and two packs of tailor-mades for each of you. I am sorry that those men died in the fire. Truly. I would have given anything to save them."

For interminable seconds, no one moved. Neither keepers nor kept, as if each were building a little more time, a little less. It would just take one thing wrongly handled. One of Nightcutt's legs slapped back and forth, as if his knee joint were rigged to an armature. Cheatham looked like he was squaring things with his maker, getting ready for the assault. One and one quarter thousand dollars a month hardly seemed worth it.

The convicts too had a little juice zipping through them. They could have charged. It would have been nothing to overrun the three state men, and storm the yard. Then what? Join Pitch in the cloudy ether, wherever that conjure man had floated? Maybe in uptown Charlotte that moment with a bag of herb and a fresh, red woman on each silk-sheathed sleeve. Pitch had not run; that was the man's story – trying to explain away sorcery. Pitch done left his body to burn to ash so fine it could be snorted, then he rode off on the currents. Nothing left of him in Coventry but a rolling pin, and a white hat hooked to a nail in the chow-hall.

The men looked through the barred window glass of the dormitory and saw the concertina skyline and Ernestine's shotgun. That is what waited for them if they bucked now. Still. To a man, they saw the cook-shack fire not so much as epilogue – it's hard to set a capstone on suffering – but confirmation of them as nothing. Ephemera. Chain-gang bodies that simply came and went, filled bunks, then filled holes. It was fear. Not said-fear, or dictionary-fear, but slaughter-fear, like the cow that does not blanch as the maul caves its brainpan. Tainted meat.

Cal recognized it, smelled it too, and he reckoned a little more of his father because at that minute he was not fearful, but calm. In the right, as if ordained. Righter than just by virtue of being a chore-man for the State, but also before

God and the devil and every damn one of those convicts spread out about him like a photograph of men snared in mid-sentence on the dust jacket of a book. Lurid and true and artificial at the same time.

He caught the eyes of Lump and Irby, two men he had always been straight-up with, standing shoulder to shoulder and he saw again in them as he looked dead into their bloodshot eyes, felt it, that same declension. When you know you have someone. Saw it in their big hands hanging lampooned at their sides like someone else's hands. And he did not want to quit Coventry. Those convicts would sell their souls for tailor-made cigarettes and a steak, and less than that. He knew again that he had them, all of them, and he felt for the first time in his life, with a twinge of regret, what it might be like to be his father.

They moved toward him, his hand still up like a wroth prophet's, walking past him from either block without looking, then out of the cellblock into the yard where the leaves had begun falling, having withered from the fire. Ezekiel came forth with a shovel, then three other convicts wheeled slop buckets sloshing with soapy water and mops into the slab alley between the blocks and began mucking it out. The last man through was Talfont. As he slumped past Cal, he turned to him and said, "Fuck you."

Cal studied him for a moment: the dull black pricks of his pupils imbedded in yellow irises, almost bluish skin, rotting teeth, the sharpened, devilish goatee, and long black hair sprouting to his shoulders from under the green state cap. A face that Cal, despite himself, could not help hating.

Fuck you didn't mean a thing to Cal. It could have been *Good afternoon* or *God be with you*. There was something too on Talfont's breath. Chemical. Maybe he had been eating deodorant sticks or swigging aftershave. He was loaded on something, swaying slightly as he sneered at Cal. There were still a dozen inmates at the mouth of the cellblock, and they all turned to watch.

"Alright, Talfont," Cal said with enough in his voice, enough in his eyes, to let Talfont know that if he moved along, it would be ignored – the epithet, the intoxication – like forgoing collection of a debt, but that Talfont would still owe him. Simply another way of communicating on the yard. Convicts and guards were all well-schooled on how to go about it.

"Mother fuck you and all y'all asshole pigs," Talfont shrieked, then spit on Cal.

Most of Talfont's saliva flew by Cal, but he its stinking spray on his face, then looked down and saw on his blue uniform blouse a knot of sputum that filled him with a loathing so deep that he smiled at Talfont. Smiled as though relieved. Then reached out and grabbed Talfont by his goatee and ripped it right off his face, leaving in its place a bloody outline, like a child's dripping, inept rendering of a beard.

Talfont flew back against the bars, his fingers crawling about his scalped, bleeding mouth. In his eyes now the defiance had slaked to outrage. Almost wonder. As if he had been party to something miraculous, as if he had been out-convicted by a free man. Cal still had part of Talfont's face in his hand, and he shook it at the stricken men stalled at the edge of the yard, then threw it down on the floor with the shit and the piss.

"You go on to chow now, boy," he said to Talfont, who bounced completely sober off the steel, and jogged after the others.

CHAPTER 80

MacGregor Gaddy needed maybe three more stones to complete his wall, now taller than any man in St. Joan's County, and impregnable. He decided to pause and have him a little smoke and a drink of whiskey before finishing. Rest now a bit. He fetched a Camel cigarette out of his overall bib pocket and lit it, then sat against the rock pile where the little mash bottle leant, and took a swallow. It was sweet and fiery, then the smoke sweet and fiery. Killdeer rushed over him, crying out, lighting in the yard to sit their ground-nests of speckled eggs, then play dead. Red canna lilies swarmed the side of the house. A listing gutter flapped against the eaves.

Elizabeth walked out the front door with a pitcher of sweet tea and cucumber sandwiches with the crusts trimmed off. Mac did not really care for them, but ate simply because it pleased her so. Unswerving in her devotion, in her wifeliness. In her Godliness. Lord, she was one to shame a man as preoccupied as MacGregor Gaddy. A wide-brim straw hat fastened under her chin with a bolo cord, a silky flowered dress that fell away from her powdered breast when she bent. Mac had never seen her in a pair of pants; and, among more things than he could list, admired her for this too. Ever careful about the sun, her skin was page white, unearthly in moonlight, though Mac had not stood between that tilted face and the moon for fifteen years or more. More, he reckoned. Her blue eyes, velvety blue like a tanager wing, shone out of her wrinkleless face, and around it fell those stray wisps of untucked hair. Ashe-blond, striking at silver.

Barefoot she came as was her habit, her feet long and graceful, white, yet stained too like tobacco browns a smoker's fingers. Girl's feet, an old woman's feet. She could walk unshod over anything. Gravel and burdock, ice, glass. The only place she favored shoes was the church-house. Her hands were long-fingered and soft, a bit of black dirt at the wrist from digging.

Elizabeth. She was a sight, and Mac was ever pleased to lay eyes on her, though, without even realizing it, he had never confided this to her, nor had he recollection of ever having told her he loved her. But he did love her. Mightily. Words, like tenderness, were things he had to let go or be bound by. He could not afford such carelessness, even now as he watched her dissipate like a puff of pollen, and his regret was just an old ache like a sore leg or shoulder that you drag along on until it flattered you like a hat or galluses.

He sipped from the bottle, sucked smoke into his lungs and realized what the wall lacked was concertina, that final inevitable punctuation. As he determined how to go about this, he spied bobbing in and out of the cedars and brake along the road leading toward Calvin's trailer a brown-clad figure with what looked like horns standing out of his skull.

The old man's skin prickled. He lifted his nose like a bloodhound and sniffed: *Fugitive convict in felon brown*. He clambered to his feet and took off after him, staying windward and out of sight until he could figure what the convict, who moved steadily along the roadside toward Calvin's door, had in mind. Mac saw the trailer, the clothesline strung in front of it, diapers rippling in the sun. Rachel's Azuretum, Sweet William and Salvia lit up along the flues leading inside. A purple windsock. No doubt the convict –

Mac saw now that he was black and muscle-bound – was headed for the trailer.

Suddenly the convict broke into a run, down the sloping road to Cal and Rachel's door. Mac made after him, but he couldn't gear up to any speed. His legs were rusted. The downslope tripped him. He flew down hard on his arm, and banged his face, inkling right off that the wrist bone was broken. Trying to summon some voice that would halt the man, he could only howl with what he knew was the ineptness of his aged body. By God, he still had the will and the fury, but his flesh would no longer mind. As he scrabbled to his knees, the left arm useless, scalding, he watched the trailer door thrown open violently and the convict disappear inside.

242

Then he heard Rachel scream. He gathered up his bones and hurled himself down the hill, falling twice more, crying out each time, despite himself, before barreling into the trailer. There was a smell in there – like creosote or charcoal, something twice burned, an aggregate of flame, yet impervious to flame. He needed Frank for this catching, some medium to speak and say what he was up against. It was more than devils. Rachel murmured, cried. The baby wailed. From the bedroom.

The convict's massive brown-shirted back was to Mac. Braided black tentacles sprung from his head. The yammering baby slumped over his shoulder like a sack of meal. Rachel on her knees in front of the convict, hands steepled in supplication as if praying to a statue, some devilish perversion of the Good Shepherd.

The pleated bodice of her gown was wet with milk. She pleaded *Please* over and over, her choking voice like dying wind, her face streaming tears. The convict had raised above her his free hand, in benediction, in execution – which, Mac could not judge. The old man shouted, but his voice creaked out in a breathless exhale. His arm hung; his face bled. The convict turned. He was bigger from the front, his shirt open, pectorals veiny, bulging, a whitish, welted gunshot scar. Another scar slashed diagonally across his upper lip. The perfect white teeth set in a smile of recognition that borrowed its cruelty from eyes so far apart, and slightly Oriental, that they seemed set at his temples. Then another terrible scar across his forehead, like a mouth, that writhed with its own pleasure and disdain.

Mac recognized him instantly, and never hesitated. With his good arm he reached for his pistol. But it was gone. That damn deputy had decreed no gun and now no gun it was. Just one arm and a body that grudged him. He lurched at the convict who, still holding the baby, stood the charge like steel, then brought one hand up to Mac's throat, pinned him against the wall and lifted him from the floor as he squeezed the life out of him.

Mac looked from the convict's face, to his mewling

grandson's, then to Rachel, who had thrown herself against the man, trying to pry him away and screaming. The four of them welded to one another like a deranged sculpture. With his feet dangling a half-foot from the ground, Mac lacked the ballast to dig in, to even kick; and with but one arm to fight, the arm of an old man – the convict man so grotesquely strong – he decided he would go on and die.

Mac felt an uncommon heat, like fire, like he was afire, and reckoned maybe hell was so eager for him that it was already cooking him. Or maybe it emanated from this devil choking him. He was thankful at least for no fear, nor wonder, that he was being punished. Rachel slid off the man's back, then wrapped herself about his legs.

"Elizabeth," Mac said with his last four syllables of consciousness. They echoed in his cranial vault like a man in the Boot calling out for mercy, and MacGregor Gaddy's last glimpse before the cell door sealed, and fire took permanent custody, was of the Eli, clamped to Pitch's shoulder, looking at his grandfather the way one might a complete stranger headed for hell, already forgetting he had ever witnessed it.

CHAPTER 81

Crowded with convicts again, the yard seemed less spooky, though still laced with smoke. The clouds swagged blackly just above the towers. It was dark as night, the perimeter lights already on. Some of the men stood in line for chow at the mess hall door.

Cal ducked under the yellow crime scene tape cordoning off the cook-shack and went inside. Dank and cauterized, about it sprawled the blackened, waterlogged effects of the dead men. In front of the wall of shadowgraphs, a lit candle at his feet, sat Father Tuesday, sipping from a bottle of wine.

"What are you doing, Father?"

When the priest turned, tears on his face. "I'm praying, Calvin."

Cal moved closer. Since the fire, the images on the wall had crystallized. There could be no mistake. They were the figures of men in the throes of agony. Limbs at impossible angles. Teeth knifing out of lurching skulls. Yet vague and impressionistic: the communion of saints, an icon wrought of fire. Cal heard something: a keening, like a faraway choir, yet it came from inside the building.

"You're drinking," Cal said.

"Yes, yes. Drinking and praying. My two favorite things."

"You don't want to be drinking."

"Wrong, wrong, wrong." Tuesday smiled and made a little laugh, though his eyes continued to drip.

"Give me the bottle, Father."

"It's sacramental wine."

"Come on. Just give me the bottle. You don't have to do this."

"But I do, I do. I am drinking the blood of Christ in honor of this great icon to suffering God has graciously granted us."

Cal cocked his ear. Singing. Unmistakable. An old work song. A hymn. Sonorous, timbrous, gathering in the bedrock.

"You hear it. Don't you, Calvin?"

Cal stared at Tuesday. He could not deny it. "Let's get out of here, Father."

Tuesday stood, killed the bottle and then smashed it against the figures on the wall.

"It's the second chain-gang coming, Calvin. The most significant religious experience I've had, and it came courtesy of the devil, though nonetheless miraculous."

"It was a goddam accident, Father."

"There are no accidents, Calvin."

"How the hell do you get religion out of it?"

Tuesday held up a finger and wagged it, smiled and staggered a step back, then sideways. "The back end of evil is always goodness. I prefer to see everything as an act of God."

"It's an act alright, and so is the one you are putting on. I need you to straighten up and get yourself to the chow-hall. I need help. Or else, get off this yard once and for all. This isn't a church. It's a prison. And that's about as religious as it's going to get."

"I weep for the men, Sergeant Gaddy. Do you understand that?" The priest's face coursed again with tears.

"Yes, I do," Calvin said.

"Let's go," Tuesday said.

"Go on. I have a couple things to see to. I'll be up in a bit."

By the light of the candle, Cal stood for some minutes studying the wall after Tuesday left. Sooty smears and stains, wisps of smoky white outlining bodies and lips, eye sockets and fingernails – like the fading apparitions in photographic negatives. There was surely a scientific explanation, but science was at a deficit when it came to explaining prison. *Pomps,* Cal's father called it. Evil begetting good, according to Tuesday, like two sides of the same coin, whatever the hell that meant.

And the singing. There it was. Faint, but again undeniable. The same singing Shoble had told Cal about on the phone the night of the fire. Like the wall of shadowgraphs – horrific and beautiful at the same time. Cal put his hand against the wall. It was nearly too hot to touch. Had it been in his power, he would have had the cook-shack demolished.

He rushed out of the building to the maintenance shack, fetched a five gallon bucket of battleship gray paint and lugged it and a long-handled roller back to the cook-shack. As the candle sputtered down to a nub, Cal slopped on the paint, coat after coat, until he could no longer see the men writhing before him. Only the singing, fading, fading, like the grizzled light in the gray sky, the candlewick drowning itself in the pool of hot wax on the cook-shack floor.

CHAPTER 82

Rachel took the old man for dead when she stepped out of the trailer to fetch Eli's diapers from the line and found him lying face up, humped in the shallow creek bed where he had crawled to drink and staunch his bloody face with mud. His eyes were wide open, attached to the deep blue sky sucking at him from its roof, uncountable miles above the sycamores that leaned across the creek. The water parted quietly as it streamed over him.

"Papa," Rachel cried, dropping her basket and hurrying down to him, Eli in a harness slung from her neck.

Figuring himself for dead, the word *Papa* infiltrated Mac's dream of the second world. It was Elizabeth's voice. He must have passed over, or merely snagged in the crossing. He had no expectations for an afterlife. Had never mistaken it for a tidier, brighter place. There would be the keepers and the kept. Coventry all over again. Pistols and chains.

"Papa," Rachel cried again.

Elizabeth. He attempted to cry out, but his voice had been cauterized in his strife with that convict devil.

Then it was Rachel's face, an inch from his. He recognized her for an instant until she shape-shifted again into his wife, Elizabeth, and then back. Calvin's wife, he told himself, and the child, the boy, little Eli, who dangled from his mother's neck like an amulet. They were safe. Or they were gone too, along with him.

Rachel lifted Mac's head from the creek water, and asked him what had happened, if he was alright.

I am dead. I will make my place here. I will not return. But there was no voice.

CHAPTER 83

Several of the tables were already occupied with their compliments of four convicts when Cal walked into the chow-hall. Many more stood waiting for their suppers, clutching trays with little geometric shapes dug into them for food, plastic silverware, and tumblers of bug juice. On the serving line with Brotherton were Nightcutt and Quick, wearing over their hands plastic sandwich bags.

Each inmate received a bony steak, an aluminum-wrapped baked potato, corn pudding, green beans, macaroni salad, a green congealed salad, a dill pickle, two rolls, two pats of margarine, and apple pie with white whipped topping – all slopped together on their trays.

Father Tuesday stood shakily next to Nightcutt and doled out to each of them two unlabeled packs of unfiltered cigarettes, grown and packaged at a big prison down east where the inmates labored in state tobacco fields. The priest smelled of wine; his eyes seeped water. As each man accepted the smokes, Tuesday blessed him, making with his hand, like a wounded bird, The Sign of the Cross: first the vertical beam, and then the transverse, whispering: "In Nomine Patris, et Filii, et Spiritus Sancti." Like a man talking in his sleep, pure gibberish, like what he spouted sometimes when saving souls at AA meetings, or the sound the wind makes on the free side of the fence when it is laying more time on you.

Brotherton had cooked the steaks frozen. Some of them were still hard in the middle and others charred. But the men ate them, and smoked their tailor-mades, mopping it all up in the end with rolls and apple pie and chain-gang coffee.

There was little talk, only the grunts and nods that they alone understood. When a man in prison sits down to eat, whatever victuals there might be on the tray supersede language. If they could live for only half an hour in the pleasure of their mouths, without having to make cheap, backstabbing words with them, then that was a portion of their existence, the only portion frequently, that they guarded from words.

If Cal could have, he would have bade them rise and break into song as he had seen them do at his father's behest – Frank leading them, the sorrow in their voices so beautiful that, even as a little boy, Cal had to take a seat after they'd finished, his legs giving way with Gospel truth, the same as when his mother sat at the piano and sang *On the Wings of a Dove*; and, if his father had not been there to shame him, all those years ago, he would have covered his face and cried and cried, as he longed to now, back in that same Coventry chow-hall, recollecting those men in the old days lifting up what was burning in their souls: *Take this hammer and carry it to the captain. Take this hammer and carry it to the captain. If he asks you was I laughin', tell him I was cryin', tell him I was cryin'.*

CHAPTER 84

MacGregor Gaddy had sustained a broken wrist and collarbone, two fractured ribs, a subdural hematoma, and his upper teeth had been knocked out. He was in the hospital two days while the doctors waited for the blood on his brain to disappear – or else they'd have had to drill a hole into his head. This was not the language the doctors had used, but this was how Mac told himself it would be. A metal bit whirred into his skull – not unlike the devils that had been nesting there like dirt daubers all along. *Go on*, he told them. *Do your worst*. But nobody heard him. He had finally let go of words as befits a dead man, and it occurred to no one to tell him that he was still alive.

But the bad blood pooled in his brain flowed back to its proper tributaries, and the doctors did not have to look inside his head like they might a stereopticon, where each panel was like a station of the cross: the ritual degradation and execution of Jesus, the convict. Through his entire ordeal, Mac never lost consciousness. He refused sleep. He waited for that devil convict.

There was one aspect of Mac's injuries that baffled the doctors – that did not line up with what looked like a fall. His throat was scorched, raw and peeling as if he had been branded. They thought he had perhaps tried to hang himself. The way he glowered out of that cowl of unkempt knotted hair, his opaque eyes like mercury congealed in their sockets, he seemed insane. None of their machines could find anything else wrong with him. No strokes. His heart was sound. Just worn-out parts.

Why he would not open his mouth and say things they simply did not know. His face, set in that spooked capitulant vigil old folks disguise themselves with, told them he had kicked in the wrong door, and it had slammed back shut on him, trapping him inside forever. He didn't know where he was or how to get out – some anomalous misfire inside his

251

skull. They asked his son and daughter-in-law if they'd like to put him in a hospital for such afflictions, or even an old folks home. Cal and Rachel determined then that they would move to the Gaddy home place, and take care of Mac.

In a blue suit, blazing white shirt and striped necktie, Calvin mooned at his father's side Every day he attended another immolated convict's funeral, hiding in the last pew, listening to the mourners keen and the red-robed choir's timbrous fury: *The head that once was crowned with thorns is crowned with glory now.* In tabernacles and missions, storefront churches and brush arbors, he listened to eulogies and testimonies. He learned that Coventry's cooks had sprung from women, that their families grieved after them just as they would the lawful, that the men in that burnt-up shack had all lived once inside their mamas.

Every day he talked to the newspaper people and told them that the investigation at Coventry would uncover each instance of wrong-doing, that full restitution would be made to the families of the victims. He put in for Captain. Saw no other way, what with the move to the big house, the money it would take to undo its decrepitude, his father finally, irrevocably mad, and now Rachel pregnant again.

CHAPTER 85

Rachel worked the yard daily, reclaiming Elizabeth's Gaddy's flower beds, the baby in his bassinet draped in mosquito bar, the grandfather like a sentinel, silent, wary, pacing small circles around his grandson. He didn't know if a dead man needed a gun to kill a conjure man, but he stole Calvin's spare service revolver nonetheless, and kept it hidden on him at all times.

Every now and then, he hoisted his walking staff toward the clouds, his silvered-over eyes scouring the tree line behind which lurked Pitch. Pitch who had not eaten in a hundred days, now aged, gray and nearly wizened, his brown clothes mere rags flapping, who bent occasionally to pick from the earth a grub or a worm, a live toad, the bleached bone of vermin, a buzzard feather to set out in configuration.

Baby Eli often woke to see his namesake, Elizabeth, hovering him like the Madonna crowned with lightning, rocking the bassinet, singing a lullaby: *All day, all night, angels are watching over me.* Then glide over to her husband, MacGregor, smooth back his hoary hair and whisper into his ear as he napped beneath one of the Pecan trees. The old man smiled in his sleep.

Eli knew his grandfather was dead. The baby watched the black man, like a wizard, move tree to tree in the woods across the pasture, charming the birds out of the branches to perch in his bony outstretched hands. It was a game Pitch and Eli played together every day; it made the tiny boy laugh and laugh. His mother, Rachel, turned at the sound of his laughter, and hurried over to kiss him, her belly beginning to slightly bow. Eli was not afraid. There was a wall his grandfather had built to protect him, and some day his daddy would be Captain.

Joseph Bathanti is former Poet Laureate of North Carolina (2012-14) and recipient of the 2016 North Carolina Award for Literature. He is the author of ten books of poetry, including *Communion Partners; Anson County; The Feast of All Saints; This Metal*, nominated for the National Book Award, and winner of the Oscar Arnold Young Award; *Land of Amnesia; Restoring Sacred Art,* winner of the 2010 Roanoke Chowan Prize, awarded annually by the North Carolina Literary and Historical Association for best book of poetry in a given year; *Sonnets of the Cross; Concertina,* winner of the 2014 Roanoke Chowan Prize; and *The 13th Sunday after Pentecost*, released by LSU Press in 2016. His novel, *East Liberty*, won the 2001 Carolina Novel Award. This novel, *Coventry*, won the 2006 Novello Literary Award. His book of stories, *The High Heart,* won the 2006 Spokane Prize. *They Changed the State: The Legacy of North Carolina's Visiting Artists,* 1971-1995, his book of nonfiction, was published in early 2007. His more recent book of personal essays, *Half of What I Say Is Meaningless*, winner of the Will D. Campbell Award for Creative Nonfiction, is from Mercer University Press. A new novel, *The Life of the World to Come*, was released from University of South Carolina Press in late 2014. Bathanti is the McFarlane Family Distinguished Professor of Interdisciplinary Education & Writer-in-Residence of Appalachian State University's Watauga Residential College in Boone, NC. He served as the 2016 Charles George VA Medical Center Writer-in-Residence in Asheville, NC.